THE CASE OF THE UNINVITED UNDERTAKER

by

Cathy Ace

The Case of the Uninvited Undertaker

Date of first publication worldwide July 2023

Cover artwork: © Four Tails Publishing
Cover photograph: © Whiskybottle
Licensed via Dreamstime.com

PRAISE FOR THE WISE ENQUIRIES AGENCY MYSTERIES

'...a gratifying contemporary series in the traditional British manner with hilarious repercussions (dead bodies notwithstanding). Cozy fans will anticipate learning more about these WISE ladies.'
Library Journal, starred review

'If you haven't read any of Cathy Ace's WISE cozies, I suggest you begin at the beginning and giggle your way through in sequence.'
Ottawa Review of Books

'...a modern-day British whodunit that's as charming as it is entertaining...Good fun, with memorable characters, an imaginative plot, and a satisfying ending.'
Booklist

'Ace spiffs up the standard village cozy with a set of sleuths worth a second look.'
Kirkus Reviews

'...a perfect cozy with a setting and wit reminiscent of Wodehouse's Blandings Castle. But its strongest feature is the heart and sensitivity with which Ace imbues her characters.'
The Jury Box, Ellery Queen Mystery Magazine

'Sharp writing highlights the humor of the characters even while tackling serious topics, making this yet another very enjoyable, fun, and not-always-proper British Mystery.'
Cynthia Chow, Librarian, Hawaii State Public Library in King s River Life Magazine

'A brilliant addition to Classic Crime Fiction. The ladies (if they'll forgive me calling them that) of the WISE Enquiries Agency will have you pacing the floor awaiting their next entanglement...
A fresh and wonderful concept well executed.'
Alan Bradley, New York Times Bestselling Author of the Flavia de Luce books

Other works by the same author

(Information for all works here: **www.cathyace.com**)

The WISE Enquiries Agency Mysteries

The Case of the Dotty Dowager
The Case of the Missing Morris Dancer
The Case of the Curious Cook
The Case of the Unsuitable Suitor
The Case of the Disgraced Duke
The Case of the Absent Heirs
The Case of the Cursed Cottage

The Cait Morgan Mysteries

The Corpse with the Silver Tongue
The Corpse with the Golden Nose
The Corpse with the Emerald Thumb
The Corpse with the Platinum Hair
The Corpse with the Sapphire Eyes
The Corpse with the Diamond Hand
The Corpse with the Garnet Face
The Corpse with the Ruby Lips
The Corpse with the Crystal Skull
The Corpse with the Iron Will
The Corpse with the Granite Heart
The Corpse with the Turquoise Toes

Standalone novels

The Wrong Boy

Short Stories/Novellas

Murder Keeps No Calendar: a collection of 12 short stories/novellas
Murder Knows No Season: a collection of four novellas
Steve's Story in "The Whole She-Bang 3"
The Trouble with the Turkey in "Cooked to Death Vol. 3: Hell for the Holidays"

PRAISE FOR THE CAIT MORGAN MYSTERIES

'…Ace is, well, an ace when it comes to plot and description.'
The Globe and Mail

'Her writing is stellar. Details, references, allusions, expertly crafted phrasing, and serious subjects punctuated by wit and humour.'
Ottawa Review of Books

'If all of this suggests the school of Agatha Christie, it's no doubt what Cathy Ace intended. She is, as it fortunately happens, more than adept at the Christie thing.'
Toronto Star

'…a mystery involving pirates' treasure, lust, and greed. Cait unravels the locked-tower mystery using her eidetic memory and her powers of deduction, which are worthy of Hercule Poirot.'
The Jury Box, Ellery Queen Mystery Magazine

'…a testament to an author who knows how to tell a story and deliver it with great aplomb.'
Dru's Musings

'Cathy Ace makes plotting a complex mystery look easy. As the threads here intertwine in unexpected ways, readers will be amazed that she manages to pull off a clever solution rather than a true Gordian Knot of confusion.
Cathy Ace's books always owe a debt of homage to Grand Dame Agatha Christie…the blend of "cozy" mystery, tragic family dynamics…
pure catnip for crime fiction aficionados.'
Kristopher Zgorski, BOLO Books

For Sue, an inspiration

THURSDAY 1st JUNE

CHAPTER ONE

Henry Devereaux Twyst, eighteenth duke of Chellingworth, was terribly worried about his sister; for more years than he could recall, Clementine Twyst had enjoyed descending upon the family seat, unheralded, with chaos following in her wake. This time? This time things were a little different. While she'd not shared her plans for a visit with her sibling, she'd taken the time to telephone their mother to announce her intentions to arrive the following afternoon, and to request that her mother speak to her brother about the family being able to dine together in the evening.

Distressed that his sister's actions felt suspiciously underhanded, rather than displaying her usual unthinking flightiness, Henry was concerned that she had something up her sleeve. Yes…the longer he thought about it, the more he was convinced that was the case.

Henry stood from his artist's stool and plopped his brush into the water pot with irritation. The painting on his easel was ruined, and that was all Clementine's fault; why on earth couldn't she just act like a normal human being for once in her life and speak to her brother like a…a…person?

'Bother!' Henry felt completely exasperated as he strode to the door; he'd left it open to catch any breeze that might waft away the unseasonable afternoon heat, but it hadn't worked. He wiped his brow with what turned out to be a paint-covered sleeve.

'Double bother!'

Having agreed with Stephanie, his beloved wife, that he would spend some hours in the artist's studio she'd created for him in the Estate's delightful Georgian folly, he now found himself completely consumed by thoughts of his wretched sister, rather than being able to enjoy the delight of creation.

From atop the little hill upon which the folly sat, he gazed down at his home, Chellingworth Hall, and then at its Dower House, where his mother lived. His eyes wandered across the expanse of the Chellingworth Estate, which was a testament to the inspired designs of Capability Brown, toward the surrounding hills and valleys of Powys. He was grateful that he was at least able to marvel at the quality of the sunlight on the verdant scene, even if he was now incapable of capturing its beauty in watercolors.

'Clemmie, Clemmie, Clemmie…when will you grow up?' He addressed the damp cloth with which he was wiping his hands, there being no one about the place who could hear him.

Cleaning his brushes as he contemplated his still new role as a father, Henry admitted to himself that his sister's lifestyle had changed somewhat over the previous few months; she'd been at the Hall more often, rather than always seeming to be hiding out at the family's London house, and she'd appeared quite keen to help with anything to do with Henry's infant son, and heir, Hugo. His wife had begrudgingly, and with more than a small amount of surprise, allowed Clementine to be an attentive aunt, and Henry had begun to hope that his sister would, if her recent actions were anything to go by, start to act in a more predictable manner. But she'd not been to visit in more than a month, and now here she was organizing secret dinner parties.

Henry pulled off his painter's smock and decided to carry his jacket rather than put it on to walk down to a late tea at the Hall; the sun was still high in the periwinkle sky and there wasn't a breath of air. Besides, Henry told himself, if any of the paying members of the public who were dragging their heels in leaving the Estate before the gates were closed at four o'clock spotted him, they'd be less likely to believe him to be the duke than if he were properly attired.

He locked his studio before sauntering down the hill and promised himself he'd give his painting another go the following day, if he could escape his ducal duties. The weather forecast was for high temperatures until the middle of the next week, which meant that at least one could plan one's days sure in the knowledge it would be dry, though Henry was keenly aware that those very conditions were making the local community jittery; sheep needed grass, and grass needed rain, and there were a great number of sheep and sheep farmers in the area, and so very little rain of late.

Sighing at the thought that the weather could never please everyone, Henry's mind turned again to his sister's unnecessarily complex undertakings just to make sure that he, his wife, and his mother would dine with her the following evening. What on earth could she be up to now? He dreaded to think…and yet he couldn't help himself.

CHAPTER TWO

Mavis MacDonald stared at her computer screen willing the information contained within the accounts she'd just been sent by her colleague Carol Hill to be different. And by different, she meant better. But the numbers were what they were, and that told her one thing: more of an effort on her part to bring new clients and extra work to the business.

Mavis had always known that the idea of four women setting up a private enquiries agency had been a risky undertaking. While the move they'd all decided to make from their office in London to the converted barn on the Chellingworth Estate in Wales had meant their running costs would decrease greatly, they'd all known they'd have to expect lower workloads, and therefore lower income levels too. Yes, Mavis silently acknowledged, the village of Anwen-by-Wye, and even the entirety of the county of Powys, was a beautiful place, but it was hardly overrun with potential clients, which meant that she – the member of the quartet who'd always taken the lead in drumming up business for the group – had her work well and truly cut out for her.

The flurry of cases over the early part of the year had dried up; all four women were underutilized, and she was now somewhat concerned about their financial situation. Mavis herself was relatively well placed, given that she lived at the Dower House with Althea Twyst, the dowager duchess, who expected nothing from her 'tenant' other than whatever care might naturally arise from the strong bond of friendship they'd developed over the past year or so. Mavis had gladly overseen Althea's excellent and now complete recovery from hip replacement surgery – always a challenge for an octogenarian – and their lives had reverted to their normal rhythm; Mavis spent most of her days either at the office or out and about seeing existing and potential clients, while the dowager 'pottered'.

She checked the watch pinned to her chest, a habit she'd continued since her days as an army nurse, then later matron at a barracks designed to care for those who'd retired from service to their country, then sighed, and pushed herself away from her desk. She had an appointment with a potential client in ten minutes and decided she'd give herself the chance to freshen up a little before the woman arrived; the converted barn was cavernous, but seemed to be almost entirely devoid of air, it was such a warm day.

'Christine, she'll be here in ten minutes,' called Mavis up the circular staircase that led from the office to the small apartment above, which provided local digs for the youngest of her colleagues.

The Right Honorable Christine Wilson-Smythe, daughter of the Viscount Ballinclare, popped her head over the balustrade. 'Okey doke, down in two, Mavis. I'll pop the kettle on,' she replied.

'Aye, a pot of tea often loosens a client's tongue when they're no' sure about where to begin,' replied Mavis sagely.

Mavis heard Christine bounce lightly down the stairs as she shut herself into the downstairs bathroom, where she combed her neat, gray bob into slightly better shape – a trim was on the cards in the near future – rubbed at a few wrinkles on her forehead, then prepared herself for what she hoped would be a meeting that would lead to a paying case.

A few moments later, as she'd done on so many occasions before, Mavis patted out the creases in the cushions on the sofa beside the coffee table in readiness for an incoming potential client. Christine had boiled the kettle, and the two women perched on the edges of their desk chairs as they waited for their arrival.

'That new frock you're wearing exactly matches the chestnut of your hair, Christine. Very becoming,' noted Mavis.

Christine smiled. 'Thanks. I'll be honest and tell you I didn't even notice until I saw it in sunlight; the lights in shops are so harsh, aren't they?'

Mavis agreed, though she reckoned the types of shops where Christine bought her clothes might have slightly better changing rooms than the ones she was used to.

'It's not unusual for a client to be late,' offered Christine.

Mavis suspected she'd been spotted as she stared crossly at the clock on the wall.

'Aye, well, being punctual is something they'd expect of us, so I don't see why we shouldnae expect it of them.' Mavis heard the irritation in her voice as she spoke.

Her young colleague nodded and forced a smile, which Mavis returned. The agency was fortunate to have Christine; there'd been several cases that had come to them because of her contacts arising both from her connections within society, and her past colleagues and acquaintances from the years when she'd worked as an underwriter at Lloyds, in the City of London.

At least Mavis knew that Christine wasn't worried about the lower levels of income they'd experienced of late; her father had inherited a penniless seat in Ireland, but he'd built his own fortune in the City, and not only did Christine have that to fall back upon, but she'd also amassed a decent personal bank balance through her own endeavors and talents. She could afford to travel between the little apartment on the Chellingworth Estate to her flat in Battersea, then on to her family's swish London house, or even to their rambling, if somewhat decrepit, Irish manor whenever she pleased. Not that she'd been there since an incident which had left her still recovering from a gunshot wound that could have been much more deadly. Mavis's experience told her that the scar which still bothered the girl would never improve, then scolded herself for thinking of Christine as a 'girl' – she was a young woman in her late twenties and engaged to be married.

'I'll boil that kettle again,' said Christine, drawing Mavis from her thoughts.

'Aye, good idea,' she replied absently, unable to avoid checking her own timepiece to see if it agreed with the clock on the wall. It did; the client was already a quarter of an hour late.

The crunching of tires on the pebble driveway outside the barn led Mavis to rise and Christine to turn, in anticipation of an imminent arrival. Looking out of the tall windows that comprised most of the walls of the building, the pair exchanged an amazed glance.

'That's a hearse, isn't it?' Christine sounded as surprised as Mavis felt.

'That it is. Which is…odd.'

'I'll get this water into the pot,' said Christine.

'And I'll get the door,' added Mavis, eager to meet whomever was arriving; this couldn't be Miss Attwater, could it? She'd not mentioned anything…funereal…when they'd spoken on the phone a day earlier, and Mavis couldn't imagine why anyone would arrive at a planned meeting with a firm of private enquiry agents in a hearse. So, who could this be?

Standing on the threshold, Mavis slapped her professional smile on her face – not the one she used when addressing recalcitrant patients, but the one she'd developed when hoping to get a client to open their heart, and then their wallet.

The woman who spilled out of the driving seat of the dusty hearse looked crumpled and frazzled; her charcoal trousers were smudged with dirt, her once-white shirt was smeared with what Mavis hoped wasn't blood, and her hair was a mat of frizzy curls with only a few strands remaining tamed within a scrunchy.

As she hobbled across the gravel, Mavis saw she was wearing only one shoe. Concerned, the retired nurse stepped forward to lend the woman a supportive arm, despite the fact she was Mavis's junior by at least a couple of decades, so in her early forties.

'Are you quite alright?' Mavis didn't care as much about who she was helping as why they might need her help.

The woman almost broke into tears. 'Yes, it could have been a lot worse. A sheep ran out across the road when I was driving here and, of course, I swerved to avoid it. But hearses are a bit unwieldy, so I ended up in a ditch. No mobile signal, of course, so I had to come up with a way of giving the wheels some purchase just so I could get back on the road. But the vehicle's alright, and I'm just a bit dirty, so that's alright too. Sorry I'm late, though. I hate being late. It's not something a person can get away with in my line of business, as you might imagine. Mind you, the dead don't care, but then they aren't the ones paying our bills, are they? Nice to meet you – I'm Louise Attwater, by the way. Was it you I spoke to yesterday? Mavis MacDonald?'

Mavis nodded and relinquished Louise's arm after steering her toward the sofa, where Christine was setting down the teapot and a plate of biscuits.

Seeing the state of the woman Christine offered, 'I've got a little flat upstairs with a proper bathroom, if you'd like to have a shower, or anything – or there's a powder room down here, if you'd like.'

Louise Attwater looked alarmed. 'Do I look that bad, then?'

'I hope that's no' blood on your shirt,' said Mavis.

Pulling at the area Mavis had indicated the woman smiled. 'Not blood, thank goodness, but there were a lot of berries on the brambles in the hedge beside the ditch, so that's probably what it is. If you don't mind me looking like this, I think it's best if we get on, because I have to get back to the office. Maybe my vehicle's a bit of a giveaway? I'm an undertaker, and there is, quite literally, a body waiting there that needs my attention, and my make-up artist is off with a nasty summer cold at the moment, so it's all down to me.'

Mavis had always admired a businesslike approach in a person, and her years in nursing had certainly allowed her to develop the sort of relationship with death and corpses that she rarely encountered in others, but even she found Louise Attwater's manner to be just a little too jolly. She told herself that the sort of humor she'd seen displayed by pathologists over the years might well be something shared by undertakers, whose habitual company also comprised, in the main, dead people.

'Black, no sugar, for the tea, thanks,' announced the potential client. 'And no biscuits, ta – though they do look tempting, I must say. I love a Bourbon, me. Oh, go on then – I'll need something more than blinking grapes to keep me going until I have time for dinner tonight. I've got to get Mr Davies-Milk's face done before I stop to eat, and we've got an early start in the morning, too.'

Mavis didn't want to get sidetracked by focusing on her potential client's clients; in any case she assumed – having spent more than a year in Wales – that the name Louise Attwater had used probably meant that the Mr Davies in question had, at some point in his life, been a milkman, there being so many Davieses in Wales that job titles, or at least life roles, were often tacked onto their name so that folks could tell one from another.

'Allow me to introduce you to my colleague, Christine Wilson-Smythe, Miss Attwater. So how can we help you?' Mavis chose to get right to the point. 'You mentioned when we spoke that you might want us to look into some "irregularities". Do you now feel able to expand upon that?'

Dabbing up crumbs from her chest with a moistened finger, and pushing her hair from her face, the woman replied, 'First of all, it's Louise, please. No one we work for ever calls me anything but Miss Attwater, so it's nice when folks are able to use my first name. And, yes, I do feel comfortable enough to tell you what's been going on, now that we're face to face, here in your office. It's a lovely place, by the way – I wish mine was as big and open as this one, but we have so much stuff to accommodate, not that that's what I really want to talk about. It's not what's happened to me, personally, as such, but it is what's been happening to a few of my clients – the ones who become my clients, as opposed to their dead loved ones, I mean. The normal way things happen when a person dies is that I get a phone call either from the hospital staff, who've usually been given my name by the bereaved, or directly from the "someone" in the family who's going to "make all the arrangements", as the saying goes. Sometimes we already have a relationship with the family, sometimes they're unknown to us. I took the business over from my mother and father, so we Attwaters have been in this line for over fifty years now, and having a name that's known and trusted makes a big difference to us when it comes to attracting business.'

'Indeed, it must do,' said Mavis as the woman paused to take a sip of tea.

'Some of them we're expecting, too; I make sure to keep an ear open for families who might need our services, and my mother set up a pre-payment scheme about thirty years back that means we've had families with the good foresight to make their own wishes for their arrangements clear when they've been relatively young. But I never ever go touting for business at hospitals or – even worse – hospices, for example. It's a line I won't cross. So when I heard about what's been going on, well…that's why I'm here.'

Mavis was still mystified. 'One of your competitors is treading on your toes, so to speak?' She wondered how on earth she and her colleagues might be able to help in such a situation; was the business of undertaking a cutthroat one?

'No…not as such, I suppose. Look, this is what's happened. About a month back I got a call from a family we've been taking care of for at least forty years; I know of them, rather than actually knowing them though, because I have to say that most people don't find it…um…comfortable to build friendships with people in our line of work. Which I suppose has a lot to do with me still being single – I've had more than a few men all but run away from me when they find out what I do for a living. One did, in fact, quite literally run off – climbed out of a window in the men's toilets at the pub where we'd met up for a blind date. Which was hurtful, and really quite embarrassing. He'd already ordered food, so I had to pay for both meals and drinks, then make it look like I wasn't crying. But I digress. Sorry.'

Mavis was glad the woman had caught herself – she was keen for her to get to the point.

Settling herself again, Louise continued, 'It was the daughter of the man who'd died who phoned me, which isn't unusual…the women, if they're around, tend to take control of funerals, I've found. Anyway, we discussed the plans for her father's cremation and interment as usual, then she thanked me for the wreath of condolence we'd delivered to their house. I'll be honest and admit that it wasn't until it happened again that it dawned on me I had no idea what she'd been talking about, and even that wasn't until a couple of weeks ago when another client thanked me for a wreath that neither I, nor anyone working for me, had delivered.'

Christine and Mavis exchanged a puzzled glance.

Louise shuffled forward on the sofa and put down her mug. 'You have to bear in mind that when I deal with clients I'm well aware that I'm talking to people who are in the throes of grief; how they grapple with their loss will vary, but I often find that I need to reiterate points frequently, or cope with changes in requests at short notice. It's why we have so many leaflets – folks can't retain information at such times. So it's not unusual for me to talk to someone who's a bit confused about things. That said, I did manage to find out from both clients in question that they'd received a wreath of condolence, delivered to their homes. They'd assumed it had come from us, because, on each occasion, a hearse had been spotted in the area.'

Mavis pressed, 'So, one of your competitors has been trying to curry favor with your potential or existing clients?'

Louise shook her head. 'It doesn't seem so – because I've spoken to them all and they deny any knowledge of sending the wreaths, too.'

Christine leaned forward, her eyes gleaming with anticipation. 'Is your world quite small? Do you undertakers all know each other?'

Louise chuckled wryly. 'Yes, you could say that. There aren't a lot of people who want to do what we do, and that means we do, indeed, all know each other. The interesting thing was that when I spoke to three other companies – people I have literally grown up with in the business – they all told me that a similar thing had happened to a couple of their clients, too. A hearse seen, a figure in a tailcoat depositing a wreath on a doorstep, and no explanation on the card left with it, just one word: "Condolences".'

Mavis was still at sea. 'So this isn't just a local thing?'

'It's local insofar as it's all happened within about a thirty-mile radius of here. Well, of Builth Wells, in any case, which is where my business is based. But what's really odd and – to be honest with you – what's really getting all of us worked up a bit, is that the wreaths are being delivered to the homes in question before the person who dies is actually dead.'

Mavis wanted to make sure she'd understood the woman correctly. 'You mean the wreaths are delivered *prior* to the person in question's death?'

Louise Attwater nodded.

'But how is the person delivering the wreaths able to predict when someone will die?' Christine sounded as puzzled as Mavis felt.

'Exactly,' said Louise. 'That's what I think you can help me with – well, help us with, because I'm really here on behalf of four companies, you see. We can't fathom it; we're all in the business of death and even we don't know when someone's going to die with that level of certainty. So how does this mysterious – and frankly creepy – "undertaker figure" do it? How do they know who's going to die, and when? So…can you help us?'

Mavis's mind was awhirl: was someone warning loved ones of an imminent death? And if they were, how could they possibly do that? The only explanation she could come up with wasn't one she wanted to countenance.

She asked, 'How many times do you and your colleagues know of this having happened?'

Louise sat back. 'That's the other thing; the more we've all agreed to broach the subject with our clients, the more instances we've found out about. Some of the clients have even accused me or the other companies of having somehow engineered the death of a loved one, because they've been alarmed by the arrival of an "early wreath". Between us, we now know of almost two dozen times this has happened – and going back at least a year. No one's put this all together until I started asking around.'

Christine spoke quietly, 'Two dozen unexplained wreaths over the past year? That sounds like…a lot.'

Mavis could tell how concerned her colleague was by the way she nibbled at the corner of her mouth after she'd spoken.

'Have you talked to the police about this?' Mavis asked.

'No need. My cousin's a policeman up in Anglesey, and he's told me they wouldn't touch it with a bargepole because nothing's "happened".'

'Except that it has, hasn't it?' Mavis mused aloud. 'Families have been frightened, then bereaved.'

'Have you and your fellow professionals considered that someone might be making the foretold deaths actually occur?' Christine ventured.

Louise slumped on the sofa just a little. 'That's something we've been around the houses about.' Sitting upright and patting the sofa, Louise's expression changed. 'Blast it, I've left my bag in the hearse. Anyway, I've brought you a list of the names of the people who've died and where they died. And when, of course. When you look at it, you'll see there's nothing any of them seem to have in common; they've died in various hospitals or hospices, and in nursing homes. One even died when he was away on holiday, I understand. So we can't imagine how anyone could be…you know…killing them.' She paused and a smile crossed her face. 'When I talked to my police officer cousin about that angle he laughed his head off. Said I'd been watching too many programs on TV about serial killers. Which I hadn't. I don't like that sort of thing at all.'

'So, you and your fellow undertakers would like us to do what, exactly?'

Christine sounded a little confrontational, thought Mavis. She made her views known to her colleague by raising her eyebrows when she gave her a sideways glance.

Mavis added gently, 'We could take the information you've already gathered and do some further digging. Maybe formulate some questions we could ask of you and your colleagues when we've had a chance to discuss the matter among ourselves. One of our number is an expert in computer data research, manipulation, and interpretation. She might be able to find out more about those who have died than you already understand. There might be a thread that links all these deaths after all.'

Louise replied, 'What we'd really like you to do is come up with the solution to the key problem: how does this "undertaker" know that a person's going to die? However – and I don't want to sound like someone who doesn't value unseen effort, which is something we suffer from in our business all the time – we don't have a lot of money to pay for your services. To be honest, it's not as though any of us are losing work because of this…we're just really curious. And, between you and me, I for one am more than a little bit freaked out by it all. It's…it's a bit spooky. And – while you might have already guessed it because of what I do – I should tell you that I don't believe in ghosties or ghoulies, or in the paranormal at all. Nor in divination of any sort. I want to know the real, down-to-earth reasons behind this being able to happen. Please. Because now that I know about it, I want to understand it. As do we all. Which is why I'm here.'

With the women having agreed that the WISE Enquiries Agency would email Louise Attwater a proposed plan of action and a quote for work by the next morning, the undertaker took her leave, still hopping about, having been unable to retrieve her shoe from the ditch where she'd ended up.

Mavis and Christine pored over the list the almost-client had given them as Mavis emailed it, and some overview notes, to Carol Hill – whom she knew would give them her immediate attention – and to their fourth member, Annie Parker. Mavis suspected that Annie would take longer to reply to her email because she was visiting her parents just outside London, in Plaistow, for a few days, and wasn't due to return to work until the following Monday. However, all four women knew how important it was to keep everyone in the information loop, because experience had taught them how, even if it was only occasionally, there were connections in, through, and around lives – allowing for some hard work to capitalize upon what some might call luck.

However, on this occasion Mavis believed that Carol might be more immediately useful because this was exactly her sort of thing – trawling through data to find connections – and she was on the spot. Annie? Mavis had no doubt she'd be able to bring her expertise to bear once she returned to work in a few days but, until then, it really was best to simply keep her informed.

FRIDAY 2nd JUNE

CHAPTER THREE

It was two in the morning and Annie Parker was sitting up in a single bed, in the room that her parents always kept ready for her, texting rapidly. The person to whom her angry thumbs were sending barbed messages was Tudor Evans – the man who was the landlord of the Lamb and Flag pub in Anwen-by-Wye, the man who was 'father' to her dog Gertie's littermate Rosie, the man who – at that precise moment – was being the biggest pain in the backside known to womanhood, in spite of the fact he was the man who was supposed to be the love of her life.

She typed rapidly.

NO NO NO U cant use any old yellow U have 2 use 1 we picked

The reply came slowly.

It looks the same.

wont match has 2 B same

Close enough.

NO must B perfect get more of same 1

Not cheep

Sorry, cheap!

not my fault you bought it should have got right 1

Annie paused. She loved Tudor with all her heart, but he did have a tendency to buy the cheapest option, when the better or best alternative cost a little more. The paint color they'd agreed upon for the snug in the pub, which was in the process of being fully transformed into a tearoom, was the perfect sunny yellow. Now she was losing her temper because he was proposing to finish the job while she was away with a cheaper paint that she had no doubt was nothing like the light, buttery hue she'd spent weeks choosing.

dont paint any more will sort it sunday night

She hoped he'd accept her suggestion. She waited for what felt like ages until she got a reply.

Already done-ish. All but finished it after I closed up tonight.

Annie wasn't surprised it had taken Tudor so long to tell her that he'd almost finished a job he'd told her not half an hour ago was something he was 'contemplating' doing at the weekend.

dont do more til I c it

Annie waited.

OK. See you at the station on Sunday. But we'll talk in the morning, alright? Gertie says hello. She's licking my ankle now.

Tudor added two emojis of a dog and a smiley face.

Annie couldn't help but chuckle.

luv 2 gert & u

Love you. Goodnight. I miss you. Tudor xx

miss u 2 ax

Annie settled into her pillow and allowed her mind to roam. The email she'd received from Mavis that evening had piqued her interest, and she'd already named the case – which wasn't even theirs yet – The Case of the Uninvited Undertaker. She felt a chill as she wondered what it would be like to receive a condolence wreath before a loved one died, then tried to think of cheerier things, so focused on the day ahead that she and her mother had planned, visiting old friends who'd been part of her childhood…

She knew nothing more until the vibration of her phone woke her.

Bleary-eyed she checked her messages. There was one from Tudor, though she couldn't understand why he'd be texting her at gone three in the morning.

Got a message from Delyth James. She's thinking of selling the Coach and Horses. What do you think?

Annie's thumbs weren't as swift as usual.

The woman wants to sell the pub shes allowed to stay empty and fall into disrepair for more than a year? To you? What's going on Tude? Do you know its three in the morning?

She took the time to use better English than she usually bothered with for texts, hoping Tudor would realize she was grappling with what was going on.

I just got a message. Out of the blue. She's asked me to phone her later on. So? What do you think?

Annie sighed.

I think we should talk to each other before you talk to her. Lets sleep then talk. How about I phone you around half seven? Everyone will be awake here by then so I wont be disturbing them. OK?

OK. Good idea. Miss you. Love you. Txx

GOODNIGHT!!!!! Ax

Annie slumped onto her pillow, wide awake. She and Tudor had talked about how wonderful it would be if the other pub overlooking the village green would come up for sale. The entire village of Anwen-by-Wye, including the Lamb and Flag pub of which Tudor was the publican, was owned by the Twyst family, except for St David's Church and the Coach and Horses. King Charles I had been well-treated by the publican of the day and ordered that the Twyst family should give the pub to the publican as a gift. At least, that was how the myth went. Of course, it was all twaddle. Had to be, because Charles I never got closer to Anwen-by-Wye than Shrewsbury, something Annie had taken the time to check into when she'd first arrived at the village she now called home. Back then, she'd been a tenant of Delyth and Jacko James at the Coach and Horses itself – and that had not been a good experience at all.

Now the woman whose father had given her the pub as a wedding present had sent Tudor a message asking if he was interested in buying the place? Annie pushed the sheets off her; it was so warm she couldn't bear to be covered at all.

Tudor had always said how much better a business he could make of the larger pub, not only because it had an extra bar and a bigger kitchen, but because it had guest rooms as well as a larger living space for the publican.

Annie had never seen the pub's living quarters, but took Tudor's word for it that they were more spacious than his own – which were tight, to say the least, especially given that Annie was spending more and more time there. And her cottage was almost as small as his flat, but with the great disadvantage that if Tudor was at hers, he wasn't on the spot at the pub in case of any problems arising, hence the pair of them spending more and more time at Tudor's.

But it was a squish for two large humans, plus two still-growing Labradors who enjoyed nothing more than running, jumping, and wrestling with each other. Before too long there'd be mayhem at the place. Annie had been thinking about how she might be able to move from her cottage to something larger in the village, or the area, but the fact that she didn't drive, that the buses were reliable but infrequent, and the critical factor that Tudor really needed to be at the pub – and she wanted to be with Tudor – meant she'd done nothing about looking for an alternative home. So maybe the Coach and Horses offered a truly workable alternative: a chance for Tudor to spread his business wings, and a bigger place for them to live as a couple.

As Annie thought of what that meant, in terms of her life and her future, she pulled the sheet up under her chin, despite the heat: she and Tudor had made a commitment to each other, albeit without specific words having been spoken. Would they take such a giant leap without anything about their relationship changing? Could they? Did she want to?

Burying her face in her pillow, Annie wondered if she'd ever sleep – then wondered why Delyth James had sent a message to Tudor at such an odd time. Maybe she'd had a few drinks, had indulged in a bit of drunk texting, and wouldn't recall what she'd done in the morning? Or maybe she was baiting him for some reason. Either way, Annie was aware that no one had seen anything of Delyth since the events that had originally drawn the WISE women to the village of Anwen-by-Wye, and everyone agreed that the infrequent attention of a management company just wasn't enough to prevent a fine example of a Georgian coaching inn from falling into an unsightly level of disrepair. The paint was peeling, drainpipes were dripping and gutters were threatening to fall away completely. If something wasn't done soon, the ancient brickwork might be damaged beyond saving – at least, that's what folks in the village had been saying, according to Sharon at the shop, who kept her finger on the pulse, her ear to the ground…and probably her backside in the air, thought Annie, exasperated by her whirling mind.

Go to sleep! Annie tried to take her own advice, but, even so, the question of why Delyth James – who she'd always thought of as quite predatory – had got in touch with Tudor at such a strange time vexed her, and led to disturbing dreams about him being chased through a forest of giant beer pumps by a woman screaming at him in Welsh, brandishing a sword made of horse brasses, as she squirted him with beer foam.

When she phoned Tudor the next morning – though she realized it was really just a few hours later during the same morning – Annie wasn't in the brightest of moods and nor, it was immediately apparent, was Tudor.

'One of our dogs managed to get up onto the table and ate half a loaf of bread during the night,' was his opening gambit. Annie inferred from his tone that he suspected her Gertie rather than his Rosie of the crime.

'Well, you'd better keep an eye on both of them then, because that much bread can upset a dog. But it's not like you to leave any food out overnight on the table, Tude. What's that all about then?'

'I was painting, in the snug, as I told you. Totally exhausted when I went up to bed, so I suppose I didn't notice it. More fool me. I hope neither of them gets ill because of it. But I'll keep an eye on them both, as you say. Now – what about this thing with the Coach and Horses?'

Annie didn't hesitate. 'What on earth was Delyth flamin' James doing sending you a message at that time of night? Do you think she'd had one too many?'

'She's in Alaska. At least, she's on a cruise ship that's sailing along the coast of Alaska. She sent another message saying that an hour later, then asked me to phone her around six-ish this evening – our time – when she'll be up and about again.'

Annie was more than surprised. 'That's even odder. I mean, she's left the pub standing empty since she upped and flounced off over a year ago, and now she's wanting to have a phone conversation about it when she's on holiday…all the way over in Alaska. That's just…well, it's a bit weird, don't you think?'

Tudor chuckled. 'You're not the only detective in the family, you know. I did a bit of Googling and it seems her father died a couple of days ago. I dare say she was already where she is now when it happened. There was a bit about it on the website of the local newspaper. Stanley Davies – that was her father, the one who gave her the pub – was quite the local figure; pots of money and wasn't afraid to dole it out supporting local businesses, it seems. Someone was waxing lyrical about him to the local rag – a bloke with an orchard near Hereford that's doing great business in the artisanal cider market thanks to an investment made by Delyth's late father.'

Annie took a deep glug of her coffee and waved, smiling, at her mother who was busy in the kitchen. 'Will Delyth inherit everything, then?'

'Down, Rosie…no idea. The article I read said the mother was living at some sort of home. Delyth was in her fifties, and the father was in his late eighties, so it's likely the mother's no spring chicken either, so maybe she's at a care home?'

'Since her father gave it to her as a gift, do you reckon Delyth didn't want to sell the pub during his lifetime? Could that be it?' It sort of made sense to Annie.

'Maybe. But, look, what I want us to think about is this: we've talked about it, and you know I've always believed I could make a go of it. But what if she wants more than I can afford? I mean, have you ever considered…' Tudor's voice trailed off.

'Tude, darlin', I haven't got the proverbial pot, you know that. I mean, yeah, I've got a bit in the bank, but I live off that. And the way things are going with the agency, I'm eating into it more and more, even though I pay hardly any rent. To be honest, I don't know where it all goes. It's not like I'm buying clothes for meself, or fancy make-up or anything like that. And we eat at your place such a lot that I can't think it's going on food.'

Tudor chuckled. 'I'm looking down at your Gertie here, with her fancy collar, her new harness, her third bed in as many months, and I know for a fact she goes through toys like they're rice paper. I bet if you take a long hard look at where your money is going, this dog will account for a lot of it. But, yes, I know what you mean. I just thought I'd check. I've got my savings, and there might be someone who's prepared to give a fit man, in his prime, a mortgage to buy a pub…in the middle of nowhere, with no existing clientele at all.'

'You've got the track record, you're only in your mid-fifties, and you're right, you're as healthy as an ox…so, yeah, they should give you a mortgage.'

Tudor sighed. 'Oh, I don't know, Annie…is now the time to invest in a country pub? The world doesn't seem to need them anymore. You know what business has been like here, and this place doesn't need the turnover that place would need to make a go of it. The Twysts charge me hardly any rent, and I get treated very well by them, to be fair. Speaking of them, I'm due up at the Hall later on – another meeting about the village regeneration scheme that I'm not looking forward to.'

'Come on, Tude – you're Hugo's godfather…a real link to the heir to the seat, and you know Iris Lewis will always back you up if there's a ridiculous proposal on the table. As will Marjorie Pritchard, once you explain to her how it'll put her nose out of joint, somehow.'

'True. But I don't want to be the one standing in the way of real progress, nor do I want it to look as though I'm only against things that will affect my business, like that idea they had of opening up a teashop in the village with staff from the tea rooms at the Hall.'

'Well, that was a stupid idea, wasn't it? All they'd be doing is diverting business from the Hall to the village, and they'd completely scupper your plans for serving teas and coffees in the snug at the Lamb and Flag. So of course you had to speak out against it.'

'But when they said they wanted to offer local beers at a small bar when they've got the Market Hall redecorated, the toilets there sorted out, and all those panels installed about the history of the village? I could tell that both Henry and Stephanie were a bit put out when I kicked up a fuss about that.'

'Come on, Tude, that wasn't just you. Constable Llinos Trevelyan even wrote to them about it, saying how unlikely it was that a licence to sell alcohol would be available for yet another location in Anwen-by-Wye, when there are two licenced premises – the Coach and Horses *and* the Lamb and Flag – within a mile of the Market Hall.'

'That was a bit of luck, wasn't it? And I already know you suggested it to Llinos; she mentioned it when she dropped in to comment on the new furniture at the front of the pub, which is very popular – by the way – with the weather we've been having. Ideal for folks who want to sit in the sun and sip a cool drink. And those umbrellas? Inspired, Annie, inspired; the rep for the brewery was only too happy to give me half a dozen, and he's thrilled that their logo is so prominent now.'

'Do you think she'll want a lot for it? The pub, I mean. Delyth.'

Tudor sighed again. 'No idea. I hope not. But who knows? Maybe if she's getting in touch with me this soon after her father's death it means she's wanted to get rid of it for a while. But I know what you've always called her, and she might be difficult to deal with.'

'I tell you what, I'll do a bit of digging around about her through today and I'll send you whatever I can find. Just between the two of us, let's call it The Case of the Predatory Publican, though I hope that turns out to be me overreacting a bit. As per usual.'

'Hope so. Right-o, but I thought that you and your mum were off visiting people today – when will you have time to do anything?'

Annie chuckled. 'There'll be breaks, while we're on the bus getting from A to B; this will keep me out of mischief…and it's for us, so it matters. Alright, my sausages are ready it seems. Talk later – and hug Gert for me, will you?'

'Will do. Love you.'

'Love you, too.'

CHAPTER FOUR

Carol Hill had been hoping for a slow start to the day because her infant son Albert had been awake and crying with teething pain for most of the night. She'd been on duty because her husband David's computing consulting had him liaising with a company based in Honolulu, so his working hours had become nocturnal for the past couple of weeks, and he still had a couple more to go before the end of the contract.

With Albert finally sleeping peacefully in his cot – if pink-cheeked and a bit restlessly – Carol poured tea down her throat in the kitchen as though her life depended upon it, which she suspected it might. The toast and Marmite helped too, but not as much as the tea. She'd been glad that things had been quieter than usual at the agency for the past little while, and was especially grateful that she wasn't needed at the office while David was sleeping during the daytime, because that would have meant taking Albert with her, which was lovely – but a real fiddle-faddle.

Now that he was properly crawling, as opposed to scooting, and even taking his first unsteady steps, Carol didn't fancy her son ranging around the barn where she and her colleagues were based; it was easier for her to keep him safe in the home over which she had complete control – even if she didn't really have control over him. It seemed that now he'd learned to get around under his own steam, he wanted to do nothing more than stick his nose into everything; Carol had never realized how potentially lethal their home could be to a child with insatiable curiosity and a perpetual desire to push his fingers everywhere, or else shove absolutely anything into his mouth, or up his nose.

Bunty, Carol's calico cat, bounded onto her lap, making the most of the opportunity to suggest she needed to be petted. Carol indulged her, enjoying the silky warmth of Bunty's fur, and loving the feeling of the tiny body vibrating as she stroked her velvety ears.

Answering her phone with a sigh, Carol said, 'Morning, Mavis.' Not giving her colleague the chance to even say hello, she continued with, 'Yes, I saw that you'd emailed me and, before you ask, no, I haven't had time to read the attachment. Sorry. Bad night with Albert. I'll read it as soon as we finish on the phone. Promise.'

'Is the bairn no' well?' Mavis sounded concerned.

Carol smiled. 'He's fine, thanks. Just teething. Asleep now. What can I do for you?'

She listened patiently as Mavis explained Louise Attwater's situation, and wondered if she'd left a window open somewhere, because she felt quite chilly.

'How on earth can someone know that people are about to die, Mavis? That's…unsettling.'

'Aye, that it is. Do you think you'd be able to at least gather data about a couple of dozen deceased people within a day of work? That's what I need to know as a matter of urgency.'

Carol was sometimes grateful that Mavis focused on business to such an extent; on other occasions – this being one of them – it made Carol wonder about how much compassion Mavis actually possessed. Maybe it was a nurse thing? The only other nurse Carol had ever known well was a girl from the farm beside the one where Carol had grown up, and who'd been at school with her in Carmarthen. There'd been a certain aloofness about her when it came to human suffering, too. Carol had, therefore, always assumed it was an attitude nurses needed to possess to allow them to do their jobs without getting too emotionally attached to patients. In Mavis's case, that aura hadn't left her, even though she'd retired from her previous profession.

Carol replied, 'It would depend on quite a few variables, but I dare say I could come up with something that might be useful.' She'd learned that simple answers were best at times like this, rather than even trying to explain how she did her job.

'Excellent. In that case, by all means cast an eye over what I emailed you, but I'll send off our proposal and quote to Louise Attwater now, and I'll let you know when I hear from her. She didn't give me the impression this was an urgent matter, and I believe she'll want to speak to the other firms of undertakers upon whose behalf she's acting before she responds, so enjoy the rest of your day with Albert, and I'll let you know if there's anything else we need.'

Carol suspected the tea was starting to kick in because she realized she couldn't let Mavis go without asking a quick question. 'Hang on a sec, Mavis. Have you had a chance to look at those figures I sent you yesterday? The accounts aren't looking too good, are they? That pot of money we built up at the start of the year has dwindled, and we're all likely to have to take a pay cut next month. Any ideas?'

Carol was surprised by Mavis's sharp response. 'Aye, well, letting me get back to a potential client would be a start. We'll talk later. Bye for now.'

Carol looked at the now inert lump of plastic in her hand. 'A quick, "Thanks for putting the accounts together so quickly, Carol," would have been nice, but there you are then.'

Placing Bunty on the floor with one hand as she pocketed her phone with the other, Carol moved toward the kettle, stalked by her feline shadow, who took up her position guarding the Aga with a swift flick of her tail.

Carol almost dropped her freshly filled mug when her phone rang again in her pocket. 'Hello?' She knew she sounded snappish, but she'd managed to get hot water on her hand and sleeve and was cross with herself.

'Hiya, it's me. Ellie. Caught you at a bad time, have I?'

Carol grinned at the familiar voice and enjoyed the chance to lapse into her native tongue. 'That's weird. I was just thinking about you, and now here you are.'

'I've said it before, and I'll say it again – we're linked in the universe you and me, Carol, my lovely. So, why were you thinking about me?'

'Oh, nothing really; just talking to Mavis, who used to be a nurse as I've told you, and wondering about how exactly you nurses manage to do what you do, day in and day out.'

Ellie chuckled. 'Because of the massive amount of money we're paid, and the way people shower us with praise for every act of mercy we perform, I expect.'

'Yeah, that must be it,' replied Carol wryly. 'Anyway, what's up? You alright?'

'I'm fine, ta, but I've got a couple of days off unexpectedly and wondered if you'd be up for a night out? Just you and me – with the prospect of me using your spare bedroom afterwards. I was thinking about staying tonight and leaving tomorrow. How about that?'

Carol groaned. 'Aw, Ellie, Albert's teething and David's working nights. I mean, of course you can come and stay, but I don't know about a night out. What about a night in? I could do a curry – and you know how you love my curries.'

Carol was surprised that her old friend didn't answer right away, and was puzzled by her tone when she did. 'You haven't got anyone who could babysit Albert just for a few hours, have you? I really, really want us to be able to get our heads together somewhere…well, neutral, I suppose. Private, you know? Not even the pub in your village – nice though it is. Somewhere where no one knows either of us, where we can just be us. I…I need to talk to you about something. Just the two of us.'

Carol hesitated. 'I could ask Joan, I suppose.'

'Good. Who's that?'

Carol smiled to herself as she pictured her neighbor. 'Joan Pike. She lives a few doors away. Lovely girl. Well, I say girl because she's younger than me, though I suppose she must be in her late twenties. Huh – yes, I think she's about the same age as Christine who I work with – though the two of them couldn't be more different. Joan's quite an old soul – does a lot of sewing, crocheting, and knitting. She likes to spoil Albert rotten. Thanks to her I don't think he'll ever go short of any sort of baby clothes – though he's growing so fast at the moment not even she can keep up with him. She might sit with Albert this evening – if she can. She's her mother's carer, see? Mobility problems. Anyway, I trust her with Albert, and David would be in his office upstairs if there were to be an absolute emergency. I'll ask her. Tonight, you said? When would you get here, do you think? Oh hang on, there's someone at the door.' Carol couldn't believe it – no one ever knocked at the front door. 'Hold on, just let me get…'

'Surprise!' Ellie was on the doorstep, beaming. She had a bottle of wine in one hand and her phone in the other. 'I knew you'd say yes.'

She flung her arms around Carol, who was feeling slightly befuddled as she hugged her friend back and stuffed her phone into her dressing gown pocket.

Ellie pulled back. 'What, not dressed yet? It's half eight – what are you thinking, woman? Come on, let's put this wine in the fridge for later, and I'll hold the fort while you make yourself gorgeous for the day. Got a pot on the go? I'll get my bag from the car later.'

Carol watched as Ellie headed toward the kitchen, and smiled; sometimes there was nothing quite like seeing a friend who was so close that, no matter how much time had passed since you'd last seen them, it felt like only a few moments ago that you'd hugged, and chatted…and planned your futures together.

Carol stage-whispered, 'Ignore the mess and help yourself to what you want. You know where everything is – and don't forget that both my son and my husband are fast asleep.' She followed Ellie into the kitchen, then added, 'I'm going upstairs to pull on some proper clothes.'

Ellie grinned. 'Don't worry about that, have a cuppa with me first. If we're on our own right now for a while I'll tell you what I need to tell you, then – when your boys are up and about – we won't have to hide from them in the pub, or wherever, okay?'

Carol was intrigued as she sat down with her chum. 'Just spit it out, then – I'm all ears. Are you alright? Nothing's wrong, is it?'

Ellie raised her tea in a toast. 'Don't panic, I'm fine. And, by the way, Janice Taylor's finished her chemo now, and they reckon she'll be alright. It's not a health problem for me, it's a work problem.'

'A problem at the nursing home?'

Ellie nodded. 'You're the only person I know I can talk to about this. And you've got to promise you won't tell a soul without asking me about it first. Well, not anyone who isn't family, or a work colleague. You know what I mean. And no names, or places, unless I say so. Right? Because what I'm about to say could ruin a person's career, or even their life; that's why I haven't said anything to anyone until now. But now I need to talk to someone I trust. And of course I trust you, but you're also by far the best person to know about this because you've told me so much about your work and the sort of people you encounter because of it – people who are bad, Carol…or maybe people who are good, but do bad things.'

Carol's tummy clenched. 'Okay, if you're trying to make me worry, it's working. What is it, Ellie? What's wrong at work?'

Ellie fiddled with a non-existent stray hair. 'You know I took the position of Sister-in-Charge at the nursing home about six months ago?'

Carol nodded.

'Well, there's a junior nurse there I don't see much of because she's always on nights and I'm always on days. I know her because of our handovers, of course, but I don't *know* know her. Anyway, one of the things that happens at a nursing home is that our patients die. It's to be expected and, for many, it really is a release from pain. When they die, all their medications are supposed to be disposed of in the proper manner which, in our case, means taking them all to a local pharmacy that makes sure they don't just end up in the oceans, or something awful or dangerous like that.'

Carol nodded. 'Sensible. And?'

Ellie placed her mug on the table and leaned forward. She whispered, 'I think the junior nurse in question isn't properly disposing of the leftover medications. I think she's pocketing them for herself. I don't want to believe she's giving them to our patients, because…well, while people do die, they aren't exactly unexpected deaths. But she doesn't strike me as the drug-dealing sort, either.'

Carol gave her friend's words a moment's thought. 'You mean you think that one of the nurses you work with is stealing drugs, and you don't know where the drugs go?'

Ellie nodded. 'Carol – what should I do?'

CHAPTER FIVE

Christine Wilson-Smythe had agreed with Mavis that she'd work with Carol if the agency was successful in getting Louise Attwater as a client. Indeed, she was keen to get her teeth into a case that might engage her more than the last one she'd worked on. That little gem had required her to keep watch on a woman who the head of security for a department store in Cardiff was convinced was shoplifting, despite the fact that they couldn't catch her doing anything amiss.

To be fair, wearing constantly changing disguises had kept Christine entertained for a while, and she'd especially enjoyed being a blonde at times, but it had taken her several days at the place to be able to finally work out what was going on. She'd managed to follow the suspect all the way from the department store to the multi-storey car park nearby, whereupon the suspect pulled several expensive electronic items from beneath her skirt – which had shocked Christine at the time.

Having informed the client of her observations, the security staff had apprehended the suspect when she'd next been attempting to leave the shop; as usual the alarm had sounded, and – again as usual – the woman had shown the security staff an item in a bag she was carrying that was branded for a different shop, close by, where 'they must have forgotten to remove the tag'. But, because of Christine's input, the security staff were able to discover that – beneath her full-skirted dress – the woman was wearing long culottes with lot of pockets she was able to access through side-slits in her frock.

The client had been delighted, the agency had been paid swiftly, and there were reassurances that the WISE women would be top of their list when they needed any future help. His finals remarks had worried Christine a little, because she hadn't thought that being a private enquiries agent would involve such mundane tasks.

Now, however, she was in her element, driving toward her London home, where she was about to spend the evening with her fiancé and parents. She'd cleared her desk and cleared her head before she'd set off from Wales, and had thoroughly enjoyed blasting out the music as the miles disappeared. Not wanting to use the phone when she was driving – and singing – she'd returned her fiancé's missed call as soon as she could, which was why she was sitting in the car park of a motorway service station waiting for him to phone her back again, the two of them having exchanged a couple of messages.

Finally, Christine's phone rang.

'Excellent, it's really you this time.' Alexander sounded truly delighted. 'Not long now, and I get to hold you in these eager arms of mine.'

'Mr Bright – you're making me blush,' mugged Christine. 'You're funny.' She giggled.

'I try. Anyway, where are you exactly?'

'Just about thirty miles from the M25,' replied Christine excitedly.

'Why?'

'What do you mean, why? Because I'm on my way to Battersea and you're joining me at my parents' place for dinner tonight. Remember?' Christine was sure he'd forgotten.

'No, that's next weekend. This weekend I'm coming to Anwen-by-Wye to take a look at that old antiques shop in the village that I've been talking to Henry and Stephanie about setting up as a sales outlet for the Coggins antiques business. We talked about it not two days ago.'

Christine's certainty wavered. They had discussed it; Alexander was right about that. Henry and Stephanie's plans had been the talk of the entire village for a couple of months, and she clearly recalled how enthusiastic Alexander had been about the idea of the antiques company in which he was now a silent partner having a chance to offload some of their pieces in a part of the world where their auction house had no presence.

But weren't they doing that next weekend? She checked her calendar, and sighed.

'You're right. I'm sorry. You and me in Anwen this weekend, then with Mammy and Daddy next weekend. How stupid am I?'

'Not stupid at all. It's an easy mistake to make. So...will you turn around and come back now? I'm about an hour away. I could meet you at the Lamb and Flag if you like. Dinner there, then back to the flat? At the barn, not Battersea, of course.'

Christine felt deflated. Hours on the road for no reason – except her own inability to differentiate one week from another. This wasn't her...this wasn't normal. When she'd been working in the City of London, she'd juggled a massively demanding career and a stellar social life; now that she was kicking her heels in a tiny Welsh village, she felt...less. Less stressed, of course, but somehow less herself too. Or was that because she was now half of a whole? Half of an engaged couple. Seemingly incomplete without Alexander to make her so.

A low-slung red sports car revved as it parked close beside her, drawing her attention. The woman driving it was about five years Christine's junior, and she leaped from the stationary vehicle like an animal. Tattoos on her bare arms were revealed by a slinky leopard-print top, and she showed perfect white teeth between her blood-red lips when she smiled at Christine as she danced past, heading to the restaurant area. To Christine's eyes the young woman looked free, empowered...and happy.

'You still there?' Alexander sounded concerned.

'Yes, still here. Sorry – just thinking. I'll see you at the pub as soon as I can make it back. Sorry about this. Of course we can go to the shop tomorrow together, and you said you were going to show Bill Coggins around the place through your phone, right?'

'That's right. See you when I see you, then. But no mad driving, okay? I want you with me safe and sound – and later and safe is better than putting yourself in danger. Love you.'

'Love you, too.' Christine couldn't be certain if she'd disconnected before she'd finished telling her fiancé that she loved him, but knew he'd understand. At least, she hoped he would.

Sighing, she began her journey back to Anwen-by-Wye – to her quiet life there, her quiet job there, and her fiancé.

When she eventually arrived at the pub, she found Alexander deep in conversation with Tudor Evans at the bar, a pint of fizzy orange juice almost empty beside him, and the two men staring at each other in a rather alarming manner. She was immediately certain she'd found them having some sort of a disagreement – a suspicion that was confirmed by her fiancé greeting her with slightly too much relief, and Tudor's curt nod, followed by him looking as though he was trying to polish his way through a beer glass.

'What can I get for you?' Alexander kissed her on the cheek.

'A pint of gin might do the trick.' Christine wasn't in the mood for banter, and she knew her tone would tell Alexander as much.

He grimaced, then chuckled. 'Okay, I dare say you can leave your car here overnight and I'll drive us back. A pint of gin for my fiancée, if you please, Tudor, and I'll have another orange juice and soda water. Oh, and two lamb stews, please.' Alexander grinned at Christine. 'That's what you fancy, right?'

Christine weighed her response then conceded, 'Yes, please, a lamb stew, and just make it a very large G and T please, Tudor. Though I'm not promising I won't work my way up to that full pint as the evening passes.'

She noticed the strange way Tudor looked at her, then he smiled broadly. 'As long as I know you won't be driving, you can have the biggest gin you want. You two go on over and grab that table, and I'll have Aled bring everything over when it's ready.'

Settling themselves at a small table beside the unlit hearth, Christine allowed Alexander to fuss over her, and to convince her that there was absolutely nothing amiss between him and Tudor whatsoever beyond a heated conversation they'd been having about the extortionate amount of money the publican was charging for what Alexander claimed was just a pint of fizzy squash.

Then they chatted about the journeys they had both taken to bring them to the place – which filled the time until Christine could finally enjoy the bitterness and sweetness of her drink in her mouth and allow herself to truly relax. She didn't tell her fiancé how she'd managed to make such good time on her trip, simply saying there hadn't been much traffic about; she reckoned it was better if he didn't realize how fast she'd actually driven.

Just as Aled arrived with their dinner, Christine checked her buzzing phone. 'Oh, that's good,' she said before thanking Tudor's helper for the food and cutlery he'd brought.

'Something to do with work?' Alexander didn't lose any time in tucking a large napkin into his shirt and arming himself to attack the bowl of stew in front of him.

'Yes, a new case. I'll be working on it with Carol. It could be…interesting.' Christine enjoyed her first mouthful of rich, glistening stew, though a few hours earlier she'd have thought it mad to be diving into a steaming bowl of anything, the day had been so warm.

Alexander paused and watched her for a moment. 'Did you even have lunch?'

Christine shook her head as she chewed. 'Forgot,' she managed to mouth, then she shrugged. When she could, she added, 'You know I really only like to eat when I'm hungry, and I wasn't then, but I am now. Besides, don't forget that I thought I was saving myself for a five-course marathon at the family pile tonight. What a twit I am. But don't worry, this weekend will be grand in any case. You and me and an empty shop – with Bill on the video phone and you two talking about bits and bobs of shop fittings and a pile of old antiques. What could be better, eh?' Even as she spoke, Christine wondered why she was being so…cutting.

She wasn't surprised when Alexander put down his spoon and said, 'Right, come on then. What's going on? Is it something I've done to make you so angry? Or is someone else to blame? Just tell me and I'll—'

Christine leaned forward and hissed, 'You'll what? Sort them out? Get one of your shifty friends to have a quiet word with them? What if I told you that old Ned over there had been making lewd suggestions to me? Would you take him out the back of the pub and give him a good going over? Oh yes, I bet you'd do it – I can see the way you're looking at him right now, so you are.' She finished off her drink and waggled her glass in the air, getting Tudor's attention and making it plain that she wanted the same again.

Alexander broke off a chunk of the soda bread on his plate and dunked it into his bowl, swirling the meaty liquid slowly, not looking at her. Christine wondered what he was thinking, then wondered why she was always niggling at him, pushing him to find his breaking point. She had to admit she really didn't know. But surely he would react? He had to, didn't he?

'So what's this case you'll be working on with Carol?' Alexander's voice betrayed no hint of annoyance as he spoke. Indeed, he smiled and winked his thanks when Aled took Christine's empty glass and gave her a fresh drink.

Christine could feel herself seething and snapped, 'So that's how it's going to be, is it? Alright then – if you want me to talk about work, I'll talk about it. It's all we seem to do these days in any case – talk about your work or mine. For once mine's quite interesting. A mysterious figure is leaving creepy wreaths on the doorsteps of houses before someone in the family dies, and Carol and I are going to work out who it is, and how they're doing it.'

Alexander stopped his annoying swirling and looked up. 'You mean they deliver the wreaths because everyone knows that a family member is about to die?'

Christine gave his question some thought as she glugged at her drink. 'Having looked at the information the client gave us, it seems the people who died were very ill, and mainly older, and some were already in hospices so…you know.'

Alexander sat back in his chair, surrendering his soaked bread to the depths of his stew. 'Still, wreaths *before* deaths. That's weird.'

Christine couldn't help but laugh. 'So it is, Alexander. So it is. And this mystery man arrives in a hearse, which is a nice added bonus.'

Alexander's brow furrowed. 'That doesn't just sound weird, it sounds…worrying. And it'll just be you and Carol working on this? So you'll be doing all the field work?'

Christine nodded. 'That's right. Carol's wonderful, but you know she's tied to Albert, so she'll do her thing at home, and I'll be the legs. Doing any face-to-face interviews, following up any leads that can't be sniffed out via a laptop or a phone.'

Alexander picked up his spoon and attacked his stew again – hunting about for his lost chunk of bread, Christine suspected. 'But what if…I mean, what if the person delivering the wreaths knows these people are going to die because they're actually killing them? Have you thought about that? That could be really dangerous.'

Christine drained her glass and stared at her stew. 'Good heavens, now why had that thought not entered my empty little head? How do you fancy being the detective and I'll just stay at home and wash your socks for you, shall I?'

Alexender dropped his spoon and pushed back his chair, scraping it loudly across the ancient flagstone floor. 'Excuse me – I need the facilities.'

Christine saw his eyes flash as he glanced down at her before he left, and could tell he was angry, which allowed her to feel just a little triumphant as she waggled her empty glass toward Aled behind the bar and indicated just how big she wanted her third gin to be.

CHAPTER SIX

Althea Twyst looked quite a picture as she descended the stairs in the Dower House to be greeted by Mavis MacDonald.

'Do you no' think that a family dinner calls for a more demure form of dress...you know, for an eighty-year-old dowager?' Mavis couldn't help but ask; she was wearing her serviceable black dress, once again.

'I have worn this on many such occasions,' replied Althea, sliding her hand down the pleats in her bottle green taffeta skirt.

'Aye, I've seen it before. But that orange wrap is new, I think, as are the red shoes and those striped tights. They are tights, aren't they?' Mavis's voice was trembling.

Arriving in the hallway, Althea smiled sweetly. 'Yes, they're all new. I feel that mixing new bits in revitalizes the old, don't you?'

'Well, the dress certainly looks different tonight than I've ever seen it before,' was Mavis's purposely enigmatic reply. 'You've had it shortened, I think.'

Althea beamed. 'Indeed. I ran a few stitches around it myself. Of course, my eyesight's not quite what it was when I used to make my own stage costumes in my years as a professional dancer, but I think I've done a passably good job of it.'

'It's evenly hemmed,' acknowledged Mavis, 'though I've no' seen you keen to show off your knees before tonight, I must say.'

Althea glanced at her reflection in the hall mirror. 'Yes, I took it up a little more than I'd originally planned, but I don't think anyone will notice.'

'Aye, well, it's hard to not pay attention to those yellow-and-green striped tights.'

'Don't you think the green matches the dress just perfectly?'

'Aye, that it does. Ach, here's Ian arriving, ready to drive us over to the Hall. Now you're certain it will be alright for me to join you all this evening? You've checked with Clementine? This dinner being her idea.'

'Absolutely, my dear, she said she'd be happy to have you there. Of course, I don't understand why she's doing all this cloak and dagger stuff, but you know my daughter…sometimes she gets so bored she has to create drama where none exists.'

'Indeed.'

In fact, that was Mavis's fear – that they were in for a dinner where drama would prevail, and she didn't care for that sort of thing…no, not at all.

However, as the evening began, it seemed to Mavis that her apprehension had been misplaced. Everyone was all smiles as they cooed over baby Hugo and sipped cooling drinks.

When the Twysts' butler, Edward, announced that dinner was ready, Henry looked at his watch, tutting.

'So Clemmie is doing her usual thing, I see. Makes a fuss about us all dining together, then doesn't put in an appearance herself. Typical.'

'She's been here since about three this afternoon,' replied Stephanie. 'Went straight to her rooms, I happen to know. You were at your studio, dear. I'm sure she'll be down to join us momentarily. Come along, let's get our son settled into his crib in the dining room. He's fast asleep at the moment so we won't even know he's there, and I do so want him to grow up with the knowledge that he was always a part of our lives, and not just shut into a nursery.'

Mavis thought she caught a slight clucking noise coming from Althea who, she happened to know, was very much of the opinion that the use of a nursery and nanny as methods of managing and controlling young children was to be welcomed rather than ignored, having employed both for her son and daughter. Mavis also noted, with delight, that Althea said nothing on the matter – something for which she was grateful.

Instead, Althea focused her attention upon her son, the duke. 'Henry, I don't think it's terribly constructive to constantly harp on about Clementine's lack of punctuality. We don't know why she's late. She might have a very good reason.'

'Thank you, Mother,' said Clementine Twyst as the party arrived in the dining room, where she was already waiting. 'Indeed, there was a very good reason for my not joining you all for drinks this evening. Though, as you can see, I myself have been quenching my thirst with this big jug of lemon barley water.' She nodded at one of the sideboards, then acknowledged Edward's solicitousness.

'What a surprise,' said Henry, sounding glum rather than elated.

'I don't like to disappoint,' replied his sister slyly. 'Ever. And I don't think I shall this evening. Now, come along, let's all get comfortable...but, before you snuggle him down in his crib, let me at least look at my little nephew.'

Clementine and Stephanie gazed down at the sleeping heir to the Chellingworth title, both beaming, and both doing their best to not disturb him. The moment touched Mavis deeply, as she recalled how wondrous her own two boys, and even her grandchildren, had been at the same age. Magical – especially when they were fast asleep.

'There's an extra setting,' observed Henry, glancing toward Edward, who appeared to Mavis to be overly involved with straightening some glassware on the sideboard, requiring him to momentarily turn his back to the party.

'All will be revealed,' replied Clementine brightly.

Henry's sigh was loud enough that no one could have missed it. 'Oh, please, Clemmie, no drama tonight. It's been too hot a day for dramas.'

Lady Clementine allowed her left hand to run across her brother's shoulders as he sat, prior to taking her own seat; Mavis noticed something catch the light, and her heart sank. A drama-free evening was the last thing on the cards, she feared. She steeled herself, and turned her attention to Althea, who seemed to be having a few problems adjusting her voluminous skirt so that she was comfortable.

Leaning toward Mavis, the dowager hissed, 'I think I've taken too much of a hem on this thing. There's not enough left to properly cover my hindquarters.'

Mavis tried to stop her eyes from rolling, but failed. 'Well do the best you can,' was all she could manage.

Althea fidgeted about for a bit, then settled down when Edward arrived with the wine, of which she happily accepted a large glass. Leaning toward Mavis, she again hissed, 'Have you spotted what Clementine's got on her ring finger? I bet I can guess what's coming. Make yours a large one, too, Mavis – we could be in for an interesting evening.'

Mavis allowed Edward to pour her twice as much wine as usual – half a glass – and tried to not sigh audibly. She feared the worst, but hoped for the best, which would probably still be a disaster.

Once all the glasses were filled – Stephanie's with elderflower cordial – Clementine tinkled the lead crystal of hers with a silver spoon and cleared her throat. 'I have an announcement.'

Mavis noticed Henry's mouth set itself into a thin line as he grunted and fingered the bottom corner of the napkin that was tucked into his shirt collar above his bow tie – thereby offering maximum protection.

Clementine held up her left hand, the large ring on her fourth finger catching the light from the chandelier. 'I've become engaged to be married.'

Neither Mavis nor Althea reacted, Stephanie looked surprised, and Henry shrugged. 'This will be the fourth time, isn't that right, sister, dear?' His tone suggested boredom rather than an accusation.

'And the last.' Clementine smiled demurely. 'My fiancé is joining us for dinner, and I hope you'll all give him a warm welcome.'

Stephanie said, 'Please, invite him to join us, Clementine. I'm sure we'll all do our best to not pepper him with too many questions as we dine, won't we, Henry, dear?'

'Indeed.' Henry's voice sounded a little strange to Mavis, but she gave her attention to Clementine who bounded from her seat and returned to the room a moment or two later – during which time it appeared that all her tablemates were incredibly thirsty.

'I'd like you all to meet Julian – though everyone calls him Jools. Jools, my mother Althea, my brother Henry, my sister-in-law Stephanie, and my mother's great friend and confidant, Mavis. I've told Jools that he's not to use "Your Grace" or anything like that, because he's family too – or will be soon enough. Right?'

Mavis was moved by the absolute adoration etched into every line on Clementine's face, which was mirrored by her fiancé's – at least, as far as she could tell. Jools towered over Clementine's short, spare frame, and whereas Clementine's entire appearance was always attention grabbing – as witnessed by her currently turquoise hair – his attire was entirely black, matching his bushy beard and eyebrows, as well as his long, curling hair. He looked like a massive bear – that was Mavis's first impression. She hoped he was a kindly one, because with his height – more than a foot taller than Clementine, and girth – certainly twice that of the duke's sister, he could probably have crushed her with one tight squeeze.

'A pleasure to meet you all.' The accent was from somewhere in the West Country – maybe Bristol – thought Mavis.

'You're next to me,' gushed Clementine, encouraging Edward to hold Jools's seat for him before accommodating her.

Once the party was complete again, Jools declined wine, accepted sparkling water, and placed his seemingly inadequate napkin on his lap with calm authority.

He raised his glass and said quietly, 'Thank you for your gracious invitation to dine. It is my great pleasure to meet you all.' His sonorous voice rolled across the silent dining room, and Mavis thought it sounded as though a great train was rumbling through a tunnel.

'You're most welcome,' said Stephanie raising her glass in response, 'as I'm sure we all agree. To the happy couple.'

The toast was taken up around the table, though Mavis couldn't help but notice that Henry responded with less enthusiasm than everyone else.

'And what does a big boy like you do for a living?' Althea had tilted her head toward the man, quite coquettishly.

Mavis wondered if Jools would be taken aback by Althea's directness, but he didn't seem fazed at all.

Within his beard – which Mavis could now see was well-groomed, lush and glistening – a great expanse of white teeth gleamed in a smile. 'I'm a blacksmith.' It seemed like an absolutely natural answer.

Althea beamed. 'Horses – or arty things?'

When Jools laughed, Mavis thought she felt the table shuddering beneath her hands.

He replied jovially, 'Arty things mostly these days, though I shod a fair few beasts during my early years. Important work, but not, as it transpired, where my talent lay. The horses sometimes worried me, but sometimes I worried them, too, and you can't be building a career with animals if they aren't happy to be around you.'

Althea sipped her wine and nodded. 'Absolutely. Whenever a certain blacksmith came to shoe the horses here – he travelled about to many stables, as one might imagine – they would pass the word, so to speak. When the time came for him to give them his attention there was a lot of whinnying, and perfectly delightful creatures would get quite uppity with him. We had to find an alternative, of course. I've always wondered if it were just our horses he had a problem with, or if they all didn't care for him.'

'It might have been his aftershave, or some sort of other product he used on his person,' replied Jools, immediately engaged. 'I was told about that and avoided all scents for a while. But, in my case, it made no difference. The folks I was working with at the time reckoned it was my size that made some horses feel nervous around me. Not used to dealing with such large human beings, you see. Afraid I was going to plonk myself on their backs, I dare say.'

Mavis was fascinated: she watched Clementine watching her mother and fiancé, and could see the apprehension on her face decrease as the seconds and moments passed.

'You wouldn't recall the man I mean, Henry, nor you, Clemmie – it was during the period when you were both away at school, I believe. He didn't last long. So what sort of things do you make, Jools? And where are you based?'

'Jools has use of a smithy in Bethnal Green, Mother,' replied Clementine excitedly, 'and he makes the most wonderfully delicate objects you could imagine. It's how we met: he was commissioned to make a gate for one of my chums – as a fiftieth birthday present – and we collaborated on the design. He's so talented. So very talented.'

Mavis hoped that Henry would resist the urge to comment that it hadn't been that long since his sister had sat at the very same dinner table and had gushed about another artist – his portraitist, no less – in the same way. But, on that occasion, Mavis happened to know that there'd been no more than a fleeting 'romance'. This attachment seemed to have taken root very quickly, and had so far borne the fruit of an engagement.

'Have you set a date for the wedding yet?'

Mavis had known the question was inevitable, but was a little surprised that it was Stephanie who'd posed it.

Clementine blushed. Jools might also have blushed but there was so little of his face on display that it was difficult for Mavis to tell.

Clementine replied, 'The twenty-first of June. At dawn, on the summer solstice. In Egypt. At the base of Queen Hatshepsut's obelisk at the temple of Karnak in Luxor.' She beamed.

'I beg your pardon?' Henry spluttered wine, mopping his chin with his napkin.

Clementine shot him a withering glance. 'You heard me. Egypt in June. This June. In just less than three weeks' time.'

Henry blustered, 'Isn't that a bit…I mean, have you really taken the time to…I mean…that's quite specific.'

Clementine snapped, 'What you really mean is – have I thought this through and have I lost my mind? Yes and no. Jools and I are agreed – that's where and when we'll be married.'

'Has that been terribly difficult to arrange, dear?' Althea sounded genuinely concerned.

Clementine shrugged. 'Well, we haven't ironed out all the final details yet, because there's a lot of paperwork and dealing with embassies and so forth to get through, but that's what we want, and we shall do whatever needs to be done to make sure that's what happens.'

Mavis heard Althea's 'ah' as more of a sigh than a comment. 'That's a shame.'

Clementine glared at her mother. 'Thank you very much, Mother. I'd hoped for more support from you.'

Althea looked hurt. 'I just meant that it's a shame I won't see you marry. I don't think I'd be quite up to June in Egypt. It's going to be very hot, isn't it?'

Clementine sat back in her seat. 'Yes, though not at dawn. But it will be magical, Mother. And you'd be welcome, of course. However, to be honest, we imagined it would just be the two of us. Jools doesn't have anyone, you see – and Henry and Stephanie have baby Hugo to think about, and...well, I didn't think you'd manage, Mother.'

Jools added, 'Everyone is welcome to join us for what I believe will be a unique and moving ceremony in Egypt, of course. But, quite honestly, our conversations about where we want to have our wedding have always been framed in an utterly selfish way. We've been honest with each other, and both recognize that a marriage is about much more than a wedding, so we would still enjoy the chance to celebrate as a group – as a family – afterwards and, of course, we hope you'll all be supportive of our marriage in the long run, not feeling you've been left out of the short little "weddingy" bit of it.' He helped himself to more sparking water.

Mavis admitted to herself that she was starting to like Jools. 'Is that a Bristol accent I detect?' Mavis dared.

'Well spotted, Mavis.' Jools beamed. 'Though I'm specifically from Filton, which we who come from there still see as distinct from Bristol itself. There's only six miles difference, and most people think of it as just a dormitory area for the city, but I'm Filton born and bred. My grandfather moved there to work for Bristol Cars, and my father helped to build Concorde, as well as other aeroplanes, of course. Metal working of some sort, or engineering, I suppose, is in my blood, you could say.'

Althea perked up. 'Bristol Cars? You like old cars? I have a Gilbern.' She sounded proud.

Jools's voice betrayed amazement. 'A Gilbern? I'd love to see it. What type is it?'

Althea sat up a little straighter. 'A Gilbern Invader Estate. My late husband gave it to me as an anniversary gift many moons ago.'

'And it still runs?' Jools sounded disbelieving.

'Indeed. I'd be happy to take you out in it, if you'd like. Oh, I say, smoked trout, my favorite. Thank you, Edward, and thank Cook Davies for me too, would you, please?'

Edward muttered, 'Indeed, Your Grace,' as he placed Mavis's trout in front of her, which she acknowledged with a nod.

'Maybe we could all talk about cars at some other time, Mother,' said Henry snippily. 'Don't you think the topic of Clementine's wedding is rather more pressing?'

'It's not really a topic for conversation, though, is it, dear?' Althea's nodding suggested she wanted Edward to top up her glass, which he dutifully did. 'The plans are in hand, and that's that. I think it's more a cause for celebration. So, allow me: to the happy couple.'

Once again, glasses were raised, and Mavis felt that the dinner progressed surprisingly smoothly from then on; conversations about modern blacksmithing, vintage cars, local trout fishing, the farm-to-table movement, and even the value of restoring rather than renovating when it came to architecturally significant buildings ebbed and flowed as a vegetable consommé, then duck, then apple turnover, were served and enjoyed – with a liberal addition of wine, none of which Jools drank, Mavis noted.

The eventual movement of the party from the dining room to the drawing room was accompanied by hearty screaming from Hugo, so Stephanie took her leave and retreated to the duke and duchess's rooms.

Meanwhile, Mavis wondered if Althea might drop off before they managed to get back to the Dower House; her eyes were glassy, and her earlier joviality had subsided into occasional rushes of chatter followed by lengthening silences.

As Henry expounded the delights of an excellent brandy to the apparently tee-total Jools, Mavis whispered, 'Shall we ask Ian to collect us now, Althea? It's getting on.'

Althea focused and replied, 'But it's only just dark. It can't be that late.'

'Gone ten, dear,' replied Mavis. 'It's almost the longest day now, you know.'

Althea nodded. 'Yes, get hold of young Ian. Edward's probably got him down in the kitchen if I know him. Then we'll get back. Good idea. I'm terribly sleepy. I've no idea why.'

Mavis could think of a few reasons, but didn't mention how much the dowager had drunk that evening.

As Edward was helping the women with their jackets in the Great Hall, Althea asked the butler, 'What's Jools's family name, Edward? I forgot to ask, and Clemmie didn't mention it.'

'I believe it's Tavistock, Your Grace.'

'Like the place in Devon?'

'I believe so, Your Grace.'

'I wonder if that's where his people come from, Mavis,' continued Althea, as the pair made their way down the steps to the car, aided by Ian Cottesloe.

'I believe he said he was from Filton,' replied Mavis, knowing that was exactly what the man had told them.

'I know, I know,' replied Althea airily, 'but I mean his long-past people, his ancestors. Maybe you could find out.'

Mavis took her seat in the rear of the vehicle, the dowager preferring the front seat. 'What do you mean? You want me to dig into his past?'

Althea turned, looking surprised. 'But, of course, dear. I can't have someone about whom I know nothing marrying my daughter. He's very charming in his ursine way – but we don't know him really, and nor does Clemmie, having only met him a few months ago. Yes, I wonder if you and the team could look into it for me, please? I wonder what Annie would call this one…The Case of the Big,

Beardy Blacksmith maybe?' Althea giggled, then hiccupped. 'Or what about The Case of the Furry Fiancé?'

Mavis sighed, telling herself there'd be no speaking to Althea until she'd had a good sleep – then noted that she'd already dropped off.

SATURDAY 3rd JUNE

CHAPTER SEVEN

Carol hadn't really enjoyed her Friday, and wondered how her Saturday was going to turn out. Albert had grizzled throughout the previous day but she'd not been able to give him all her attention because of Ellie being in the house. Then, when David appeared to have his 'breakfast' around teatime, having slept all day, she'd not had a chance to chat to him about what Ellie had told her regarding the nurse at her place of work before he'd had to disappear into his office.

By the time she and Ellie had settled to a curry and a bottle of wine on Friday evening, Carol had been a bit overwhelmed, overtired, and feeling utterly inadequate: she hadn't been the best mother she could, nor the best wife she could, nor the best friend she could – and she'd done no work at all.

The only saving grace was that it appeared Ellie was happier to talk about old, joyous times than dwell on her suspicions about her colleague for most of the evening. Then, just before she headed off to the spare room, Ellie had said bluntly to Carol, 'I bet you lot could work it all out and save lives on the streets, or maybe even at the nursing home,' which meant Carol hardly slept at all.

Now? She was sitting in her kitchen as the sun came up. It wasn't even five o'clock, and already she had a list of questions noted on the pad in front of her – questions she was determined to get Ellie to answer before she headed off that morning, back to her flat near Cardiff, and back to the nursing home where there may, or may not, be a drug dealer, or a serial killer on the loose.

On the next page of the pad, Carol drew up a list of questions about the dead people she had to investigate for the WISE agency. She'd told herself to think like that about the people whose families had received wreaths of condolence, unbidden, because she didn't like to think of them as ever having been living.

Sitting back, with Bunty squished onto her lap, purring, Carol wondered why she felt that way. Was her work making her become less emotionally attached to the people upon whose behalf she was investigating? Or was this case featuring the unknown wreath-deliverer just so unsettling that she was trying to distance herself from how this specific job was making her feel?

'Surely a nurse who's stealing leftover drugs and might possibly be dealing them on the street is more worrying than an unidentified undertaker leaving flowers at front doors, isn't it?'

Bunty's eyes narrowed, but she didn't answer Carol.

'Fat lot of good you are,' added Carol.

'Do you always talk to Bunty in the middle of the night, in the kitchen, all alone?'

Carol jumped, sending Bunty darting from her lap and heading for the living room, right between the legs of her husband who was standing in the doorway.

'Hello, *cariad* – oh you gave me a fright. How long have you been standing there?' Carol rose to peck David on the cheek. 'Fancy a cuppa? There's a fresh pot.'

David pecked back. 'That would be great. Thanks. Just time for a ten-minute break before we all meet up again.' He looked at his watch. 'I know why I'm up this late – or is it early? – but what about you? Are you okay? Albert alright?'

'Our son is magnificent – and sleeping soundly, thank goodness, and I'm fine too…though I do want to talk to you about something that Ellie's told me…but it can wait, for now.'

David's brow furrowed. 'Ellie? What's up? Man trouble?'

Carol tutted. 'I can't believe you said that. Ellie's a professional with a full life and a demanding career. You know she yomps up mountains, and plays musical instruments, and gets involved with her community in umpteen ways, yet you automatically go to "man trouble" when I say I want to talk to you about her. I've got to say I find that a bit disappointing…and, to be honest, not at all like you.'

David poured himself a mug of tea from the pot, adding milk – which always made Carol cringe because she was very much a milk-in-first tea drinker.

Both sitting at the table David said, 'You're right. That wasn't me, was it? And, to be honest, I would say I don't know why I said it, but I do…it's this bloke I'm working for in Honolulu. He's…well he's a bit of a dinosaur when it comes to world views, and he keeps goading me into agreeing with him all the time. He's my client so, you know, I sort of have to go along with it all. Maybe it's rubbing off on me.'

Carol replied, 'I don't like the sound of that. Isn't there any way you can get him to tone it down? Or put him right, somehow?'

David chuckled. 'You heard me say he's my client, right? How can I tell a client he's a complete buffoon when it comes to his views about women – and so many, many other things – without him dumping me? You know we need the money, especially while your income from the agency is on a bit of a downswing.'

Carol half-smiled. 'That's a difficult one. I know I was the boss at our last company, and I had to oversee a huge group of people working across many disciplines, and in loads of countries – but I was in a position where I could point to behavior as inappropriate when I saw it. I even built in a whole set of training modules people had to work through as part of their career development. And when I was dealing directly with clients, I suppose they were guarded in terms of what they said to my face, because there I was, a woman – and a Welsh one at that, with an accent that some types like to believe means a person is as thick as two short planks – telling them how they should run their business, and they were paying me to do so. But, yes, I know there were lots of comments behind my back, and not just from clients, but from the people who paid my salary and bonus too.'

'Any tips, then? Any language I can use to try to stop him going on and on about things in such a hateful manner? Because that's what it seems to be – the man sounds angry all the time, about almost everything. It's really wearing.'

Carol tilted her head. 'How well do you know him? As a person, as opposed to as a client, I mean.'

David sipped his tea before replying, 'Not well. He got hold of me through our Los Angeles office...through Dave, you know?'

Carol nodded. 'With Dave in LA, Davy in Australia, and you in Wales, do people assume you have to be named David to be a part of your little unofficial software-troubleshooting cabal?'

Her husband grinned. 'One, not a cabal but a handy grouping of professionals; two, David is just about the best name in the world in any case; three, you're not answering my question.'

'Touché,' Carol replied, taking her husband's hand in her own. 'Advice? Well, I've still got access to those online courses you "should" have taken as a requirement of your employment under my oversight, so I'll send you the link and you can trawl through those as a starting point. There's one particular session on dealing with difficult people in the workplace I vaguely recall, which could help, but – to be honest – I put those courses in place about five years ago, and the world's moved on since then.'

David sighed. 'You're not kidding.' Brightening, he added, 'And, for us, it's moved in wonderful and positive directions, so I'll focus on that. And – to return to the original point – I'm sorry I said such a stupid thing about Ellie. What's her non-man-related problem? And I don't mean that to sound as patronizing as it probably did.'

Carol weighed her response; she wanted a meaningful discussion with her husband about a deeply worrying situation, but was mindful that he had a meeting looming. 'It'll keep until we've got longer than we have now, *cariad*. How about you top up that mug and go and get settled for your next meeting, eh? I, too, am a woman with an incredible range of professional skills, so I'll sort it...though I'll value your input when we've got the time to talk. And, no, that's not meant to sound patronizing, either.'

Exchanging a kiss, Carol and her husband parted company, and Bunty slinked back into the kitchen to – apparently – check if there was a lap that needed to be sat upon, which there was.

Carol stared at her notes again. Knowing she'd need to access information that wouldn't be readily available from people in offices in the area until Monday morning regarding the undertakers' case, she set that to one side and gave her attention to Ellie's problem. She wondered if Annie would refer to it as The Case of the Suspicious Sister, or maybe The Case of the Naughty Nurse. She then decided that the latter sounded too much like a Carry-On film, and not as serious as the case demanded it should be, so Ellie, the Suspicious Sister, it was, then. As she thought of her chum Annie, visiting her parents near London, Carol knew she'd be the best person to talk to about the case, but knew she didn't want to disturb her during her few days off.

She also knew that Mavis didn't like it when any of them took on non-paying work – which this would surely be – so gave some thought to how she might sell the idea to her colleague. Then Carol realized that Mavis could make all the difference: she had a nursing background, could go to the nursing home as a carer, under Ellie's wing, so to speak, and might be able to work out what was going on by doing a bit of undercover observation.

Carol topped up her mug, knowing she was onto something. Now all she had to do was come up with a way of getting Mavis to agree to such an undertaking, given there'd be no money in it, when they also had a real client with a bank balance they were prepared to dip into for the WISE women's efforts.

'Right then, Bunty,' she said, petting her darling cat, 'let's give this some serious thought, shall we?'

CHAPTER EIGHT

'Why did you say we'd do this so early?' Christine was bitterly regretting her overindulgence of the previous night.

Alexander replied, quite heartlessly to Christine's ears, 'If you say, "I'm never drinking again" once more, I think I might stop finding it funny. You really have only got yourself to blame, my darling. I love you dearly, but, sometimes, you really go on what you Irish would call "a tear", don't you?'

Christine couldn't be bothered to get into an argument, so simply replied, 'Not looking for pity, just peace. So please fill my thermal mug and drive quietly – no revving or taking corners too abruptly, thank you. I really don't think I could cope. But making a plan for nine on a Saturday morning is early.'

Alexander picked up the coffee pot. 'I'd suggest pouring this straight down your throat if I thought it would help, but it won't. In my defense, nine o'clock works for people who have other things to do on Saturdays, and you know that means Bill and me, because we both run businesses that are, essentially, operating seven days a week. Even if my construction sites are closed at the weekends, they're still my responsibility, as are my tenants. And the antiques business? So many members of the public can only bring their items to the warehouse in Chelsea on a Saturday or Sunday that it's the weekends that are busiest for incoming items, even if the sales are held midweek. See? Saturdays are just like any other day. And it's often the same for you with your investigations, right? So I know you understand, really.'

Christine harrumphed as she dragged her feet through the pebbles of the driveway outside the barn. 'Yeah, I know,' she grumbled, clutching her coffee and cursing the noise of the stones, then stepping more lightly.

The couple met Bob Fernley at the boarded-up shop overlooking the green at the heart of Anwen-by-Wye just before the appointed hour. Christine liked Bob – not that she'd ever really had much to do with him but, whenever they'd encountered each other, he'd been efficient and knowledgeable – two qualities she knew to be essential for any Estates Manager. In his role representing Henry and the Twyst family, Bob Fernley took his responsibilities seriously – though Christine had spotted him sinking the odd pint or five at the Lamb and Flag, overseen by his wife Elizabeth, who'd more-or-less run Chellingworth Hall after Althea had moved into the Dower House, and before Henry had married Stephanie.

This particular morning Bob looked especially keen to get going; he was wearing his usual beige trousers but without the addition of his ever-present green, quilted jerkin – and his thin arms were poking out of a short-sleeved shirt, which Christine thought made him look somehow vulnerable.

'You look as though you're expecting another warm day, Bob,' she observed, wondering why she herself felt so chilly; it was a beautiful morning, without a cloud in the sky.

'That's what they said on the forecast last night, and I believe them,' he replied jovially. 'My wife suggested this shirt because I got a bit too hot and bothered yesterday. She also made me wear sun protection. I thought that was what sleeves were for, but there you go. She's not got as much to do these days – not since Her Grace married His Grace and took over the running of things at the Hall – so she likes to spend a bit more time looking after me, I suppose.'

When Alexander replied, 'You can't beat the love and oversight of a good woman,' Christine spluttered coffee.

As Bob fiddled with the lock of the shop door, she whispered, '"The love and oversight of a good woman"? Have you met us? We're Alexander and Christine, neither of us with an unblemished past, nor – in all probability – an unblemished future. Am I supposed to start telling you what to wear now?'

Alexander whispered, 'Just doing my best to bond with the bloke, Christine. You know how it is – old school tie, and all that.'

She grunted, 'Well, I don't know about Bob, but you didn't go to school very much, let alone wear a tie if you popped in there – so a bit less of the "old boys"' networking, and a bit more of you and me getting this done, right?'

'There you go,' said Bob as he flung the door open, 'not rusted shut, just needed a bit of a jiggle. I've been popping in from time to time, and we've had the chaps from the Hall coming in to make sure it's well-maintained overall. Can't have any eyesores in the village, after all, can we?'

'The sign outside has gone,' noted Christine.

Bob nodded. 'Yes, His Grace asked us to remove that once the last tenant…um…left. Were you thinking of renaming it? It used to be called A Taste of Time.'

Knowing that would be up to Alexander, Christine didn't comment, but focused on the place itself. She'd never been into the shop when it had been run by the now absent Tristan Thomas, and was surprised by its size. 'It goes back a long way, doesn't it?'

'That's to allow for deliveries to be made from the road that runs behind it,' replied Bob.

'Is the road easy to access?' asked Alexander.

'Yes,' replied Bob. 'When you come off the main road, through the copse, you can either drive into the heart of the village, or you can do what I dare say you do when you go out to the Estate – you take the road to the left, past the old Market Hall out to the road to Chellingworth Hall itself. But you can also turn right, and there's a road that runs along the houses that back onto the duck pond, which then leads around to the old school and the village hall. That road gives access to the back of this place. Come on, let's go through and you can see for yourself.'

The rear double doors of the shop were encouraged to swing open, letting the warm air and morning sun stream in. Dust floated like fairy glitter, and Christine discovered she was, indeed, looking across the road at the old village school, which looked a sorry sight, even bathed in the bright sunshine.

Bob must have noticed the way she was squinting at the low, rectangular building with its pebble-dash walls and peeling green paint. 'I don't know why they don't do something with that place. I understand that there aren't enough children in the village to warrant a school any longer, but the education lot should keep it in a better state than it is.'

'Is that not part of the Chellingworth Estate, then? Like the rest of the village is?' Christine was surprised – she'd always believed the Twysts owned everything, except for St David's Church which she knew belonged to the diocese, and the Coach and Horses pub.

'They lease it from us – from the Estate. Local education authority,' replied Bob. 'Nothing we can do about it. It's a right old mess but my lot aren't allowed anywhere near it. That playground looks more like a field nowadays; used to be a nicely laid bit of tarmac, that did. Anyway – at least we keep the village hall looking tidy. Which pleases both Their Graces, I know. Though I don't know how Her Grace expects us to win that "Prettiest Village" award with that eyesore.'

'Is Stephanie going to push for that then? I thought she'd given up on the idea. I heard that the village social committee was against it.' Christine had been chatting to the duchess about it just a few days earlier.

Bob shrugged. 'Last I heard she was. Her Grace, I mean.' Christine suspected that Bob rarely used Stephanie's title when he was talking to those who worked on the Estate, but did so when certain people – like a chum of the duchess – were present.

'So what do you think?' He asked the critical question.

Inside the shop, Alexander was pulling open doors and tossing aside dust sheets. 'There's still a bit of stock here, I see, and the place is in generally good shape. This rear entrance is a game-changer for loading large objects, and the windows offer two excellent display areas. I think my partner will be impressed. But it'll need a good clean out, and a fair bit of decorating before we could open up. And we'd have to get the stock delivered, of course. But then – if we go ahead – the big question is…who would run it? I can't do it, of course –' he shrugged at Christine – 'and it's not as though we're rolling in staff at the place in London who'd be either willing or suitable to run a shop in a Welsh village.'

Bob Fernley was nibbling his lower lip. 'So would this person be here full time?'

'Probably not,' replied Alexander. 'To catch most customers through the season when Chellingworth Hall is open I'd say opening around ten, and maybe closing around four. And maybe shut on Mondays and Tuesdays. Not sure yet. It might have to be a sort of suck it and see arrangement. But they'd need to be good with the finances, and the stock management. And I suppose it goes without saying that they'd have to know their antiques, and be good at dealing with customers. After all, we would actually want to sell the stuff.'

Bob nodded. 'Yes, His Grace has been talking to me about how he wants to decide which items they don't want to keep, that they find around the Hall as they go through this inventory-taking exercise that's got us all a bit topsy-turvey. Then we're going to send them to one of the barns, where my blokes who keep on top of maintenance work are based, so things can be restored, as needs be, then they can come here. Is that how you understand it?'

Alexander nodded. 'Yes, mixing the Coggins stock with the Chellingworth items is the plan. And I hope it'll work – for both our sakes, because getting this place sorted won't be cheap.'

Bob laughed. 'Tell you what, if you want to see "not cheap", then come and have a look at what we have to do up at the Hall. All this needs is a bit of commercially available paint and wallpaper and it'll be as good as new. None of this having to get cloth specially woven to recover a precious chair, and don't talk to me about those plaster ceilings, nor the blessed chandeliers. Still, it's what the visitors want, and it's what they'll get – along with everything being up to all the health and safety codes, too.'

'True,' replied Alexander. 'That's something at least my colleague Bill knows about. I've promised I'll show him around via video on my phone – would you like to meet him?'

Bob checked his watch. 'Go on then, but I've got to be away in half an hour. When's he expecting you?'

'About a quarter of an hour from now, why?'

Christine noticed that Bob Fernley was doing the lip-nibbling thing again. 'Well, I've been thinking…and I don't like to speak out of turn, but I was wondering if my Elizabeth might be the right person for you, to run this place, you know?'

Christine was surprised. 'Really? Doesn't she have her hands full up at the Hall – and looking after you, of course.'

Bob shook his head. 'Hates to not be busy, and she knows antiques inside out – she's been at the Hall for donkey's years and loves everything there so much that it's become more than her hobby, see? And she's good with money, and even a dab hand at shifting heavy bits of furniture…though I do tell her off about that, I must admit. But I could always send someone down if there are especially massive pieces to be handled. She could manage everything else, I'm sure.'

'Want to give her a ring and talk to her about it?' Alexander sounded far too casual about it all, to Christine's ear. 'If she likes the general sound of it, maybe she could get here before we talk to Bill – see how everybody feels about everything all at once, eh?'

Christine didn't know how any of this was going to work out: she'd always thought of Elizabeth Fernley as the more caustic half of the couple, and couldn't picture the woman being cordial, or effective, when it came to selling to customers. But she told herself it wasn't her problem.

An hour later, everything was sorted: decorative themes and finishes had been agreed; placements for electrical and connectivity upgrades had been worked out; Elizabeth Fernley would be onboard from the start, with flexibility when it came to opening hours – to be agreed later.

However, the name of the shop was still to be decided; Alexander was insisting upon having the Coggins name in the title somewhere, because both he and Bill felt it critical that the shop would be seen as an extension of their business. Bob Fernley had no say in the matter, but kept asserting that, 'Their Graces had some ideas', so Christine offered to phone Stephanie to chat about it. Bob also mentioned that he had a good working relationship with a professional signwriter in Cardiff who could create a name-board – which everyone agreed should be mounted in the same fashion as a pub sign, swinging on an arm above the door – in less than a week. Meanwhile, orders would be placed, cleaning and decorating would get underway, and the hope was to have the shop fully stocked and open within three weeks, before the end of June – allowing them to capitalize upon the tourists who would visit the area during the summer months.

As he closed up the shop again, Bob commented to his wife, 'If this isn't proper summer yet, I can't imagine how hot it's going to be then. This is more than enough for me.'

'Hence my request for as many fans as possible in the shop,' said Elizabeth, adding quickly, 'though, of course, being careful to not do anything that would adversely impact antique woods, glues, paints or veneers.'

She was reiterating a point Alexander had been keen to make earlier, noted Christine, who still couldn't warm to the woman, though had to admit she'd obviously impressed Alexander with her efficient air and knowledge about antiques in general. It had become apparent that Elizabeth had a particular interest in porcelain, which Alexander was happy about; Christine knew that he and Bill always found it difficult to 'shift pots' as they referred to it, but both had agreed that smaller, lower cost items might move well in a village shop.

Having ignored three calls from Carol while all the faffing about at the shop had been going on, Christine checked her text messages as Alexander and the Fernleys exchanged farewells, only to find that the third one was all in capital letters, so obviously needed a response.

'I'm popping over to Carol's place,' she called, heading across the village green. 'I'll let you do your thing, and I'll pick up my car at the pub later. See you back at the barn for lunch?'

Alexander agreed, and she headed to see her friend – who clearly had something urgent to communicate.

CHAPTER NINE

Carol had seen Christine and Alexander, and Bob Fernley – then Elizabeth Fernley – go into the old antiques shop, diagonally across the green from her own house, ages and ages ago. She couldn't imagine what they were all doing in there. Christine had annoyingly ignored a few calls, and three messages, but now – finally – there she was making her way toward Carol's house. Opening the kitchen door, Carol ushered her in and introduced her to Ellie, who was hanging on just to meet Christine.

She could tell that Christine was surprised to see Mavis also sitting at the kitchen table, and was only too happy for Ellie and Mavis to bring her colleague up to speed, as she gave her son the attention he needed.

By the time the teapot had been emptied, and refilled, and an entire packet of fig rolls had been devoured – everyone commenting as they nibbled that they'd probably regret eating so many – Carol had settled Albert in his playpen, and he was doing his best to play nicely with his stuffed animals, though she knew he would much prefer to be staggering around from one set of adult legs and knees to another, being applauded for his efforts as he went.

'So, if I've got this right,' said Christine at last, 'Ellie suspects a junior nurse – whose name she won't tell us – of removing supplies of drugs originally prescribed for now-deceased patients at the nursing home where she's sister-in-charge. She's no idea what happens to the drugs, but fears the nurse might be selling them, or – though it's unlikely – administering them to patients with fatal results. Correct?'

Carol, Ellie, and Mavis all nodded.

'That's a bit…heavy,' observed Christine.

'It's criminal,' said Mavis, 'and I believe – despite what Ellie has been told by a family member who is a serving police officer – that this should be brought to the attention of the police service in the area where the nursing home is located.'

Ellie stood. 'I can't. Not yet. What if I'm wrong about her? What if I'm totally off the mark and she's not doing anything at all? I could ruin her life. Even the sniff of a scandal can follow someone for years, especially in nursing. It can completely alter the trajectory of a promising career. I won't do it.'

Carol said, 'Calm down, Ellie. Look, Mavis, I can see both sides of this: you're right that if this nurse is breaking the law, she should be brought to book for it, but Ellie's also right that she might not actually be doing anything wrong at all. Which is why I've invited you all here. You see, I think the best thing is for us to gather evidence – evidence that could be used to charge her, or clear her.'

Mavis put her empty mug of tea on the table precisely in the middle of her coaster. 'And how do you suggest we do that?'

Carol smiled sweetly. 'I suggest you do it, Mavis. I've talked to Ellie about it and she says there's a way it could work: you'd go with her today and join the night shift at the nursing home as a trainee care assistant. They're always desperate for people, and you'd not only know what you're doing when it comes to the caring bit, but you could watch the nurses on the night shift in case there's something…amiss.'

Carol didn't know how to take Mavis's astonished look: was Mavis surprised that she'd come up with such a good plan – or such a stupid one?

Mavis spoke slowly. 'There's one major problem I can see with such an idea.'

Carol waited to hear what it was, as did Christine and Ellie.

Mavis poured herself another mug of tea. 'You've said that these drugs that walk out of the nursing home do so after a patient has died. Is that correct, Ellie?'

Ellie nodded.

'Which means I could end up undercover for days, or even weeks. And that's no' something I can do. As you all know, we have a paying client who'll need me to work on their case, and I have meetings planned with a couple of potential clients next week – as well as an appointment to meet with Rhodri Lloyd, to keep him sweet and to see if he's got anything we can help with. That's on Friday. I couldn't miss that.'

Carol silently acknowledged that Mavis had made a good point: there was no way to know when one of Ellie's patients might die, thereby potentially setting in motion the unnamed nurse's actions.

Ellie surprised Carol when she placed her hand on Mavis's. 'You were a nurse for quite a while, weren't you, Mavis?'

'Aye, I gave many good years to the service of those who were serving our country.'

Ellie nodded. 'And Carol told me that when all you women met, you were the matron at the Battersea Barracks, caring for retired servicemen and women. So I'm guessing you've attended a great number of deathbeds.'

Mavis stared into her tea. 'Aye. Too many, I dare say. And I've no real desire to attend any more, thank you.'

Ellie sat upright. 'That's not quite what I meant, Mavis. What I meant was this: those of us who care for people over time, especially those close to the end of their life, we get a sense of when their time is coming close. Wouldn't you agree?'

Carol wondered if Mavis would ever stop drawing in breath she sighed so heavily. 'Aye. That we do.'

'Well, I happen to know that one of our patients is at that point right now, Mavis. She's been worn to nothing by her pain, and she's barely hanging on. I've already phoned up to check on her this morning, and she's still alive, but only just. I…I wouldn't be surprised if she didn't make it to morning. Her entire family is visiting her today. Well, all but one son.'

Christine said quietly, 'That's a shame. I mean it's a shame that she's dying, of course…but it's also a shame that one of her sons can't get to her to say goodbye.'

Ellie drew her hand away from Mavis's. 'Oh, he can. He just doesn't want to. Or at least, he's chosen not to. Hasn't seen her once since she was moved to us from the care home. Lives in London. Just can't be bothered to put his mother before his various family and personal thises and thats.'

'I don't understand,' said Carol. 'Wouldn't everyone want to...well, no, I suppose I can't say that, can I? I mean, who knows what sort of mother she was...if she's deserving of his attention. No – I won't judge, because I don't know. You might have met a frail woman who's sympathetic and vulnerable, Ellie, but she might have been a horrible person earlier in her life, and he might be quite right to stay away from her. I mean, how would you know?'

Ellie replied quietly, 'Her six other children, and their families, have all planned a visit. It's him – he's the problem...not her.'

Mavis sighed. 'You're both right, Mebbe. She's his mother, she gave him life, and might have dedicated her every moment to his happiness. Or she might have been a tartar who made his entire childhood and youth a misery...and maybe even only his, of all her children, for some reason we cannae fathom. But Carol makes a good point: when we meet people in their later years, it's always hard for us to judge what they were like as a younger person. As I walked the corridors at the Battersea Barracks, I saw innocent faces, green serge proudly worn, the brightness of polished brass buttons and buffed boots on parade...and I had to remind myself that the majority of my charges had taken the life of at least one person during their active service years. I was overseeing the twilight years of men and women who'd been trained to kill for their country, and yet, there they were, just as vulnerable as your patients, Ellie.'

'Good grief, Mavis,' said Carol, 'what with one of our clients asking us to find out who this person is who's going around leaving wreaths at houses before anyone's died, and now you two talking about possible killer nurses – and even killer patients – I'm glad it's a warm day, because I'm feeling chills up my back.'

Ellie asked, 'What's that about wreaths?'

'No' your problem, dear,' replied Mavis, 'and let's not be diverted from our conversation. You say you have a belief that a death is imminent, and you think that might be tonight, or tomorrow. In that case, I agree to join you at your nursing home for a couple of days. If it's down near Cardiff I'd rather not drive back here after my shifts, so I'll assume you can put me up, comfortably, somewhere.'

Ellie stared at Carol, looking panicked. 'I suppose I could sleep on the sofa bed in the living room so you could have the bedroom in my flat. How about that?'

Mavis stood. 'Clean sheets, of course. I'll be away to the Dower House to pack a bag. I'll be able to leave in two hours – would that suit? All I need is your address, and the name of the nursing home so that I can do some cursory research, and I'll drive myself. I'll meet you at the nursing home an hour before my shift is due to start, and you can introduce me to everyone. I suggest you get on and finalize arrangements for me to join the staff as quickly as possible.'

Carol tried to not smirk as Ellie looked amazed. 'Yes. Right. Thanks. It's the Ty Coch Nursing Home. It means Red House. Here's the address, and here's mine.' She scribbled on a piece of paper Carol handed her.

'And is it?' Mavis took the paper and read it.

'Sorry – is what, what?' Ellie looked bemused.

'Is the nursing home a red house?' Mavis's expression suggested she thought Ellie to be very stupid indeed.

'Oh, yes. I mean no. It's got a red front door, and it's built from brick, but the brick isn't the very red type…just sort of…um…brick-colored…' Ellie's voice tailed off.

When Mavis had left, Carol stared at her friend. 'I bet none of your junior nurses would have recognized the person you became when Mavis gave you what we all call "her special look". Scary, isn't it?'

Ellie grinned and nodded. 'I felt like I was fourteen and she'd caught me smoking at the bus stop. Is she always like that?'

Christine and Carol exchanged a knowing glance. Carol said, 'No, not always.'

'But she can turn it on like a tap,' added Christine. 'And off again, thank goodness. I've always imagined it's a nurse thing. Have you got a "special look" for when someone's done something stupid, Ellie?'

Ellie rolled her eyes. 'No, I do not. Though…well, I have heard a few rumors that I have eyes in the back of my head.'

'Which might, on this occasion, be to our advantage,' said Carol, then her phone rang. She answered it immediately, surprised to see that it was Mavis. 'Hello, did you forget something?'

Mavis snapped, 'I need you to find out everything you can about a Julian, also known as Jools, Tavistock, of Filton. Age about fifty – or maybe even sixty, it was hard to tell. Don't speak to anyone else about this – this is between me and you. I should have done it but can't because I'm helping your friend. Let me know what you can as soon as possible. And I'll phone Louise Attwater to tell her you're taking the lead on the undertaker case. Get Christine and Annie involved as you need. Goodbye.'

Carol stared at her phone.

'Was that Mavis?' Christine sounded puzzled.

Carol nodded.

'What did she want?'

'Just to say I'm leading on the undertaker case, and I'm to call on you and Annie as necessary. That was all.' She stood and said, 'Just got to pop to the loo. Back in a tick.'

As Carol hovered outside the kitchen door she sent herself an email containing the information Mavis had just barked at her, completely mystified, but knowing she really had no choice but to do as she'd been asked.

CHAPTER TEN

Annie Parker loved her parents, Eustelle and Rodney, dearly, but was glad she'd be leaving the following day. Three days with them was about all she could cope with – but she did her best to make the most of every moment with them. Having left home at sixteen, she'd never shared more than a few days at a time with them as an adult, and she found even the temporary loss of her independence to be almost too much to bear when she was under their roof; her mother couldn't do enough for her, and her father treated her like a princess, but that didn't really suit Annie.

At that moment, her mother was in her element, sitting chatting with the other women in the hairdressing salon with her daughter – the detective – at her side. Annie knew that everyone who met Eustelle was immediately made aware of what her daughter did for a living, and she was delighted that her mother was so proud of her, though she wished she could have been just as proud when she had been the receptionist at a large firm of Lloyds' brokers in the City of London.

Her mother's hairdresser had given Annie the usual head massage and slight trim that kept her almost non-existent hair in good form, tight against her shapely head. Now she knew she had at least another hour to wait while Eustelle's complex treatments were undertaken, so she sat and watched.

When required, Annie dutifully responded that, yes, she did really know the duke and duchess of Chellingworth, and yes she did live in a thatched cottage in Wales. Photos were circulated, to prove these claims, and she finally got her phone back, which allowed her to spend some time checking the social media accounts of one Delyth James or, as Annie was now happily calling her, the Predatory Publican.

She picked up quite a lot of insights because it seemed that Delyth didn't understand the concept of privacy, and was happy to show the whole world what she was doing, and with whom, at almost every hour of every day.

Annie became more than passingly familiar with the menu items offered by several fancy restaurants on a swish cruise ship and saw rather more cocktails and glitzy outfits than she'd ever wanted to. One of her main thoughts was that she couldn't imagine how much luggage Delyth had taken on her Alaskan cruise, which she'd begun after what had been an apparently tortuous journey from Heathrow to Vancouver to board the ship.

'What you squinting at, child?' Eustelle was behind Annie, looking at her phone, still wearing the plastic cape illustrated with tiny palm trees that she'd had draped over her shoulders two minutes after they'd arrived at the salon.

'Just checking my socials,' replied Annie nonchalantly.

Her mother shrugged. 'If you say so, child. Not long now, then we can have a bit of lunch and do a little shopping, how about that? There's some fabric they're keeping for me at the market that I want to collect. Your father needs a new lining in his good jacket, and I'm sure I can do it myself.'

Annie was completely convinced her mother would make a wonderful job of her father's jacket, because she was a woman who could turn her hand to almost anything.

'Right-o, but don't worry about me,' she said lightly, 'I'm fine here. You go and finish that cuppa they brought you, and I'll just do this quietly.'

'If you're phonin' Tudor, you give him my love, won't you?'

'I will.'

Annie gave her attention to Delyth James's Twitter feed, which wasn't as information-rich as her Facebook posts, so gave up after a while, and decided to send some notes to Tudor, sharing what she'd learned.

Annie checked her watch; it was gone two. The Saturday lunchtime rush – such as it was – would be over, and Tudor would probably be up in his flat having a spot of lunch himself, with the dogs at his feet. She decided to phone him instead of sending an email.

Pointing at her phone to her mother, Annie stepped outside the salon to make the call; the chemical smells inside were getting to her. Outside there wasn't much of a breeze, but it was cooler and less humid than inside, and even the constant flow of traffic was a blessed break from the din of dryers and chatter she'd put up with for almost two hours already.

'Hello, Tude, it's me. How're you doing?'

There was a muffled sound.

'Hello?'

'Sorry about that – I said I'm walking the dogs, but Gertie just tried to get at a duck. We're at the pond. It's hot. Even the ducks can't seem to be bothered to try to waddle away from the dogs, hence Gertie lunging for one.'

Having spent the vast majority of her life unable to imagine the attractions of a duck pond, Annie was surprised at the ache that she felt as she pictured Tudor, Gertie, and Rosie beside the pond in Anwen-by-Wye. A bus hurtled past her, causing a gale, and she had to chuckle; her father's career as a bus driver was what had made her current life – her whole life – possible, so she thanked the bus, and told herself she'd be able to walk around the village with Tudor and the pups in just a couple of days, or maybe even on Sunday evening.

'So what's up with you?' Tudor sounded more focused. 'Eustelle and Rodney alright? You having a good time?'

'Lovely, ta. Mum hasn't stopped feeding me, and Dad? Well, he's just being Dad. Quiet, but strong, in his own way. We left him to clear away the breakfast dishes bemoaning the fact he now only reads his newspapers on his tablet instead of in paper form – but he agrees with Eustelle that it's better for the planet that way.'

'Give them my best.'

'I will. But, listen, Tude, I've got some news about Delyth and I want to tell you before you talk to her.'

'Don't panic. She sent me a message to put me off until tomorrow. Going on some excursion or other.'

'Yes, she's being taken on a sledge pulled by a pack of dogs across a glacier.'

Tudor sounded puzzled. 'She's what? How do you know that?'

'Delyth was raving about it on Facebook. Apparently it's the most expensive excursion you can do – involving a helicopter to get you there and back, and a four-course lunch served with champagne out on the glacier itself. Kept going on about "seeing the wonders of nature". Didn't mention how her jaunt might have an impact on it.'

'Good grief, that sounds like a terrible waste of money to me, but there you go, it's hers to spend, I suppose.'

Annie peered into the salon window – her mother was laughing and a stylist was, finally, teasing her hair into shape.

'Well, I don't know about that. But listen, what I do know is this: Delyth and Jacko James got divorced, which is understandable, I suppose, and now she's got another bloke in tow. She's still going by Delyth James online but she's planning to marry this one, from what I can gather. His name is Raymond and he's French. Not bad looking, to be fair, and he runs a winery in France…which she keeps talking about as though it makes a fortune, but I've looked into it and it's not doing very well at all. Ripe for takeover, the trade news says, or it might just go under altogether unless he gets an injection of cash for some new equipment.'

'So you think she might be selling the pub to put some money into the business this new bloke of hers runs?' Tudor sounded hopeful.

'Maybe. And that could be good, or bad.'

'How d'you mean?'

Annie replied, 'Well, look at it this way – if he needs a certain amount to get his business sorted, she's going to be looking for that certain amount. It might be a small amount, or a larger one – but it might be that she'll only sell the pub if that amount is what she gets.'

Tudor sounded thoughtful. 'Yes. I see what you mean. The amount she wants might not have anything to do with the real value of the pub at all – it might just be whatever it is he needs. Could be a problem. I'd have thought that running a winery was a risky and expensive business. Oh heck. Maybe that's that, then.'

Annie could tell he needed to be picked up. 'Oh, come on now, Tude. Let's look on the bright side – she might not need much at all. So that could be in our favor.'

'You're right. Hang on, Annie – no, Rosie, come here now. Good girl. Good girl. No – you come here, Gertie. Come. Gertie. Come! Good girl.'

Annie loved listening in.

Tudor said, 'Anything else?'

'Delyth will drink any sort of tequila cocktail you can imagine, is absolutely not a vegetarian, and will – no doubt – post umpteen photos of her blessed yomping across a glacier before you talk to her. You should take a look at her Facebook feed – it's all public. Everything. You'll see Raymond on there – they're not shy of taking a selfie or two…hundred. Oh, and she mentioned her father's death, too. Do yourself a favor and watch the video of her crying about it – before they show it at the Oscars next year.'

Tudor chuckled. 'You've not warmed to her, have you?'

'Didn't when I met her, haven't now. You know I have to be honest, Tude. And listen, I'm actually being kind, because if I started talking about her eyebrows, well, then I'd just be betraying the sisterhood.'

'Eyebrows? Did you say eyebrows?'

'Yes. She's got those giant, heavy ones that look like two slugs crawling across her forehead. You know the sort I mean. And she's not as young as she'd like to think she is, so they look absolutely bizarre. But, there, it's her face, so she can do what she wants with it, I suppose.'

'No comment.'

'Clever man.'

'Listen, you're talking to a bloke whose own eyebrows look like two drunk ferrets staggering across *his* forehead, so I haven't got a leg to stand on…like the ferrets.'

Annie giggled. 'You've no idea how funny you are, do you, Tude? Bless. Anyway…that's all I've got about our Delyth: cashflow troubles for the new man, spending money like a drunken sailor, and questionable taste in beauty treatments – speaking of which, I think I'm about to be taken shopping by my mother. She's at the till, paying, and she's looking a picture. There's a dinner and dance at Dad's domino club tonight – well, the partners of the members are invited, which really means all the wives and girlfriends, and there's a pig roast in the car park and a DJ. Given the weather it'll all be outdoors, and I'm allowed to go too because one of Dad's mates has a wife who won't come, so I can have her ticket.'

'Take photos, please?'

'Nah – you know me, never met a camera I didn't want to turn away from.'

'Please?'

'We'll see. Talk later – or tomorrow, when I'm on the train, alright? Oh – picking me up won't clash with you phoning Delyth, will it?'

'No. I told her I'd do it around eight, and we should be back from the station before that. I love you, have fun.'

'I love you, too. Give Gert a hug from me.'

Eustelle Parker did, indeed, look a picture as she emerged from the salon, and Annie told her so.

'Just you wait till you see what I'm wearin' to that party tonight, child,' was her mother's spirited response.

Annie couldn't imagine, but suspected that for once, given her new hairdo, it wouldn't involve a hat.

SUNDAY 4th JUNE

CHAPTER ELEVEN

Marjorie Pritchard was making a beeline toward Carol, who feared escape might be impossible – everyone was trying to leave church at once and she and Albert were trapped in the pews, David having managed to sneak out before the crush began.

'Just the person I wanted to see,' said Marjorie with delight. 'I said to Sarah that you'd know all about it.'

Carol greeted Sarah Hughes warmly, a woman she admired a great deal, who was not only managing to continue with her career as a teacher, but also raising two energetic boys. She smiled as broadly as she could at Marjorie Pritchard while trying to stop Albert from wriggling out of her arms.

'Such a big boy, now, isn't he?' Marjorie cooed into Albert's face, which Carol could see was upsetting him.

'Still so young and innocent, not like mine,' said Sarah, turning to try to spot her two sons as they made their way from the vestry, where Carol imagined they'd have got rid of their choir robes. 'Lovely voices, but oh my word, the trouble they can cause. Excuse me, there they are now. Must dash.'

Carol nodded sagely, recalling exactly what trouble they had – on occasion – caused in the village. 'What will I know all about, Marjorie?' Carol didn't want to get stuck nattering for longer than was absolutely necessary – she knew David wanted to get home to be able to snatch a few hours' sleep.

'The hearse,' replied Marjorie calmly. 'It was up at your place on Thursday. I saw it turn onto the road to the Hall, but no one saw it there, so it must have gone to your barn.'

Carol was deeply puzzled. The only thing she knew about any hearse was the one that had been delivering unsolicited wreaths. But she knew she couldn't mention a case to Marjorie – it would be all around the village in about an hour.

'I don't know anything about any hearse – but I wasn't at the office all last week, I've been working from home.' Carol hoped she'd supplied a sufficiently neutral answer to allow her to escape.

Marjorie Pritchard's face suggested she'd just sucked a lemon. 'Oh dear, still having to work from home? That husband of yours just can't cope with this one, can he?' She nodded solicitously toward Albert, who was doing his best to rip off his mother's nose.

Carol wasn't having that. 'David's currently contracted to overseas clients, which means he's working all through the night. We're a team, Marjorie – a parenting team. Albert's the main focus of both our lives.'

Marjorie looked deeply satisfied. 'Yes, I said it was something like that to Sharon at the shop; those lights are on in that upstairs room all night, you see. So it was either that he was working there, or something else was going on.'

Carol dreaded to think about the variety of possible 'something elses' that might have been raked over by Marjorie and Sharon during one of their gossip fests at the shop, so set the thoughts to one side and made sure she kept smiling as she did her best to sidle out from between the pews.

'So you didn't see a hearse, but maybe one of the rest of you did,' continued Marjorie, refusing to be swayed form her original digging. 'No Mavis this morning, I see. That's unusual for her. I hope she's not poorly. The dowager relies upon her so much, now that all her lady's aides have left.'

Carol sighed. Marjorie really was very good at wheedling information out of people, possibly even as good as Annie was – if rather more obvious about it. 'I understand that the Newburys moved to be closer to family in Cheltenham,' replied Carol, annoyed with herself that she was giving Marjorie much-wanted information, though she couldn't really see the harm in it, 'and Mavis is fine, thanks, just busy doing something…somewhere else.' That was enough.

Marjorie's eyes glinted. 'Oh – is she off doing something terribly dangerous, somewhere? What you women get up to is really thrilling, isn't it? And useful, too. I mean, look how you helped me out with that spa place. Wonderful, you were. Is she off doing something like that? Like you were, undercover, then?'

Carol could feel herself sliding down a slippery slope, so slammed on the brakes. 'Not really, Marjorie, something quite mundane. Now, if that's all, I really should try to catch up with David, and Albert needs a bit of a nap before lunch.'

Marjorie looked crestfallen. 'Oh well, there you are then. Only I was saying to Sarah that it must have been the same one, see, because there wouldn't be two in one day, and she only caught a glimpse of the one at her place before it shot off.'

Carol's head swam. 'What? Sorry. I mean *pardon*? I don't understand. More than one what? When? And what's it got to do with Sarah?'

Marjorie's lips pursed as though Carol needed telling off for being so dim. 'The hearse that delivered the flowers to Sarah's house. On Thursday. She only saw it as it sped off – which I don't personally think is a very nice thing for a hearse to do, to be honest with you. She doesn't know who sent the flowers, see – so I said I'd ask you lot about the hearse that I saw going to your place, because there wouldn't be two hearses in a place like Anwen-by-Wye on one day, would there? It has to be the same one. So you might have known who sent the flowers.' She spoke as though her explanation was perfectly straightforward.

Carol paused where she was, her mind settling cogs into place. 'Sarah received a delivery of flowers from someone in a hearse – flowers she wasn't expecting?'

Marjorie nodded. 'She brought the wreath with her to church this morning to check with Reverend Roberts if they'd been meant for someone else – you know, maybe somebody wanted them put on a grave outside to mark some sort of anniversary. He said he'd check his records after he's said goodbye to everyone at the door, though he thought it unlikely.'

Carol made a real effort to extricate herself from the pews and managed to get into the aisle. 'I'd like to see the flowers, and Sarah,' she said, striding out as much as was possible given that she was holding a wriggling toddler. She had a very bad feeling about the turn events had taken.

Marjorie followed her, not quite managing to keep up, calling, 'She left the wreath in the porch, and said she'd see me outside – because I told her I'd ask you about the hearse.'

Carol found David, handed off Albert, called over to Sarah, then picked up the wreath; she felt she had no time to lose.

Both Marjorie and Sarah seemed puzzled by Carol's interest – and, possibly, her intensity – but she couldn't let herself care about that, she needed to find out as much as she could.

She examined the wreath first. The roundel of many types of flowers – some vividly colored – surprised her; she'd expected something much more traditional. This looked almost jolly, with its yellows, pinks, and oranges. Next she peppered Sarah Hughes with questions that clearly took the woman aback: no, there wasn't anyone who'd recently died in her family; no, she wasn't aware that anyone in her family, or even that she knew, was close to the end of their life; no, she hadn't been able to find anyone who'd ordered the flowers; and – finally – no, she wasn't able to give Carol a detailed description of the person who'd left them.

'I was coming home from work and I spotted him outside the house. He left what turned out to be this wreath of condolence at our door, jumped into his vehicle and shot off – he literally vanished around the corner. Short bloke. Black tail coat, you know…like the Victorian style undertakers wear at funerals. I dare say I'd have guessed he was an undertaker – or maybe a wedding guest – if I'd seen just him on his own, but the hearse-type car? Well, that's a dead giveaway, isn't it? Oh – sorry, I didn't mean to make a joke about…bodies.' She stifled a smile.

Carol was on the case. 'What do you mean by a "hearse-type" car? Marjorie told me you'd seen an actual hearse.'

Marjorie smiled weakly.

Sarah looked at Marjorie with venom. 'The car he got into looked like a hearse – long and black, with big windows in the back. But I couldn't see the whole thing because he'd parked around the corner…as I told Marjorie.'

Carol gave the matter some thought. 'So might it have been an older type of estate car?'

Sarah replied, 'Yes, I suppose it could have been, but, you know, there were the tails, and the black car, and the wreath…so maybe my brain made a bit of a leap. I get that. Maybe there wasn't much about the car that was hearse-like, after all.'

Carol knew that Sarah was sharp and intelligent – and had no doubt that the woman understood the way the psyche can create a whole that's greater than the sum of the parts; it was the sort of thing that school teachers had to grapple with all the time, when children jumped to conclusions rather than following a logical path.

'May I take the wreath with me?' Carol was bemused by the surprised look on the womens' faces.

Sarah hesitated. 'I'd like to wait until the reverend is sure the flowers weren't meant for someone here in the graveyard. He's probably inside checking…oh, there he is now. Any luck, Reverend?'

The Reverend Ebenezer Roberts looked glum – which Carol knew to be the way his face hung when it wasn't doing anything in particular.

He replied with his usual mellifluous tone, 'No record of any date during the past or forthcoming week being the anniversary of anyone's death who resides in our graveyard. There was a Mr Selwyn Richards of this parish who passed on June second, 1973, but his remains are at the graveyard in Brecon, not here, so I think it's unlikely to be him. I'm afraid I cannot be of more help.'

Carol wasn't surprised, but felt unable to put Sarah Hughes on full alert: this might simply be a case of a wrongly delivered floral tribute rather than a prediction of a death within the family. But, even so, Carol wrestled with her conscience, and decided her course of action.

She said, 'Alright then, if I could take the wreath, that would be wonderful, and how about I find out what I can from my colleagues about the possibility that a hearse visited the barn on Thursday? I'll let you know if I find out anything illuminating, Sarah. Right then, I'd better get Albert home because he needs food, and he'll grizzle until he gets some.'

She swept along the path to the lychgate where her husband and son awaited her arrival, then whispered to David to not ask anything about the wreath she was carrying until they got home, which they did in double-quick time.

Carol knew what she needed to do: she had to get in touch with Christine as soon as she could; she needed to talk to Louise Attwater, because she needed guidance about the best way to deal with the problem at hand; then she needed to get Sarah Hughes on her own, so she could deal with the situation as sensitively as possible.

With Annie still in London, and Mavis off at Ellie's nursing home, Carol was going to have to rely upon Christine. A close neighbor had received a wreath – an occurrence that had predicted a death within a family a couple of dozen times already – and she didn't want anyone within Sarah's circle to die, let alone 'on her watch', as she saw it.

As they approached their house, Carol said to her husband, 'Sorry, David, but I think we'll have to make it a very quick lunch, and you napping with Albert this afternoon, because I need to do everything I can to help a neighbor who might be about to lose a loved one.'

David stared at his wife, then replied, 'Okay, I'll cope. But you know you're going to have to give me details over lunch, right? Because what you just said is a bit scary, to be honest.'

Carol smiled, though she didn't really feel like it. 'I know what you mean, *cariad*, but needs must.'

David muttered, 'Ellie having Mavis working at her place because of some sort of suspicions she's got about one of her nurses, and now a neighbor "maybe" losing a loved one? This job of yours sounds a bit too deadly at the moment, Carol. But talk me through it all, and maybe it'll sound less worrying.'

Carol hoped it would, but feared it might not.

'I preferred it when you were working on The Case of the Purloined Pickles,' her husband continued. 'This sounds more…well, all a good bit darker.'

'I shall explain everything as we eat,' said Carol grandly, trying to make her face grin wickedly, but – she suspected – failing.

CHAPTER TWELVE

Christine gazed at the face of her fiancé, who lay beside her, fast asleep. Alexander Bright looked perfectly peaceful. Innocent. And even happy.

The Alexander she'd fallen for had always worn an expression of alertness, like an animal constantly reassuring itself that its environment was safe, or else was hunting for its next prey. He'd had an edge to him, that immediately told you that being with him would never be boring, or routine; an edge born of a questionable background, some extremely dodgy dealings, and the challenges of having grown up the son of a white, alcoholic mother, and an unknown, but obviously black, father on a council estate in Brixton where he was found to be unacceptable to any of the gangs who operated there. He'd forged his own path and had reinvented himself – leaving behind his reputation as a reliable courier serving the criminal fraternity in South London, to become a successful businessman heavily invested in various social housing projects.

She loved that about him – that he'd risen above so much adversity; that he'd literally created himself from nothing. She admired him for it too – and even for the fact that he still operated within the shadows, to a certain extent, whenever he needed to. She'd fallen for a good man doing sometimes shady things in order to achieve admirable ends.

Even as she thought it, Christine caught herself.

I'm thinking of him being that way as something that's passed…gone. He's comfortable now – safe. This antiques shop? Just another example of how he's becoming…normal.

Not wanting to disturb him, Christine gently pushed herself away from Alexander, watching that his breathing didn't change, so that she had time to study him as she contemplated her feelings toward him.

In many of the conversations since their engagement had been announced, Christine's mother had warned her off trying to change

Alexander – urging her to understand that she'd never be able to do it. What her mother had seemed unable to grasp was that Christine didn't want to change him – she loved him because of who he was, not in spite of it.

But now? Now he *was* changing – though she was sure it had nothing to do with her.

'When I married your father, I married a man with a title but not a penny to his name,' her mother had said. 'I knew that wouldn't last, though, because he was a driven soul – that much was obvious from the moment we met. And, even though he knew I didn't care for wealth or the good life, he put his heart into doing everything he could to build a business that's provided the funds we needed to give you and your brother the education and upbringing we didn't have. Look at me, Christine – I'm little Dierdre Wilson, a girl from the Irish countryside who fell for a man she'd no idea was a viscount. Indeed, I don't think I even knew what a viscount was, back then.'

Christine admitted to herself that the way her father had built his life, having started with nothing, and the way that Alexander had done the same – though both in very different ways – was something that had not escaped her notice, nor that of her mother.

'He's devilish handsome, is that Alexander,' her mother had said, after having first met him.

Maybe it was the little bit of the devil in him that attracted me?

Christine studied the ceiling. Was her fiancé now too saintly to be truly attractive? Was he following too straight a path for her to believe that – at any moment – a possible detour toward danger might be taken, with all the excitement that might offer?

Christine wished with all her heart that she knew the answer to that. She was young, intelligent, successful, worked with wonderful people and had a fiancé who adored her. But she still wasn't truly happy.

What was wrong with her?

Unable to lie still any longer, Christine rolled out of bed as carefully as she could, and padded out into the small sitting room, pulling a robe around her shoulders as she went. She felt the cloth snag on the lumpy scar tissue that was her daily reminder of the injury she'd sustained during a dangerous bit of gunplay that had – unexpectedly – taken place at her family home in Ireland. Even as she felt the tug, and that strange numb-but-sore feeling of the area where she'd been shot, her mind flashed back to that day: Alexander and his hired heavies lying in wait for the person she'd unmasked as a very bad man, doing very bad things; there'd been an electricity in the atmosphere that day – an electricity she missed.

Not that she ever wanted to be shot at again – once was more than enough for that sort of thing. But she missed how Alexander's presence and actions at the time – launching himself at her assailant to save her – had made her feel.

She shook her head. *Do I need to feel like a princess, and he's my knight in shining armor coming to save me, so I can be happy? Grow up, Christine – you're a woman, not a child.*

Alexander emerged from the bedroom mumbling, 'You alright? Is it very late? It looks late. I should have had my run by now. Shall I make coffee?'

Alexander pecked her on the cheek and was already in the small kitchen reaching for the beans he would grind – to perfection, for the coffee he'd make – which would be fantastic, to accompany the scrambled eggs on toast he'd pop in front of her – which would be fluffy, buttery, and delicious.

Christine stood behind him as he fussed, and put her arms around him, hugging his wonderfully broad, muscular back. 'Shall we go for a drive in the Aston today? Just for the hell of it. Put your foot down…frighten the birds in the hedges and the sheep in the fields with the roar we make?' She giggled.

Alexander chuckled. 'Maybe not, my love. I've promised Bill that I'll have a video call with him today to agree that first lot of stock for the new shop, and Henry was muttering something about wanting me to take a look at a Georgian press they've found in some disused room up at Chellingworth Hall – he's not sure if it's wildly valuable, or just a bit of old tat. Though the chances of any tat coming from that place are slim, I'd say. More likely to be the genuine article, I'd have thought. Oh – and we've decided to go with the paler of the two greens we were talking about for that one area of wallpaper, did I tell you?'

Christine felt her body sag.

'No, you hadn't mentioned that. It'll be grand, I'm sure.'

CHAPTER THIRTEEN

Mavis MacDonald had slept for much longer than she'd meant to, and was still exhausted. As she peeled herself out of Ellie's bed – which was very comfy, as it turned out – she felt every muscle scream, then uncramp.

You're no' as young as you once were, Mavis told herself as she stretched, hearing her back crack.

A soak in a hot bath wasn't possible because Ellie's bathroom only offered a shower stall, but Mavis let the hot water run down her back until she began to feel guilty about using as much as she had. Snuggled into comfy clothes – which she welcomed, despite the warmth of the flat and the sun streaming through the open windows – Mavis made herself a breakfast from the supplies Ellie had marked for her attention in the fridge. A sausage sandwich wasn't the sort of thing usually served for breakfast at the Dower House, so she enjoyed every mouthful, and was almost tempted to make herself a second – but thought better of it, because she knew she'd regret it later in the day; she had a great deal to do, and would need all her faculties to be sharp, not dulled by too much stodge.

As she'd driven from the nursing home to Ellie's flat at the end of the night shift, she'd made an audio recording of her impressions and findings, which was the method she intended to employ on this case, thereby saving the time needed to actually write notes. The little plastic holder on her dashboard allowed her to make voice recordings hands-free, and she felt perfectly capable of speaking as she drove, even when she was – as she had to admit she had been – quite exhausted.

Grateful to have been able to call upon her previous years' experience, Mavis had at least been able to lift patients properly, as well as understand the roles of all the pieces of equipment needed to help those who needed it with bodily necessities, and as a means of giving them a comfortable night's sleep. Even so, she'd still been surprised, then alarmed, at what was expected of the care assistants in the facility. She'd imagined there'd have been much higher staffing levels, and then told herself she was finally seeing what life was like for a nurse, or a carer, outside the armed forces – which she'd thought was leanly staffed as it was.

Her professional hat was off to the people she'd worked with the night before, and she was impressed with the level of care being provided at the place. Unfamiliar with either local authority-run or private nursing homes, Mavis had arrived with much trepidation, but had left knowing that all her charges were being well tended to in terms of their health, and general wellbeing. She'd said as much in her audio notes, and was relieved to have been able to do so. Ellie, it was clear, ran a good team: there was clarity about roles, and expectations; there was clarity about routine, and how to deal with uncommon occurrences; there was a good team spirit, despite the fact it was obvious that everyone she'd met was operating at the very edge of their emotional and physical capabilities. Mavis had recorded those observations, too.

But as for spotting a junior nurse who might be acting in an unlawful manner? That was where she was still at sea. Her first problem had been that her duties didn't allow her to watch either of the two junior nurses on duty much of the time – but at least there were only two, so her focus could be trained upon just them.

One was a mousy girl, of the type Mavis had encountered before: Veronica Daniels had probably become a nurse to do good, and was finding that her storybook image of the job wasn't even close to the reality. Mavis had seen Daniels interacting with a few of the patients with tenderness and compassion, but she was slow, and Mavis immediately realized that the girl – for that was what Mavis thought of her as, because she was only in her mid-twenties – would find it hard to keep up with caring for all the patients for whom she had responsibility.

The other one? A totally different kettle of fish: Wanda Gorman was in her mid-thirties, blunt – verging on the rude – and absolutely efficient. She spent less time with each patient, completed her tasks rapidly, and left them with the job done. However, Mavis feared that the feeling on the part of the patient would have been that they'd been 'seen to' rather than 'nursed'.

Mavis put her dishes to drain and made herself a mug of tea – a strong one. She knew about the balance that nurses needed to strike, and the challenges they faced when dealing with patients who needed higher levels of attention – or demanded it, at least. If she were in that home as a patient she'd not be happy with either just Veronica nor Wanda attending to her – she'd want someone who was a bit of both, and that was the rarity that made a really good nurse. That was the type Mavis had always tried to be: efficiency balanced with compassion – a tough challenge. But no one had ever told her – nor any nurse who'd ever trained – that it would be an easy job.

Mavis picked up her phone to make a fresh recording, this one designed to comprise a summary and action points she planned for Ellie, Carol and – if necessary, in the long run – for the police.

Her understanding of what was needed in order to lift a case to the level of a police investigation had been developed over the past year or so, in no small part as a result of lengthy conversations with Chief Inspector Carwen James, who knew his onions when it came to his job, and wasn't shy about telling Mavis how to do hers – to be better able to allow him to do his, to be fair.

Mavis hooked her hair behind her ears and started to speak – only to be immediately interrupted by her phone ringing.

'Hello, Carol, what can I do for you?'

Carol spoke rapidly and with some stress discernable in her tone. Mavis gave her colleague her full attention, her alarm growing as Carol told her about the wreath that had been delivered to Sarah Hughes's home.

Mavis said, 'Our client, Louise Attwater, did indeed arrive at our office in a hearse – a fact I dare say I should have mentioned to you – but yes, you'll be right to clarify that with Sarah. I wish you luck when you interview her properly – and as far away from Marjorie Pritchard as possible, too. One thing – if Sarah was on her way home from work, might her boys have seen something, if they were already home from school?'

'I don't think so,' Carol replied. 'Sarah picks them up on her way back to the village, so they'd all have arrived together.'

Mavis was surprised; as a girl she'd walked a mile or so from her home to school, in Scotland, and that in some terribly inclement weather through the winters. She sighed as she realized the world had changed, meaning that children now needed to be delivered and collected, especially if a walk to school meant using some narrow roads and lanes, with no protection from the traffic. She'd been fortunate to have had the use of safe streets and a gaggle of chums to walk with, her best friend living next door to her.

Taking her chance, Mavis sought more insight into Ellie, Carol's childhood friend.

Carol told her, 'We were joined at the hip, though not literally because her family's farmhouse was about two miles from ours, even though our parents' farms abutted each others'. We'd meet where our lanes joined up, then walk to the main road together to get the bus. I dare say we came over as very exclusive to the other kids in our class and school; we didn't need to say certain things to each other, see, because we both knew what it felt like to have parents who worked twenty-four hours a day, every day of the year – or at least had to be prepared to. Lambing season was nuts, and we both got that; we'd basically had to fend entirely for ourselves at weird times since we were little, and we saw that as normal, whereas a lot of the kids in our school came from more suburban areas, so they had no idea what our lives were like. I dare say they thought we were both a bit feral – which we probably were. But we turned out alright.'

'What drew Ellie to nursing?' Mavis was always interested in knowing that.

Carol was hesitant. 'I was never sure. I was always good at maths, and she was always good at English, but how that led her to want to become a nurse, I don't know. She just did. And, to be honest, we drifted apart a bit for a good few years, after we both left home to do our own things. We didn't really pick up our connection again until – oh, about four or five years ago, I reckon. I was just taking over as the head of systems and she had just been appointed as staff nurse at a nursing home in North London. We managed to meet up a few times and it was lovely to see her again…all grown up.'

Mavis nodded, then said, 'I see…' She then continued, 'She's got a good setup, Carol, I should tell you that. And, now that I've seen how she manages her responsibilities, I have more faith in her concerns…which I suppose is both a good and bad thing. I believe that if she has suspicions they are probably based upon something she cannae quite put her finger on, but maybe I can spot it. The patient she thought might die yesterday was still alive when I left this morning, though I also agree with her assessment of that situation; I might have an opportunity to find out what happens to the medications prescribed to a deceased patient very soon.'

Carol replied, 'I feel weird saying "Good Luck" to that, but you know what I mean.'

'Yes, quite,' Mavis agreed. 'And I wish you the best with the undertaker case; please keep me informed. I have every faith you'll handle the case, and the contact with the client, most appropriately – but also agree that what we had considered to be a case without a great sense of urgency about it has now become more pressing. I'll try to speak to you tomorrow – possibly about this time, or later. The workload of a carer is challenging, especially now that I'm getting on in years – it's more suited to those who are younger than me, without the weakness of body I seem to be suffering from these days. Well, we're none of us as bonny as we once were, I dare say – now I'll be away. Ach, no – what about Julian Tavistock? I'll be speaking with Althea next, and she's bound to ask me. Anything?'

Mavis was surprised that Carol didn't reply immediately, and was further taken aback by her tone when she did. 'Honestly, Mavis, I haven't had two minutes to myself – or even for my family, today, so I haven't got anything. Who is he, anyway? If Althea's going to be asking about him, is this something to do with her? Any clues? Starting points at all?'

Cross with herself that she'd let the connection with Althea slip, Mavis replied, 'No worries, my dear. Yes, there is a tangential connection with Althea, but I think it's best if I don't steer you at all on this one. Just let me know what you can, when you can. I'm sure tomorrow will be fine. Bye for now.'

Mavis disconnected before Carol had a chance to reply – or complain; a technique she'd found useful on many occasions. Then she stared at her phone. She didn't like the sound of a wreath having been delivered to a villager, and shared Carol's concerns. But she also knew she had to focus on her own case, so hesitated before phoning Althea, because she expected the dowager to fuss, and be entirely focused on the question of her potential future son-in-law's background. Mavis knew only too well how the woman became fixated upon one thing, and was just like her aged, but still playful, Jack Russell, McFli, in many regards: when he got hold of – well, almost anything really – he would never let go, except on his own terms.

CHAPTER FOURTEEN

Althea Twyst sat quietly at the dining table at Chellingworth Hall, gazing at her grandson in his crib with delight. He really was a much better behaved baby that either Henry or Clementine had ever been. She wondered if she was complimenting Stephanie on her good parenting often enough, then decided that was something one could overdo so easily, so said nothing.

Clementine's fiancé was being witty about something to do with bronze – though she'd lost focus for a few moments and couldn't recall how his story had begun, so smiled politely at what was obviously the punchline – if her son's too-hearty laughing was anything to go by.

She desperately wanted to know if this man was the right one for her daughter; Clementine had, indeed, become engaged to be married on three previous occasions, and all three of the men in question had turned out to be completely wrong for her – a decision that Clementine had found herself making after certain facts about them had been explained to her.

Althea sighed too heavily, and drew the attention of her daughter-in-law.

'Are you feeling quite well, Althea? You look a little tired. Missing Mavis, I suppose.'

Althea rallied. 'Not at all. I very much enjoy her company, but she has her responsibilities, as we all know, so I'm quite used to spending time alone.'

Jools sounded genuinely interested when he asked, 'So what are Mavis's responsibilities?'

Clementine replied, 'I told you – she's a detective.'

Jools looked surprised – at least, that was what Althea saw in his eyes, which were about his only visible features.

He said, '*She's* the detective? I thought she was...well, it would be understandable if I...um. *She's* the one you told me about who helped to unearth your family history, and save the family name, and so forth?'

Clementine nodded. 'She did. She works with three other women, as a team. Is Mavis off doing something daring, Mother?'

Althea tried to not show that she was disappointed that Mavis hadn't gone into any details about her latest job.

'I can't say.' Althea thought that was as good a reply as any. Then she decided to add, 'But I happen to know she's digging into someone's background…someone who might have a few things they'd rather people didn't find out about. In their past.'

She smiled sweetly at Jools, then turned and said to her son, 'Henry, do you think we could have some more windows open, please, even Jools is looking a little pink. It's rather warm in here this evening.'

Henry nodded. 'Of course, Mother. I agree. Edward, would you, please? Though not the windows at this end of the room, as they might cause a draft for Hugo in his crib.'

'With pleasure, Your Grace.'

Stephanie said, quite innocently thought Althea, 'Mavis is terribly good at getting to the bottom of things, you know, as are all the WISE women.'

'The WISE women?' Jools looked at Clementine with bafflement.

'Oh yes,' his fiancée replied, 'I don't think I told you about that. You see, Carol's Welsh, and lives in the village – ever so good with computers; then Christine is Irish, and Mavis is – as you saw – Scottish, and Annie's English. Proper Cockney, she is. From Mile End. Christine went to the same school I did, though about twenty years after me, then worked in the City, as did Annie, and Carol; they knew each other from their time there. And Mavis was a matron at an army hospital or something when they met her; they were investigating the death of Christine's uncle. Then they all decided to become proper detectives.'

Althea added, 'It was a little more complicated than that, dear. They all did training courses and that sort of thing to start with. And then, of course, your dear brother invited them all to come here to investigate me, and they stayed.'

Jools almost choked on a mouthful of peach sorbet.

Althea chuckled, 'Yes, well you might choke, Jools. Henry got them to come here to find out if I was losing my marbles, because I'd seen a dead body that disappeared. Didn't you, Henry?'

'Mother –' Henry folded his napkin with great vigor – 'we have spoken about this on several occasions, and have agreed that everything turned out for the best in the long run. I did what I felt was necessary at the time, and our community has gained significantly because of it. The women of the WISE Enquiries Agency are a boon to the area in many ways.'

Jools had given up on his dessert, it appeared, and was shuffling in his chair. Althea noticed him squeezing her daughter's thigh.

Clementine said, 'I promised Jools a turn around the walled garden before the light goes completely, I think we should go now.' She looked at her watch. 'Yes, now would be a good time.'

Althea was surprised by the alacrity with which Jools was on his feet and helping Clementine to hers; she found it remarkable that such a large man should be able to move so swiftly and deftly.

With farewells exchanged, the couple left the dining room. Once the door was closed, Stephanie remarked, 'They seem very happy, don't they? Though Henry and I were wondering about the wisdom of their plans for a wedding in Egypt. How do you feel about that, Althea?'

Althea had entertained many thoughts about not just the planned wedding but the marriage after it, too, and struggled to find the best words to use.

'I believe that the right people will find each other, to be wed in the right way, and to live their married life in the way that suits them best. Have they mentioned their plans for their marital home at all? I wondered if Clementine and Jools intend to live here, or at the London house, or maybe at the lodge in Scotland. That might suit a blacksmith, as might here – though she mentioned his using a smithy in London, didn't she? She's not said anything to me about it, you see, and one doesn't like to pry, or interfere.'

Althea chose to ignore the surprised look that crossed her son's face at her comments, and gave her attention instead to Stephanie, who replied, 'Neither of them has said anything to either of us. Though I have to say, the idea that the pair of them might move in here hadn't occurred to me. Had it occurred to you, Henry?'

Now Althea paid attention to her son, who was becoming pink around the gills. She placed her napkin across the lower part of her face as though wiping her mouth – which allowed her to hide a smile.

Henry sounded alarmed when he said, 'No, the thought hadn't occurred to me either, dear. Though I cannot imagine she'd think that…not the two of them…not for any real length of time. Surely not.'

Althea had quite enjoyed the sport of watching her son have his in-laws living at Chellingworth Hall for a few months, but that had worn thin after a while. Now she could feel his apprehension afresh: Henry hated having anyone living at the Hall save himself, and those who absolutely had to be there.

Having dropped a couple of cats quite successfully among the pigeons that evening, Althea asked Edward to inform young Ian that she was now quite ready to be driven back to the Dower House.

CHAPTER FIFTEEN

'Thanks for agreeing to see me this evening,' said Carol as she settled at the table in Sarah Hughes's huge, and truly lived-in, kitchen. 'Are the boys in bed yet? I hope I didn't disturb them when I rang the bell.'

Sarah laughed. 'Those two in in bed at this time? No way. First of all, it's still light, despite the time and, secondly, neither of them has finished their homework so they're both doing that at the moment. Fine teacher I'd be if I didn't make sure they'd done their homework at the weekend. Though I have to admit that it's not unusual for them to be doing it at the last minute. To be honest, I usually don't even think about it until I sit down to do my lesson planning for Monday on a Sunday evening; I don't give my pupils at the infants' school any homework, you see – oh no, I'm the one who gets to do all that. And when I sit down to do mine, I remember the boys have theirs. Is Albert with David? Doing alright, is he? He's a big boy now, isn't he?'

Carol agreed that her son was, indeed, a big boy for his age, but didn't want to get sidetracked, so said simply, 'Look, Sarah, there's something I have to tell you, and something I have to ask you – but you might want your husband here to hear all this, too. Is Steve about?'

Sarah looked puzzled. 'He's in the garage, fiddling about with the mower. As he said, it's so dry at the moment that he hardly needs to cut the grass, but it's bound to rain some time, isn't it, and then he'll want it to work. I can give him a shout if you like, but…well, what's this all about, Carol? You're being very mysterious. Is this anything to do with that wreath you were so interested in?'

Carol nodded. 'Yes, it is – but I really do need to speak to the both of you, if you don't mind.'

Sarah Hughes looked worried as she stood. 'Alright then. You wait here. Back in a tick.'

Carol composed herself as she waited and took in her surroundings. Such a wonderful, big kitchen, and so much more updated than the one at her house – which she loved, but it felt smaller and smaller, these days. Sarah didn't have an Aga, but she did have a large oven and a dishwasher, which Carol thought would be bliss; she'd never had a dishwasher, and wondered if they were as life-changing as everyone said they were. Before she'd had time to become as covetous of Sarah's six gas burners as she was of her dishwasher, the Hugheses came to settle themselves at the table, and Sarah brought a fresh pot of tea.

'Sorry about the hands – I'm a bit oily,' said Steve Hughes, whose sandy hair and freckled complexion had always entranced Carol; being very fair-skinned herself she was pleased to know at least one other person in the village who looked as though they might burst into flames if the sun ever touched them.

'No worries,' said Carol, then began.

She'd spoken to Louise Attwater and had received clearance from her to tell the Hugheses about the mysterious wreaths, and what had followed. As Carol explained the situation, a look of disbelief shifted to anxiety on her hosts' faces. When she'd finished, Carol paused, letting it all sink in.

'But I don't know of anyone in the family who's ill,' said Sarah, sounding panicked. 'What if it's one of the boys and we don't know anything about it? Oh my God, that wreath was left here on Thursday. I'll be back in a minute.' She dashed up the stairs, where Carol had no doubt she was double-checking that both her sons were hale and hearty.

Steve scratched his chin. 'She's right – there's no one. I can't imagine what this is all about. Maybe this wreath we got was just badly addressed – meant for someone else entirely. That's got to be a possibility.'

'Ty Mawr, The Green, Anwen-by-Wye is quite a specific address, Steve,' said Carol. 'And you're certain that no one's contacted you about a delivery? There haven't been any odd phone calls or so forth? And what about Sarah's own family? Are they all…quite well?'

He shook his head. 'Sarah's family have all gone. There was only ever her mam and dad and they both passed away a couple of years back. So sad; her father had early-onset Alzheimer's, and her mother knew she'd lost him years before he finally went. As it turned out, she died about six months before him. Heart. Sarah thinks the strain of loving someone who usually didn't know who she was took its toll on her – but, to be honest, I'd rather we didn't talk about that if we don't have to because it still upsets her. So you see, there can't be anyone about to die because there isn't anyone…except us. Which is worrying.'

Sarah retook her seat, sighing. 'They're both fine. As am I, and you – right, Steve?'

Steve nodded.

'What about your side of the family, Steve?' pressed Carol. 'The wreath was delivered to the house – so it might have been meant for you, not Sarah. She was first home, so she was the one who found it.'

'My family?' Steve looked shocked. 'Right. Of course.' He pulled his phone out of his pocket, stabbed at it a few times and nibbled his lip as he waited.

Carol did her best to not stare as she listened to his side of the conversation, with some long pauses between his comments.

'Hello, Mam? Yes, it's me. Oh, nothing really. I didn't wake you, did I? Good. No, no, nothing to worry about. Yes, we're all fine, thanks. I just realized I hadn't phoned you back about that thing we were talking about. Yes, that's right, the program on TV I was talking about. Right, yes, that was what it was called. Oh, you didn't? Sorry. Dad thought it was what? Oh heck – no I didn't mean to shock him. Yes, right. But you're both okay, are you? In fine form, as ever? Yes. No. Well, yes, your back, of course. And Dad's too, now. Well, it would be, after doing all that, wouldn't it? Yes. No. Yes, she's here beside me now, doing her setting up for school tomorrow. Doing their homework. Oh yes, I know I did. You always tell me that, Mam. But listen, now that we've got that sorted out, I'd better go and look in on them, just to make sure they aren't playing those video games of theirs. Yes, the ones you sent them for their birthdays. Yes, they are a bit violent, Mam, but not too bad. Yes, I'd tell you, of course. Right-o then, I'll phone again soon, yes, I love you too, and Dad. Yes, I'll tell them. Night night.'

He disconnected. 'They're fine. Thank heavens. And, other than them, there's no one. Well, if you leave out my father's wastrel brother Ernie, that is. No one's heard from him, nor of him, I don't think for years. Ostracized due to his inability to stay out of the reach of the long arm of the law, was Ernie. I never met him, and certainly never called him "uncle", though he was, of course. A good bit older than my dad – who was, apparently, "a mistake". His father wouldn't have him in the house once he turned eighteen, and my dad was only about eight at the time, so never really knew him. I suppose you could say he's family – but only in terms of blood.'

Carol tensed. 'And do you have any idea where Ernie might be, these days?'

Steve shook his head. 'Not a clue. Dad had no way to keep in touch with him, and I've only ever heard stories about him. What I've just told you about him is all I know.'

Carol pulled out her tablet, got the password for the Wi-Fi from Sarah and started to tap. 'So, Ernest Hughes, right?' Steve nodded. 'And his age?'

Steve stared at the ceiling. 'Dad's seventy-two, so eighty-two-ish.'

'Born where? Do you know?'

Steve and Sarah exchanged a glance. She said, 'Your lot's always been in Caerphilly, haven't they?'

Steve nodded. 'As far as I know, Caerphilly. That's where Dad grew up, anyway. I don't know if his parents were living there when Ernie was born, though.'

'I'll try it, but it could turn out to be a common name. I don't suppose you know your paternal grandmother's and grandfather's names, do you? You see, if I could track down a birth record for the right person it might make it easier to find out if there's been a recent record of death.'

Steve picked up his phone again, and Carol listened to another pause-filled half-conversation. 'Sorry to bother you again, Mam. Yes, everything's still alright. It's just that Sarah and I were having a bit of a natter and I realized I couldn't remember all my grandparents' names. Yes. No. Yes, all of them. Okay – so yours were Samuel Probert, and Elizabeth, nee Howells. Oh, I didn't know that, no. And Dad's were…oh, yes, Gwynfor Hughes, I remember that now, and Arabella nee Swinburne, like the writer but no relation. Right. Yes – very helpful. Yes, still doing their homework. Oh, very soon I should imagine. Yes. Thanks again, Mam. And Mam, just a quick one for Dad, if I may. Yes, I know he doesn't like to talk on the phone – yes, you can ask him for me. See, I wondered if Uncle Ernie's name was actually Ernest. Did he have any middle names? And did Dad have any idea what became of him?' There was a particularly lengthy pause. 'Yes. No, I suppose not. Oh yes, I couldn't agree more. Absolutely. No way at all. Thank Dad. Talk soon. Love you. I will.' He turned to Carol. 'Did you get all that?'

'Bits.'

Steve said, 'Ernie was Ernest, with no "a", middle names Edward and William, born and raised in Caerphilly. I can give you that address because it's the house Dad grew up in and I've seen it often, but, no, my father's got absolutely no idea what happened to him. Sorry.'

Carol beamed. 'Don't worry, please. You've given me a lot more to go on than I've had sometimes. It might even be that – if he was in trouble with the law, as you said – that could help too, in a strange way. I'll work on it all as soon as I get home.'

'This has all left me feeling a bit shaky, if I'm honest,' said Sarah, draining her mug. 'If this wreath thing is foretelling a death in the family – which is creepy enough in itself – I'm going to be on pins until we know who that is. Steve's parents are lovely, and we couldn't bear to lose them. The boys never knew my father, see, because he was…ill, and they lost their gran a couple of years back. So, please, Carol – do whatever you can? And, Steve, why don't you drop over to your Mam and Dad's after work tomorrow? You could stay the night there, and I could keep an eye on the boys here. Alright?'

Steve Hughes looked surprised. 'If you think I should.' Carol could sense his hesitation.

She said, 'I'm going to leave you now. I'm sorry to have unnerved you this way; I promise I'll do all I can to track down your uncle as part of our overall investigation into every element of this case. And, yes, we'll also be working on finding out who it was who left the wreath, which might throw some light on the whole matter, too.'

Carol took her leave, and Steve showed her out. 'I understand why you had to do this,' he said, 'but please do let us know as soon as you have anything? Sarah's not usually this…sensitive. It'll be the anniversary of her mother's death in a few weeks, so maybe that's on her mind. Anyway – my regards to David and Albert. Night now.'

MONDAY 5th JUNE

CHAPTER SIXTEEN

Mavis was sipping tea, hoping it might possess some magical quality that would give her the energy she needed; it was gone one in the morning, she'd already put in a solid six hours, and she kept telling herself that the second half of her shift had to be easier than the first half.

With all the patients now, finally, asleep, she'd at least had the chance to eat a sandwich and gulp down a vat of tea. Though, unfortunately, she'd been so busy she'd had hardly any time to observe either Nurse Gorman or Nurse Daniels, both of whom seemed to be as frantic as herself.

And now, here she was, washing up her mug as Wanda Gorman flopped onto a chair beside the sink in the staff room, moaning loudly as she rubbed her left foot, from which she'd removed her shoe.

'That's swollen,' observed Mavis.

'You're a real Sherlock Holmes, aren't you,' snapped Wanda.

Mavis didn't bat an eyelid.

'I twisted it at the playground with my son yesterday afternoon,' Wanda continued. 'Not my ankle – oh no, I couldn't do something that simple. I had to go and twist my big toe. Stupid sandals. They might have been as cheap as chips, but they were about as useful as chips, too, for chasing after an active four-year-old. Daniel. My boy. I tripped, twisted my toe, had to get up and keep going to stop him from running onto the road. Stupid child. Lovely though, just not very aware of anything around him.'

'I didn't know you had children,' said Mavis. 'I have two boys of my own. And grandsons, too. They're a challenge, to be sure. As are girls, of course – but in different ways.'

'Only the one boy for me, and he's enough of a handful on his own, thank you very much. Besides, his father's not in the picture any longer, and I've hardly got time for my work and Daniel, let alone the chance of meeting another adult human being, so I think that's that for me. The biological clock is ticking, and I don't want to be one of those women who's taking their kids to infant school with a walker.'

Mavis didn't say anything.

Wanda continued, 'The word on the grapevine is that you used to be a nurse. Not that anyone needed to tell me that. I can always spot when someone's been trained. Where were you?'

Mavis saw no reason to lie; besides, she'd learned that sticking as closely as possible to one's truth worked best when working undercover – easier to keep track that way. The two women chatted for a while about the similarities and differences between the duties of a nurse when tending to members of the armed forces as opposed to the general public, and about geriatric needs in particular, something of which both women had experience.

'And did you choose to work with the elderly for any special reason?' Mavis wondered how Wanda would reply.

'My nan, I suppose,' said the tall, broad woman, brushing crumbs from her lap. 'She lived a hard-working but healthy life, then broke a hip and went downhill from there. I was in school at the time, and I couldn't understand why breaking a hip was like a death sentence – it made no sense to me. I could tell she wasn't being helped as much as possible when I visited her in hospital. Mam was in bits – couldn't get anything done about anything, though. Nan died, and I thought that if I became a nurse I could do better for people like her. I know things have changed for the better in the last twenty years or so, but there's still not enough money to go around, and I do get it that there have to be priorities, but…oh, I don't know. My foot, and I'm tired, and – well, I don't want to put you off doing what you're doing, but I dare say you've worked out how stretched we are. You're one of the best trainees we've had; I can tell you what needs doing, and I know you'll do it. I wish everyone was like you.'

Mavis took a chance. 'You mean Nurse Daniels?'

Wanda Gorman looked over her shoulder at the closed staffroom door and nodded. 'I could, and do, jump over her head. I mean – there's caring, and there's getting things done. There's no point in being liked by all the patients if you're not giving them their meds when they need them, is there? Chatters on for hours, she does, which is lovely, but not real nursing, is it? More for the carers, that – which is not to say it's not important, but there needs to be a proper division of effort. She'll probably miss her meal break again tonight because she won't leave Charlotte Thomas's bedside. Mind you, we'll all be—'

The alarm which signalled the need for an emergency resuscitation sounded, stopping their conversation dead.

'That's probably her now,' said Wanda as she stood. 'I said she wouldn't make it to the morning.'

Mavis was also on her feet and at the door. She was surprised that Wanda wasn't at her heels when she turned to look for her.

Wanda shook her head. 'Don't panic – Charlotte's got a DNR, so there'll be no attempts made to bring her back. The family's all been, apparently. But, there, they don't need to be here for this bit, do they? A blessing in a way; Charlotte's been here for almost two years, becoming less herself as every month passes. Nice woman. Had seven kids, if you can believe it. Seven! I'm surprised she wasn't batty. And sixteen grandkids. And two great-grandchildren. They've all been here, so I hear, which is lovely. Well, all but one son, anyway. And they all knew she was as comfortable here as we could make her. But there comes a point when it's bound to happen. And now? You don't need to come with me this minute if you don't want to.'

'I'd like to, if you don't mind,' said Mavis. She added, 'I like to say goodbye, if you understand me.' She didn't at all, but couldn't think of another way to insert herself into the picture immediately after a death had occurred.

Wanda replied, 'No skin off my nose,' and sauntered to Charlotte Thomas's room, acknowledging the doctor's arrival as she did so.

Mavis saw Nurse Daniels hovering at the bedside of the deceased as the doctor pronounced death as having occurred at one thirty-eight a.m. All the machinery in the room – of which there was a great deal – was switched off. The silence was almost overwhelming.

Wanda spoke softly to Mavis, 'You can leave it for the day shift if you prefer, but the normal thing is for us to prepare the patient for the family to visit, if they want, which would be your job. Given the time, I dare say we'll hold the call to them until later this morning. Sister Ramsey can do it; she's always all over us about us doing our jobs, well that's one I don't envy her, so she can have it.'

Mavis detected a note of something less than warmth when Wanda spoke about Ellie, and decided she'd follow that up, but took her big chance to remain involved by replying, 'It would be my preference to show my respects to the deceased by making this room a more fitting and welcoming place for her family to visit, should they choose to do so. It'll no' take me long. Am I to assume there'll be no post-mortem? I won't be doing anything invasive, of course, but do I need to allow all the attachments to remain on the body?'

Wanda shook her head. 'No, you can go ahead and remove all of those. The patients here are all under the direct care of our doctors, and her passing isn't a surprise to any of us. Nor the family. The remains will be released to them pronto. Which means there's likely to be someone else in this bed tomorrow night. I'll let you get on with it, then. And don't let Veronica give you any grief; she likes to boss people around doing this, which is about the only time she's ever on top of her job.'

Mavis kept the frisson of professional interest under control, and smiled sadly as the doctor and Nurse Gorman left the room, allowing her to finally focus her attention on Nurse Veronica Daniels, who was still hovering in a corner, with an expression on her face that Mavis found both curious and inappropriate: behind her large spectacles, she looked like an owl about to swoop on something she'd spotted as prey.

CHAPTER SEVENTEEN

Carol was at the dining-room table before dawn, hammering at her laptop while Albert was still asleep, and she imagined David was doing much the same thing at his workstation in the spare bedroom – aka, his office – above her. As a family, they certainly made the most of every square foot of their lovely Georgian home, but Carol couldn't help feeling a little pang of jealousy when she recalled the open space of the Hugheses' kitchen, and the equally spacious rooms she'd glimpsed when she'd been there the previous evening.

She pondered that the Twysts had invested in an extensive remodelling of the house the Hughes family rented from the Chellingworth Estate, and wondered if that was because it was a house that had clearly been built in the early twentieth century – so probably not a listed building. Her home was an example of early Georgian architecture, and over three hundred years old, so protected against the sort of gut-job that had probably been performed on the Hughes house.

Carol sighed, glanced lovingly at the clean lines of the cube-shaped room she was sitting in, and delighted in the fact that, when viewed from the village green, her home had the air of a doll's house: perfectly symmetrical, with an elegant stone facade, embellished with the smallest amount of refined detailing. She really did love it – but it had its shortcomings, which were becoming more and more apparent as time passed. The separate rooms meant there were lots of opportunities for privacy, and different types of décor, but she was now realizing that she actually had to be in the same room as Albert to be able to keep an eye on him. She wondered how that would work out when he was able to roam more freely; would she have to keep him shut into whatever room she was in? She sighed and refocused: she didn't have time to dwell on such things – she had more pressing matters at hand.

She'd already found the birth records for Steve Hughes's uncle, Ernie, and was trawling through death records, knowing that if he'd died very recently she was unlikely to find anything anyway; it could take some time for records to be discoverable on the databases to which she had access, due to a myriad reasons. Having had no luck, she checked other online sources, looking for reports of a death, rather than an official record of it.

She felt a pang of guilt immediately following her rush of delight upon finding a brief report of police having been called to a static caravan park near Brecon, where the remains of a man of about the right age had been discovered in his home. The discovery had been on Friday morning, when a neighbor by the name of Archie Hammond had found the deceased. He'd gone to the caravan belonging to his close – though unnamed in the story – friend to check on him, because he hadn't been seen since the previous Monday, and the fact he hadn't arrived at a gathering at a social club on the Thursday evening, was very unusual – if not unheard of – for him. The author of the piece had stated that the local police had not released the cause of death.

Carol held her excitement in check as she tracked down details of the social club in question; she found a list of members and lots of photographs online, and – yes! – there he was: not Ernie Hughes, but Ed Hughes. Known as Hughsie. He shared the freckles his nephew sported, as well as what Carol could now recognize as a familial long, lean body type, still apparent despite him being in his mid-eighties. Although the story about the deceased man in the online newspaper had not named him, she was now convinced this was Steve's uncle.

She read, with interest, the information beside the photograph of the group of men just setting off to watch Cardiff playing football a couple of seasons earlier, which told her that Ed Hughes and his best friend Archie Hammond hadn't missed a match in many years, and that Ed was the one who'd pushed for the social club to always arrange for a coach to take members to the games. It also mentioned that he'd been responsible for encouraging others to join the social club, swelling its numbers, and allowing it to become a significant donor to local charities, due to its ability to raise funds from within the community. The social club in question shared a name with the same static caravan park mentioned in the newspaper article.

So, Uncle Ernie/Ed had already been dead when the wreath had been delivered to his nephew's home – unless he'd actually died between the wreath being delivered around teatime on Thursday and the discovery of his body on Friday morning. The article didn't mention when he'd died, only when he'd been found, but he'd not been seen since the Monday. That was food for thought, and something new; Carol pondered if it changed the way she had to think about this phantom wreath-deliverer.

Had he already known about Ed's passing on Thursday? How could he, if the body body hadn't been found until the next day? Unless…

Carol felt a chill as she, once again, considered the horrible idea that the wreath-deliverer was more than just that – that they maybe had a hand in the deaths they were 'foretelling'. She shook herself, like a wet dog. There was no point dwelling on that – she had to press on.

Right – what next? Carol checked her watch; she still had hours to go before the dreadful prospect of telling Steve Hughes about his uncle's death would become a reality. Or should she say nothing at all? She couldn't be *certain* that the man they'd found in the caravan was, in fact, Steve Hughes's uncle; would telling them cause Sarah and Steve unnecessary consternation? Or would it put their minds at rest that maybe Steve's parents and their two sons – as well as they themselves, of course – were no longer 'at risk'?

Carol huffed and puffed, and decided that more tea was needed, so she ambled into the kitchen and flicked the kettle on. Bunty was curled beside the Aga – as was the norm – and Carol pictured her son sleeping soundly above her, while her husband worked diligently in the bedroom across the hall. The house seemed to sigh along with her as she looked out of the window at the sunrise – the start of what was forecast to be another warmer-than-average, dry day. Carol knew that would be lovely for those able to enjoy it, and torture for those for whom the lack of rain was a real problem – like her parents just outside Carmarthen who needed to be able to feed their flock without having to spend money, when there should be grass aplenty.

As she pictured the life her parents had always led – one of constantly worrying about the weather, their animals, the house possibly falling down around their ears and the grinding shortage of cash – Carol counted her own blessings, and silently thanked her father and mother for the sacrifices they'd made so that she could take full advantage of her abilities by attending university. By leaving home at eighteen, she'd never contributed to the family income, and they'd accepted, supportively, that there was no possibility that the business – the farm – would continue to be passed down the generations, as it had been for a couple of hundred years.

Feeling the weight of guilt creep onto her already burdened shoulders, Carol did her best to shrug it off, reminding herself that her parents had always engrained in her that they wanted the best for her – and that now those hopes and wishes extended to Albert, too. She pictured his life as the son of a sheep farmer in the modern agricultural landscape, then as the son of a computer software specialist whose clients were dotted around the world, and a private investigator – which made her chuckle, as she wondered how that profile would be viewed by his teachers and classmates once he was old enough to attend school.

And that was another thing: the local school now wasn't very local at all; not enough children meant the catchment area for schools was vast, so driving Albert back and forth would become her reality. How would that impact her potential work pattern?

The kettle boiled, and Carol made a fresh pot of tea, telling herself that her reverie should stop, and she should focus again on the data she already had about previous recipients of mysterious wreaths. Which would allow her to put off thinking about what to tell the Hugheses until…well, until she could at least talk to Annie about it. Carol knew she could rely upon her old chum and now colleague to have good instincts, and she was due to have returned from her parents' home the evening before, so Carol reckoned she'd be able to talk to her around half-seven – because Gertie's requirements meant that Annie never got a lie-in. In fact, Carol reckoned that if she sent Annie a text, she might drop in for a cuppa, and that would make the catch-up all that much more social, too.

She sent the text and listened at the bottom of the stairs: not a sound from Albert, and nothing from David, either.

Right, back to it, Carol.

CHAPTER EIGHTEEN

Annie woke to a good face-licking from Gertie, and the deafening birdsong of the countryside. She'd slept badly in Plaistow – now being completely unused to the city noise that had once been her lullaby – and had clearly made up for that lack of sleep by being late to rise, if Gertie's frantic attempts to wake her were anything to go by.

'Come on then, Gert, let me actually get out of bed. And let me get into that bathroom – yes, me first, then you.'

The lack of any garden space at Annie's tiny, chocolate-box, thatched cottage meant she always had to make herself decent before taking Gertie for a 'walk', and now the days were light so early, she knew that even more people would be looking out of their windows, even if they weren't out and about themselves.

She peered out of the tiny window in her bedroom to see Joan Pike pushing her mother around the green in her wheelchair. Joan and Doris were a common sight – the daughter would usually push the mother twice around the green just before lunch. However, with the weather being so hot, and with Doris being a martyr to her hay fever, as well as suffering from mobility issues – despite the fact she wasn't actually much older than Annie – the pair were out and about very early every morning these days. Yet another reason to have to make herself look presentable; they were always turned out like something from a bygone era, with both of them always smartly attired in clothing that Annie understood was all handmade by the talented Joan herself.

Gertie's desperation became easier to understand when Annie saw what time it was; she'd been right to insist that she and Tudor spent the night in their own homes, because he'd never have let her sleep in this long. There again, she reminded herself, it was still before eight, and she wasn't, technically, due at work until nine, so once she'd seen to Gertie, she'd have time for breakfast, then a quick check-in with all her colleagues to find out if she really needed to go to the office at all.

A text from Carol that had come in just after six that morning was the first thing she saw when he checked her messages as she followed Gertie across the village green. She looked over at her friend's house; obviously everyone was up and about because all the curtains were open, as well as all the windows. Carol had invited her for tea, and Annie was gasping; her only hesitation was that she had Gertie with her, and she and Bunty hit it off like…well 'oil and water' suggested some sort of peaceful co-habitation, and that wasn't what happened when she took Gertie to Carol's house. Not at all.

She texted back, saying she'd take Gertie home to feed her, then pop over. She knew that once Gertie had taken care of her ablutions, and stuffed herself, she'd probably nap, so didn't worry about leaving her in the cottage on her own for a while.

Carol had a fresh pot of tea on the kitchen table when Annie arrived; Albert was in his playpen happily chewing what Annie suspected had once been a stuffed cloth fire engine, though she could only guess that because it was red; David, apparently, was in the sitting room watching something he'd recorded the night before while eating what smelled like curry. It wasn't a smell that was enjoyable so early in the morning, but Annie knew that this was David's temporary dinner time, while he was contracted to the client in Hawaii.

'I can't tell you how much I've missed you,' said Carol as she poured tea and shoved a piece of toast in Annie's direction. 'Marmite's there, jam's in the cupboard,' she added. Annie grabbed the Marmite, wondering what was coming.

She gave her attention to her toast. 'Well, I've been away for all of four days, Car, so I can't see that. Thanks for not interrupting my time with Eustelle and Rodney, but – come on, doll – fill me in, while I fill me face. Thanks for the toast, by the way. If another piece magically landed on this plate, I wouldn't complain – I'm starving. All Mum's food has stretched my stomach I dare say. You talk, I'll eat.'

Carol talked while Annie managed to eat three pieces of toast; they'd just started a second pot of tea when David's head appeared at the door.

'Business or personal?' He grinned at Annie. 'Always best to check before I interrupt,' he added.

'Both,' replied Carol. 'You off to bed now?' Her husband nodded. 'We'll be quiet. I've been thinking I might take Albert up to the office today – and I'll chuck his playpen in the back of the car, to keep him safe. I might be able to get more done there – and I could give you a lift, if you like, Annie. Gertie and Albert will be fine together there, won't they?'

Annie nodded. 'Maybe I should get a playpen for Gert, like Bertie's. Have a good sleep, Dave. We'll all be fine, and the empty house will mean that no one will hear you snoring.'

Annie chuckled as David replied with a quick, 'Oi – I'll have you know I do no such thing, whatever my wife might say.'

It was Carol's turn to laugh. 'Annie was here last week when you were doing your impersonation of the *Flying Scotsman* upstairs, so you haven't got a leg to stand on with that one, *cariad.* Sleep tight – see you around six-ish, okay? For breakfast.'

'Goodnight…or should that be good-*day?* No idea – just stay safe, and I hope you achieve what you need and want to.' He blew kisses toward his son and wife, then left.

Annie observed, 'You found gold with that one, didn't you?' Her friend nodded. 'Like me and Tude. He's my chance for…well, not all of this, of course –' she nodded toward Albert – 'but for happiness, our way.'

Carol leaned over and hugged her friend, which Annie enjoyed. 'No one deserves it more than you, Annie.'

Annie felt all warm inside, and it wasn't the tea and toast. 'Ta, Car…but, come on, enough about me, let's get back to Sarah and Steve Hughes. Yes, I think you should tell them, even though you're not a hundred-percent sure, but – look – we've been nattering here so long that you might be able to get hold of someone who could really help. If this old bloke was found just outside Brecon, how about you give our favorite Constable Llinos Trevelyan a ring and ask her if there's anything she can tell you that's not in that report – maybe when he died, how he died, or if there's been a positive ID? Even if she can't, you could pass on what you've found out so far to help them out.'

Annie saw Carol's ears turned a bit pink at the suggestion. 'Of course – why didn't I think of that? Sorry – my brain's in a swirl, but I don't seem to be thinking of the most logical things at all. Of course, I bet she'll help. I'll send her a text, though, because I never know if she's at work or not, and I don't like to disturb her professional or private times, really.'

Annie watched as Carol texted scarily quickly. *If only my thumbs were that agile*, she thought, *I'd never need to use abbreviations, and mine would look like Tudor's – as though an actual adult human being had typed them…one who understands the role of capital letters, correct spelling and grammar, and even punctuation.*

Almost as soon as Carol had placed her phone on the table, it rang. She picked it up. 'It's Llinos,' she said, smiling before she'd even answered.

Annie listened to Carol's side of the conversation which wasn't overly long; she reckoned her friend had been typing even faster than it had appeared, because she didn't need to give Llinos any information at all before she said, 'Oh dear. Yes, I see. No, of course not. Yes, that's really helpful. No, of course not, I'll leave it to you. Yes, I think Steve's parents will take the news okay; there was a rift many years ago, and the brothers weren't close. No, I won't. The case? Ah well now, that's something it's just taken me two pots of tea and three pieces of toast to explain to Annie, and she had the original briefing notes. There are sensitive areas involved, and I don't think it would have a direct bearing on this death…though, to be honest, I can't be totally sure about that…but, of course I'll tell you what I can. Of course, whenever it suits you.'

Carol put down her phone and said to Annie, 'It's pretty certain it's him. His caravan, in any case, and initial belief is that it is Steve's uncle Ed. Doing dental checks next. The police will tell the next of kin – Steve's father – and I'll let them pass the news within the family. The nature of the death is still being viewed as "unexplained". The police are investigating, so Llinos wants to know what we know.'

'What do you think it means, Car? Has The Case of the Uninvited Undertaker just taken a turn? Do we now think they might really be a killer, not just a deliverer of wreaths?'

Carol shook her head slowly. 'To be honest, I don't know. "Unexplained" could mean anything. Llinos said – well, you know what the weather's been like the past while, and I dare say we can both imagine what this heat would have done to the temperature inside a caravan, and no one had seen him for five days. She said…well, it wasn't easy to work out how long he'd been dead. Hence the need for dental records.'

Annie pulled a face. 'Ta – you know I'm still eating, don't you? Anyway, tell me more about this thing Mavis is working on…or shall I help you get ready for us to go up to the office and you can fill me in on the way? I could pop over to get Gert and her away-day bag, then come back and give you a hand getting this thing – by which I mean the playpen, not Bertie himself – into the back of your car. I'll only be ten minutes.'

The plan was agreed and it was still not quite nine o'clock, so Annie felt she was doing her best for the company, and she'd even started her working day a bit earlier than planned.

CHAPTER NINETEEN

Mavis couldn't believe she was still awake, and yet she was, and she couldn't leave her car, nor the car park, until Veronica Daniels did – that was a certainty.

She'd done her respectful duty to the late Charlotte Thomas and had cleared everything from the room that smacked of medical intervention, leaving the woman freshly washed, as well-coiffed as possible, and looking peaceful in her bed. She'd also taken an opportunity to check on Charlotte's medications in what had somehow become an unlocked cupboard; it contained a range of strengths and types of painkillers – including a surprising amount of opioids – the usual raft of treatments for heart, blood pressure, and circulatory problems, and even morphine. Mavis knew how to assess medications rapidly, and made sure to take a lot of photographs, as well as a couple of other steps.

The cupboard in the room in which the remains lay was still untouched when Mavis found yet another reason to 'pop back in' just before her shift ended, but she didn't have a good reason to remain on the premises when the day shift arrived, something about which Ellie Ramsey was aware: the pair had swapped texts for the past hour.

Ellie had finally revealed to Mavis that it was, indeed, Nurse Daniels she'd originally suspected – and they'd agreed that Ellie would take up the watch over her upon her arrival at work, knowing Mavis had to leave. She would alert Mavis to any 'developments'.

Mavis had changed out of the cotton trousers she had to wear at the nursing home and into a serviceable skirt. *Thank goodness I didnae have to suffer the outfits they wear these days during my years on the wards*, she thought, pleased to be comfy once again. She'd also availed herself of a thermal mug of tea before leaving, but that was almost empty, and still Veronica Daniels hadn't emerged. Mavis was beginning to wonder if the nurse was going to hang about until Mrs Thomas's family members arrived, which they had said they would before ten.

Now it was twenty past nine, and nothing had happened – then a text from Ellie alerted Mavis to the fact that Veronica was about to leave and that, yes, as if by some miracle, the drugs' cabinet in the Thomas room was now empty.

Mavis was completely focused on looking out for Veronica when Wanda Gorman knocked on the window of the Morris Minor Traveller, threatening Mavis's coronary health and wellbeing.

She wound down her window and feigned confusion – which didn't require a great deal of acting skill. 'Hello, Wanda – I thought you'd left ages ago,'

'I'm surprised to see you still here, too. Are you alright?' The nurse looked quite concerned.

Mavis was momentarily distracted by the sight of Veronica Daniels coming down the long ramp adjacent to the front entrance. 'Oh yes, I'm fine, thanks. When I knocked off, I decided I was a bit too tired to drive straight away, so I caught forty winks. Right as rain now. Must be off. See you tonight, Wanda.'

Wanda stood back as Mavis started the car, revved the engine, and engaged her slightly clunky gearbox. 'Alright then, as long as you feel fit to drive. Bye for now.' She waved as Mavis moved the car slowly enough across the car park that she was able to follow Veronica out onto the road, where both vehicles turned left.

Mavis knew that Ellie's flat was to the right, and was comfortable with the route to and from there, but she didn't know the area well, so was glad she'd had her trusty GPS app open and ready to go when she began her journey. Her phone sat in its holder on the dashboard in front of her, the little car on the screen diligently replicating her route; she appeared to be making her way from the north of Cardiff to the west of the city, skirting the center itself. Mavis's concentration was pushed to its limits as she followed Veronica's car which was – thank goodness – a burnt orange metallic finish, with one grey door panel, primed and ready for painting.

Mavis noted that Veronica was slowing, then the young nurse made a series of turns into smaller side streets. The area Mavis found herself in was a council estate, built in the 1920s and '30s, by the looks of it. Relatively large homes had been built along broad streets in what had obviously been a planned community; the medians were wide, grassed and treed, and most of the houses were semi-detached. Mavis had certainly seen council estates in much worse condition, and she noted as she followed Veronica that many of the houses had obviously been privately purchased – the exterior décor of those being quite different to the brick bottom half and stucco or pebble-dash upper half of the original housing stock.

Mavis pulled alongside the kerb about fifty yards behind where Veronica had done the same thing, and she grabbed her bits and pieces, ready to get out when Veronica did. She pulled on a black bobble hat with a knitted peak, and a black jacket which reversed to a blue one. Knowing that she'd look overdressed for the weather, but not having any alternative ways to disguise her appearance should Veronica spot her, she exited the car and locked it, keeping an eye on the gate Veronica had entered and the path along which she'd walked.

Mavis sauntered lazily along, waggling her phone about as though she were trying to get a signal when she passed the house in question; she was, in fact, taking photographs of the house and Veronica's car outside it. She continued to the end of the street where she snapped a photo of the street name, then retraced her steps, only to have to stop when Veronica left the house and returned to her car.

Mavis's sudden interest in her phone allowed her to hide her face as Veronica drove past, then she ran as fast as she could to her own car, jumped in, and followed again.

Veronica went through a similar process three more times, all within the streets of the estate. Mavis managed to photograph every home the nurse had entered, and didn't believe Veronica had spotted her.

One thing Mavis noted was that each time Veronica entered a house, it seemed to be the least well-kept one on the street. A couple of her calls had been to houses where rubbish was strewn across the small front gardens, and there were boarded-up windows, or panes of glass missing in the front doors. Yes, the seediest houses on the street. Mavis recorded a few hurried phrases to remind herself of these facts later on.

What are you up to, my girl? Dealing the drugs you stole from the nursing home? Are you delivering to people who'll supply the street? Are these houses you're entering all being used by squatters – living among the other tenants and residents?

Mavis continued to make audio recordings as she drove behind Veronica yet again – wondering how long the woman would continue to spread poison around what appeared to be a perfectly normal, pleasant neighborhood.

Risking leaving her car with just a scarf over her head, rather than the hat – which was starting to feel far too hot as the day warmed up – Mavis was approaching a house Veronica had entered when she became aware of a bicycle approaching from behind. This was something else she'd noted about the estate; youths on bicycles seemed quite happy to use both sides of the road, or even the pavement, as they whisked along, wearing hoodies rather than safety helmets. She turned, ready to smile with confusion at whomever it might be and make pantomime actions with her phone. But she didn't have a chance. She heard a slight grunt and glimpsed a face that was covered by some sort of mask poking out from a hood, then…nothing.

CHAPTER TWENTY

It took Annie and Carol rather longer than they'd expected to be able to set out for the office, due to the fact that both Gertie and Albert had other ideas: Gertie had decided to throw up her breakfast, leaving Annie with a big clean-up job, and in a panic about Gertie's wellbeing; Albert, on the other hand, had managed to get himself into a bit of a mess with a brand new sack of cat litter, which he'd found during a moment of inattentiveness on Carol's part – so she'd had to clean up that mess, then her son, then get out of the house.

Thus it was that the pair found themselves on the road to the barn with an irritated child and a dog who was feeling very sorry for herself at almost half ten in the morning.

'No worries, Car – we'll be able to crack on when we get there,' said Annie as cheerfully as she could as the pair jollied Albert and Gertie along – him in his car seat, and Gertie in her travelling crate – which wasn't a place she ever enjoyed being.

Carol sighed. 'Yes, I know you're right. Oh – is that my phone, or yours?'

Annie fished about in her pocket. 'Mine. It's Tude, I'd better take this. Sorry. You keep going, and you can catch me up with what Mavis is up to when we get there. Hello, Tude – what news?'

Tudor said, 'Can we talk?'

Annie glanced at Carol. 'I'm in Carol's car, on the way to the office. You alright, doll? You sound a bit off.'

'Not really. I spoke to Delyth last night. Eventually. She named her price. No way I can afford it, so that's that. Sorry. At least you can get some sympathy from Carol…and how about we make a plan to have dinner in my flat tonight? Aled can cover for an hour – it's Monday, so it'll be quiet.'

Annie felt completely deflated. 'Oh no. Sorry, Tude. You're sure she won't change her mind?' She was hoping against hope that Delyth might, because she knew what a difference it could make to the couple's future.

Tudor sounded utterly despondent. 'It didn't sound like it, and…well, I told her she was being foolish, that no one would pay what she was asking, and she said that was how much she wanted and she was sure someone would pay it. I don't know how she's managed it out on that ship she's on, but – somehow or other – she's got wind of the village regeneration kick that Henry and Stephanie are on, and she reckons the pub will be an attractive proposition…for someone with very deep pockets, by the sound of it. I…well, I might have mentioned that what she was doing sounded a bit greedy to me. So, no, I don't think she'd reconsider. Not for me.'

Annie smiled weakly at Carol, who was concentrating on pulling up outside the barn as close to the door as she could get. She motioned to Carol to go ahead with Albert and that she'd follow on with Gertie, then Albert decided to show how strong his lungs were.

'Sounds like you've got your hands full there,' said Tudor glumly. 'I'll let you get on, and we'll talk about it tonight, eh? Just the two of us, and our girls. How's Gertie, by the way?'

Annie decided that Tudor didn't need to hear about projectile vomiting, so said simply, 'She's fine. A bit quiet, but you know she doesn't like her crate very much. She'll be here with me for the day, and she'll be pleased to see Rosie this evening. Seven o'clock alright for you?'

'Lovely. See you then.'

'Right-o, seven it is. And Tude – don't let this get you down. We can make the Lamb and Flag into the best pub it can be – pub *and* tea and coffee shop, that is. Right?'

'Of course. You're right. Love you.'

'Love you, too.' Annie disconnected and swore liberally at Delyth James, in her absence, then turned and spoke to Gertie. 'That stupid, greedy woman has made Tudor very unhappy. Me too. We could have made a go of the Coach and Horses, we could. I had the new décor for those little guest rooms all sorted in my head, Gert, and I had big plans for the bars. I knew she'd be too greedy. She really is a Predatory Publican, that one...didn't I tell you that, Gert?'

Gertie's head tilting suggested to Annie that she agreed with every word, so she was rewarded by being let out of her crate, allowed to relieve herself, and even got a treat. Annie immediately wondered if was a good idea, given what had happened when Gertie had eaten her breakfast.

Gertie's delight at arriving in the familiar office allowed Annie to relax a bit; if her pup was that happy to sniff about in every corner, she probably wasn't really ill at all – she'd just been sick, for some reason or other – possibly because she'd guzzled her food too fast.

Pleased to see that Albert was settled in his playpen, and that Carol had already put the kettle on, Annie settled at her desk and woke up her computer.

'Everything alright with Tudor?' Carol asked sympathetically.

Annie chuckled. 'Oh yes, just tickety-boo, ta. Not.' She proceeded to tell Carol about Delyth James's surprising messages, and unsurprising greed.

Carol made some truly supportive comments – then hugged Annie, which really helped. She hadn't told Carol about all her plans, but knew her chum would have joined the dots for herself; that pub could have provided Annie and Tudor with a home they could have shared, but now they were both stuck in their own tiny places, having to move between them – with Annie often not being quite sure where she'd left certain things like favorite clothes, or toiletries.

She tried to sigh away her frustration, and said, 'Come on then, I need to know what's going on with Mavis before we make a start on this undertaker case – which I have now officially named The Case of the Uninvited Undertaker, by the way. Spill. Tell me what Mave's been up to.'

As Carol talked, Annie drank one mug of tea, then another. Her surprise at what she heard was matched only by her certainty that she'd eaten far too many Bourbon biscuits and couldn't even remember having done so, she'd been so transfixed by Carol's story about her old chum Ellie, and Mavis's agreement to help.

Startled by a terrible retching sound coming from the bottom of the spiral staircase, Annie looked over to see Gertie in distress. She leaped to her feet, Carol behind her, then stood back as Gertie threw up something she didn't much fancy examining.

'What on earth is that?' Carol sounded curious rather than horrified.

'I don't know, Bourbon biscuits by the look of it, I'd say. They're bad for her – how on earth didn't I even notice her sneaking them off the plate.'

'I don't think she did,' said Carol. 'The wrapper's in there too – I think she got to our stash.' She pointed at a cupboard door that was swinging open, and a mound of packets of biscuits inside.

'They were all neatly piled up, earlier. I think your Gertie's worked out how to open that door. Just as well David's coming out here to childproof the barn next weekend; he said he'd do it so that I don't have to keep Albert trapped inside his playpen all the time, but it looks like the locks and magnets he'll be fitting will keep Gertie out of places she shouldn't be getting into, too.'

Annie's tummy wasn't feeling too good – she loved Gertie, but found it difficult to deal with all her bodily functions, especially this sort.

Half an hour later Gertie was clearly still feeling a bit sorry for herself, though at least the office floor had been cleaned up. Annie could see that Carol was giving her son a bit of attention, which Annie reckoned was only fair, since it had really been Carol who'd done most of the clearing up, and so forth. Annie focused on Gertie, who was sitting quietly beside the sofa, in the shade – which wasn't the norm for the usually active pup.

Her mind was racing; Gertie was her first dog, the only one she'd ever had. She wondered if a bit of throwing up was normal, but really didn't know – and some Googling had left her more confused than ever. She'd already found a vet in Brecon with an emergency clinic, but wondered if she was overreacting. She just didn't know.

Trying to pacify herself as she petted Gertie, she asked, 'So are we due to hear from Mave, or what?' Annie wasn't sure. 'And what about Chrissy? Where's she this fine, sunny morning?'

Carol was distracted but replied, 'Christine's up at the Hall – something to do with Stephanie's thing to make the village prettier. And Mavis? Well, yes – I'd have thought we'd have heard something from her by now. Actually, that's a bit odd. Can you check emails while I see to Albert for a couple of minutes – he needs changing.'

Annie could see that Gertie was resting comfortably, so she checked her emails, texts, and phone messages – but there wasn't a peep from Mavis. Next, she accessed the business cloud account, where she found a host of items that had been uploaded by their colleague.

When Carol returned with a much happier-looking son, who seemed quite content to then lie in the sun that streamed through the windows onto his playpen, Annie said, 'Mave's been busy – everything's on the cloud. I dare say we should listen to it all.'

'Listen?'

'Audio recordings, and a shedload of photos. I dare say it'll all make sense when we've waded through it.'

Annie noticed that Carol hesitated.

'What?'

Carol appeared suddenly sheepish. 'Annie, Mavis wanted me to take the lead on the undertaker case, and I really haven't got much done – except to establish that Steve Hughes's uncle is dead, and that he died around the time the wreath was left at the Hugheses' home. If you could go through all Mavis's stuff, then summarize it for me, I could get something done on the other case. She'll have my guts for garters if I don't – you know what she's like when it's a paying client as opposed to a bit of a freebie for a friend.'

Annie nodded. 'Yeah, you're right. And she's right, too – because if we don't have paying clients actually giving us money, we all know what that means. I'll do this, you do that. And – just so you know – I'm thinking about taking Gert to the vet this afternoon, if she doesn't perk up a bit.'

Carol looked surprised, which made Annie feel that she was, in fact, overreacting to Gertie's problems.

'Am I being an annoyingly nervous first-time dog-owner? You grew up with animals – sheep and dogs – what do you think?'

Carol bent to stroke Gertie. 'She's your friend, as well as your dog, and…well, let's be honest, she's a bit like a child to you. Yes – I know you try to not think about her that way, but it's really only natural. I grew up with dogs, but they were working dogs, not really pets, like this little one.' She beamed at Gertie, who wiggled her brows above sad-looking eyes.

'But they were still dogs,' said Annie.

'Yes, but it was different. So – if you're worried about her, then you should take her to the vet. But I do think the reason she just threw up was because she'd eaten a packet of biscuits with bits of the wrapper too. Frankly, getting that out of her system was the best thing that could have happened. But as for why she was sick this morning? I don't know, and by the sounds of it neither do you. So – yes, take her. We both want to be sure she's alright. I don't want to push the similarities too far, but with Albert being my first child, I had to come to terms with the balance between anxiety and being able to cope with all the little ailments he had during his first year. I think I've come to grips with that a bit better now…but remember what I was like when I didn't know he was starting to teeth?'

Annie had to chuckle. 'So what you're saying is that I'm probably being overly concerned, but I should have a professional vet tell me that – for a price – rather than me just being worried to death and banging on about it to you, right?'

Carol also smiled, and gave Annie a much-needed hug. 'Yeah, something like that. Have you got to make an appointment?'

Annie checked her phone. 'It says I can take her in as an emergency – but maybe I'll just give them a ring to check on that. Then I promise I'll get back to Mave's stuff, and shut up about Gert.'

Carol made her way to her desk as Annie poked at the screen on her phone.

'Never feel you have to apologize for taking care of someone, Annie – even if that someone has four legs and fur.'

'Ta, doll…oh yes, hello, can I talk to someone about my Gert, please? She's been sick twice, and I'm worried there's something really wrong with her.'

CHAPTER TWENTY-ONE

Alexander Bright looked more than a little irritated. At least, that was what Henry thought. The man had been as sweet as pie at the beginning of the meeting, but now he looked quite irked, and Henry really couldn't fathom why.

Everything had been going so well: the shop in the village was to be redecorated to Alexander's wishes; the timetable everyone agreed was achievable meant it could be open before the really busy part of the season; even the name had been agreed – Coggins and Chellingworth Fine Antiques.

True, it wasn't that snappy, but both Bill Coggins – via Alexander – and Henry himself had felt it best if the names of both the interested parties were employed, thereby ensuring customers could have twice as much trust in the purchases they would be making. However, the inclusion of 'Fine Antiques' as opposed to just 'Antiques' had taken more discussion than Henry had felt it warranted. Eventually, he had carried the day with his point that – of course – those buying something associated with the Chellingworth name would, and should, expect *fine* antiques as opposed to the common or garden variety.

Henry looked to his wife, who had just joined the meeting. It was clear to him that she'd spotted Alexander's less than pleasant mood, and she also appeared nonplussed.

Christine Wilson-Smythe was studying her nails, mute, and only Henry's mother dared make eye contact with Alexander.

It surprised Henry that when Alexander finally spoke, he sounded nonchalant; he certainly didn't look it. However, what he said made no sense to Henry. At all.

'But Althea, I don't see how a passing comment you overheard at church yesterday, about Marjorie Pritchard's feelings, should be allowed to rob us of this chance.'

Henry decided to get to the bottom of things, realizing he'd missed something vital. 'Please explain, Alexander. Stephanie's just joined us, and she doesn't understand what's getting you so hot under the collar.'

Henry knew of the man's reputation, but really thought he was a good sort, all in all. However, his current excitable state was making Henry uneasy.

Alexander forced a smile at Stephanie, then Henry. 'The dowager has just informed me that Marjorie Pritchard will not be supportive of Elizabeth Fernley being the person who works at the antique shop. Which seems…ridiculous. I have discussed things with Elizabeth and she's not only keen, but seems ideal. Now, because Marjorie Pritchard is against it – for some unknown reason – Althea believes we should be swayed by her opinion rather than mine.'

Henry was even more confused when his mother replied firmly, 'It's not just Marjorie, but Sharon, too. At the shop. Because of her mother.'

He noted that both he and Alexander sighed in much the same way, at much the same time. When Alexander looked at him on this occasion there was a pleading in his eyes, rather than irritation.

Henry decided to be the better man. 'Once again your words have not made anything clear, Mother. Please – for all our sakes, could you explain slowly, with all the background, so that we can better understand your concerns.'

He saw his mother harrumphing at him – silently, thank goodness – but knew she was going to help when she straightened her shoulders and sat forward in her seat.

Althea addressed her son. 'I'm surprised you don't know, Henry, because it's something one would have hoped that you, as duke, would have been aware of, but I understand that there are others here who might not be aware of the background, though I warn you it goes back a few years.'

'That would be most helpful, Althea, thank you,' said Alexander.

Henry noticed that Christine finally raised her head and gave her attention to his mother, who was preening, just a little.

Nodding graciously at her audience, Althea began, 'I can't be sure exactly when it started, because no one ever can be about these things, but it came to a head when Mair Jones sold the shop in the village. She felt it was all she could do, I suppose. However, Marjorie Pritchard refused to budge, and things were always rather awkward after that.' Althea nodded, and smiled.

Henry was still at sea, and he could tell from the looks on the other faces at the table that he wasn't alone. He reached into his wife's lap and squeezed her hand.

Stephanie rose to the occasion. 'Tell us, Althea – even if you don't know when it really started – what was the root cause of Mair Jones selling the shop?'

Althea replied, 'The rumors about Elizabeth Fernley, of course. All highly inflammatory, and no one ever knew how they got started, or when – as I said – but Elizabeth blamed Mair and Marjorie, which I dare say was understandable, the pair of them having earned their reputation as irredeemable gossips over decades.'

Henry was starting to panic; he didn't want anything salacious to be said about his trusted Estates Manager's wife. Not in his home. It wouldn't be right. 'Without going into the detail of what the gossipmongers were saying, Mother, could you tell us exactly how this impacted Elizabeth?'

Althea nodded. 'She was hurt, then angry, then she went to the police.'

'The police?' Henry was alarmed – things had gone that far?

His mother replied, 'They said they couldn't do anything, and that it was a civil matter, so she got hold of a solicitor who sent letters to both Mair and Marjorie threatening them with legal action if they didn't stop spreading rumors about her. The interesting thing was that when word got out about those letters, Mair found that not quite as many people were coming into the shop. Embarrassed to be associated with her, you see. Afraid they'd be drawn into some sort of legal argy-bargy. Which was why she sold up – to that young couple who were not at all suited to running the sort of business that's needed at the heart of a village. I said they'd not do a good job of it, and was proved right. I do think things are much more settled with Mair's daughter, Sharon, back at the place where she grew up. She's not her mother, but she's not far off.'

Henry was surprised that Christine's tone was so acid when she said, 'She's almost as bad as her mother, Althea. Gossip is Sharon Jones's stock in trade, as we have discovered on more than one occasion.' Her tone had, thankfully, moderated when she added, 'Though, to be honest, I think she does it because she's a bit bored. And she often means well – though things don't always go the way she'd hoped they would.'

Unprepared to leap into what he felt might still be treacherous waters, Henry gave his wife's hand another squeeze.

'So – and correct me if I'm wrong here, Althea –' Stephanie nodded toward her mother-in-law as she spoke – 'what you're saying is that you believe Marjorie Pritchard is speaking out against Elizabeth Fernley as a suitable candidate to run the newly refurbished antiques shop in the village as some sort of retribution for Elizabeth having threatened her with legal action several years ago. Would that be the gist of it?'

Althea nodded. 'Yes, she'll scupper the plans to get her own back, I believe, and she might have already got Sharon on her side in this matter, because it's also reached my ears that she's been telling folks that Elizabeth's been a bit dithery when she's been seen out and about. Of course, the rumors about Elizabeth at the moment have not yet reached the levels they once did, but I think that's more to do with the fact that she's a few years older now, so no one would believe those things about her in any case.'

Henry was cross with himself that he couldn't help but wonder what on earth the original rumors about Elizabeth Fernley had been, and felt he had to focus on the present, and speak up.

'And yet here you are, Mother, putting Marjorie's completely baseless claims to our meeting, as though we should act accordingly, by suggesting to Alexander that he shouldn't employ Elizabeth at the shop because of the trouble it would cause.'

Althea wriggled. 'I said no such thing. I told him there'd be trouble; not because Elizabeth wouldn't be good at the job, but because you'd be placing Elizabeth and Marjorie within spitting distance of each other – and they might end up doing that very thing. Elizabeth's out here all the time at the Hall, and hardly ever goes into the village, except to go to church, of course – though she stopped even that for a while…with very good reason. If she's in the village every day, at the antiques shop, so close to Marjorie's home, well…who knows what might happen. I want you to all be aware of the facts. That's all.'

Henry and Alexander exchanged a worried glance.

'Food for thought, then,' said Alexander quietly.

'Maybe it's something that should be confronted,' said Christine, finally appearing to have become engaged with the conversation. 'Look, I've heard Sharon justify her "exchanging and passing on of information" within the village, and – to be fair – she has a point. Villages everywhere operate the same way – there's always a hub, and in Anwen-by-Wye that's the shop. I wasn't here when the shop was run by Sharon's mother but if her reputation is anything to go by I'm not sorry about that. So, since she's moved away, and all this happened years ago – what four, five years back?' Althea nodded. 'There you are then, maybe by confronting it – by putting Marjorie and Elizabeth in the same room, let's say – this could all be cleared up.'

'They're in church at the same time every Sunday,' said Althea. 'They ignore each other. Pointedly.'

Henry saw Christine roll her eyes as she said, 'Alexander, do you think that Elizabeth is the right person for this job?' He nodded. 'Does anyone think she isn't – aside from the Marjorie thing?' Everyone shook their head. 'So do it. Get them to talk it through. We can't all go around keeping our heads down because we're too afraid to stick them above the parapet our whole lives. That's not living, that's existing, and that's not fair. Life is for the living, for everyone.'

Henry was confused; he felt as though maybe Christine had wandered from the point a little – either that, or she had something else on her mind, because her words seemed to suggest a much bigger picture than a bit of local gossip that was several years old. He also spotted the strange looks she was getting from her fiancé.

'Christine's right,' said Stephanie with confidence. 'I'll invite both women for tea, and we'll air it out. We all want this shop to do as well as it can – and it's high time that old grievances were set aside. Do you think I should involve Mair or Sharon Jones as well, Althea?'

Althea shrugged. 'I don't believe Sharon was ever involved in what happened originally, and as for Mair? As you all may or may not know, she's living a few miles away now, and fills her days with good works. Some might say it's her way of giving back to a society from which she took so much – with her gloating and gossip. Nowadays she's always at some sort of bedside or another…she's a hospital visitor, giving her time to those who need one. Though some might say she's just gone and found herself a captive audience for her poisonous words.'

Henry remarked, 'Mother, that's not an appropriate comment, I think you'll agree.'

His mother's expression suggested she thought it entirely appropriate. 'Will not.'

Henry was shocked. 'I…I think you should. I do not care for gossip, and some remarks are so close to gossip as to be almost the same thing.'

Althea shook her head sadly. 'No, they aren't, Henry.' Her son spotted the twinkle in her eye that he knew to be a danger signal. 'That's like saying that a series of contradictions and an argument are the same thing – and that's been sorted out for us by the best brains in the world. Try Googling *The Argument Sketch*, Henry – it might bring a smile to even your face.'

Christine chuckled aloud. 'I bet it won't.'

Althea replied, 'I bet it will.'

'Won't.'

'Will.'

'Won't.'

'Will.'

Henry's head turned from woman to woman; they were sitting across the table from each other, grinning.

'This is infantile,' he said, sounding cross, which he was.

'My dear boy,' said his mother, 'laughing at absurdities is never infantile – it's a worthwhile escape from the pressures of life. You should try it some time. Well done, Christine, you've raised my spirits enormously; I'll be quite back to my usual self once I've heard from Mavis – and am so pleased to see that even your generation finds what is now worryingly referred to as "classic comedy" to be worth enjoying. You've not heard from her, have you? Mavis, I mean; I've not had a peep from her since yesterday morning, and that's not like her at all. And she didn't tell me what she was up to either. Also not like her. I'm feeling rather anxious about it.'

Christine was still smiling, but less so, when she replied, 'Possibly just busy, and tired. I can't say exactly what she's doing, but she'd be asleep now, because she's working all night. I'll check with Carol and Annie, and we'll let you know. Alright?'

'Thank you, dear.'

Henry had been unaware that his mother hadn't heard from Mavis. However, while he was fully cognizant of the deep friendship the women had developed, he couldn't understand why not being contacted by somebody for just one day would get anyone into a tizz. He sighed.

'By the way, has a name for the shop been decided in my absence?' Stephanie was checking her watch.

'Coggins and Chellingworth Fine Antiques,' replied Henry, still not feeling the name exactly rolling off his tongue.

Stephanie paused. 'Really? *Fine* antiques? Do you not think that might be off-putting to those seeking a bargain? Don't we want to attract the people who come to visit this place? Tourists. Their profile isn't the sort that goes for fine antiques, nor tatty old bric-a-brac either, to be fair. We need something engaging...descriptive, too. What about Anwen Antiquities and Curiosities, curated by Coggins and Chellingworth? We've agreed we're going to be supplying the shop with items we want to get rid of, Henry, and we've also agreed those are not likely to be the most valuable, classical pieces. And Alexander and Bill have mentioned smaller, lower-cost items that come into their auction house, so we could entice folks in with a promise of things that are out of the ordinary as well as old – then have a variety of pieces at different price points to suit all budgets, but with a suggestion that the stock has been carefully selected, not just thrown together. And I do rather think we should have the name of the village in there – even if we use the shorter version, to make it a bit snappier.'

Henry was surprised by the enthusiastic response from Alexander. 'Excellent idea, Stephanie. Spot on. If only you'd been here earlier, we could have saved a great deal of time.'

'Indeed,' said Christine. 'Sounds perfect to me, Stephanie. The "curiosities" bit is a good draw and suggests browsing. And the use of the word "curated"? Brill. Well done.'

All eyes turned to Henry, who replied, 'As Alexander said, spot on.'

'Then it's agreed,' said Stephanie, rising from her seat – leading Henry to do the same, to pull back her chair.

Alexander also rose. 'I'll let Bob Fernley know, so he can get in touch with his signwriter, and we'll get that part moving too. An excellent meeting. And thanks for agreeing to speak to Marjorie and Elizabeth, Stephanie.'

'May I attend that little get-together, too?' Althea was still seated, and looking as innocent as a baby.

Henry saw his wife's entire body tense.

She replied steadily, 'If you're sure you want to do so for the best of reasons, Althea, of course. You're always welcome.'

Henry noticed the glint in his mother's eyes when she said quietly, 'Excellent. Thank you. Now – I think I'll visit that daughter of mine and her fiancé before I leave. And it's such a lovely day, maybe Jools would like to have a good look over the Gilbern when Ian brings it around to drive me home. I do so want to get to know a potential new family member a little better.'

Henry picked up on the term used by the dowager. 'A "potential" new family member, Mother? I rather think Clemmie's made it perfectly clear that she and Jools have not only set a date for their wedding, but are deep in the throes of making all the appropriate arrangements.'

'Of course, dear. But, as we're all aware, I'm sure, "There's many a slip, 'twixt the cup and the lip".'

'Good grief.' Henry made sure to mutter his words under his breath, and hoped his mother hadn't heard them…though she usually did. *Ears like a…thing with ears that always hear everything,* he thought to himself as he joined his wife to visit their son in his room; a feeding, changing, and burping, was due, and he was ready to stand by and gaze with wonder at the two loves of his life.

CHAPTER TWENTY-TWO

Carol could feel the panic in the pit of her stomach. Mavis would expect her to have made much more headway with The Case of the Uninvited Undertaker than she had done, and she was keen to make up lost ground. Annie had only been able to get an appointment at the vet at two o'clock, so she'd given her and Gertie a lift back to the village where Tudor had made arrangements for Aled to cover at the pub while he provided transportation to the clinic in Brecon.

The journey back to Anwen-by-Wye had been tense; Carol knew that Annie was cursing the fact that she didn't drive, and wondered if love for Gertie might finally spur her into coming to grips with the focus and coordination that were critical to be able to learn – abilities which Annie claimed to be lacking.

Deciding it was pointless to drive back out to the office, Carol installed herself and her son in the kitchen, then got hold of Christine, who was finally back at the barn after her meeting up at the Hall.

At least Carol had a plan, and all she needed was an extra pair of hands and eyes – and a brain, to make sense of what she was reading – which Christine said she'd be happy to supply.

'Hiya, nice to see you. Right-o, let's get on,' said Carol when their video call went live. 'I'm emailing you the reworked list we got from the client. I've already made some headway, as you'll see. I'll hang on until you've got the document open in front of you.' She watched as Christine glanced at the spreadsheet she'd sent.

Christine smiled. 'Oh, good work, Carol – this information is really well organized. Name, age, date of death, place of death, name of recipient of wreath, and date they received it, undertaker who was used, place of interment/cremation, date of interment/cremation. Good job.'

'Thanks. There were a lot of blanks, but I've managed to fill in all the information except for a few bits, as you can see. Louise Attwater is our point of contact. The group of undertakers she's representing has made it clear that there's to be no direct contact between us and them – and some of them haven't come back to her yet, which means there are still some gaps in our knowledge. As you can see, Clayton Bros. haven't given us the info about dates or places of cremations or interments yet.'

Christine nodded. 'It looks like everyone on the list – the deceased ones – died in either a hospital, a hospice, or a nursing home, all within about thirty miles of here. Ages? Mainly elderly. Is that a fair assessment?'

Carol nodded.

'Putting in the addresses really helped there, Carol, thanks. But what about this one? Alan Ridley was the deceased, his date of death is here, as is all the rest of the information except for where he died. You've put a big question mark. Why's that?'

Carol sat back in her seat. 'That wasn't one of Louise Attwater's clients. She said Alan Ridley was on holiday when he died, and she didn't know where. She said she'd check with the undertaker who handled the arrangements and get back to us. I still haven't heard anything.'

Carol watched as Christine stuck out the tip of her tongue and let her eyes wander. *Her thinking face,* thought Carol, waiting patiently.

Eventually, Christine said, 'How does this list of places where people died stack up against a list of *all* the hospitals, hospices, and nursing homes in this geographic area? Until I know that I can't say more.'

'Great minds think alike. I sent you that full list too – it's the second document. You'll see that almost every place on that list is on our list too. The deaths we're dealing with aren't grouped, or bunched, or concentrated in one area, or even in one type of institution.'

Christine read, her brow furrowing. 'Alrighty…that's not much help then, except that it might be, in that there's no favor being shown by our Uninvited Undertaker. Nice title for the case, by the way; I dare say this means that Annie's officially named it for us.'

Carol nodded. 'She has, and she'd be helping us too if it weren't for Gertie.' Carol checked her watch. 'She should be with the vet now. Maybe we'll hear something soon.'

'Hope she's alright. Gertie, I mean. Well, Annie too, of course,' added Christine hurriedly. 'Carol, there is something here, and I'm sure you've spotted it, but all the dates of the delivery of a wreath are very close to the dates of deaths. Mainly they've been delivered the day before a death. I'm right, aren't I?'

'You are, and I had noticed; though I don't know what it means. The fact is, the wreaths were still delivered *before* the deaths, never afterwards. Which is what's so puzzling, and quite chilling, about this case.'

Christine shook her head. 'There isn't a pattern here at all, is there? I mean there are no clusters of dates, no grouping of deaths at one place or another. Do we know if any of the deceased, or their families, were connected in any way? Memberships of clubs, hobbies, past military service…that sort of thing?'

Carol sighed. 'I've done what I can online, but I fear we're only going to be able to establish that by speaking to each surviving family…which would be a massive job, and would demand more than a little delicacy.'

'You're not wrong…and…well, I've got to be honest…I don't fancy doing that. But – needs must, I suppose.'

Carol replied, 'I did have another thought; why don't we start with those most used to dealing with death, on the basis that they might be most prepared to talk about it?'

Christine nodded. 'Grand idea. I could phone all the hospices and find out if there might be roving members of staff who work, or have worked, at multiple locations. Try to track down someone who might recall the deceased and find out what they remember about them. We might get some insights that way, I suppose. And at hospices…well, they have to be willing to talk about death and the dead, don't they? Has the client said we can explain what's been happening – or is that a big no-no?'

'Not a big no-no, but don't mention the fact that it's the undertakers who are our clients; they don't want their names linked to this, given that they don't really understand what's going on.'

'Fair enough. I'll start now, and keep going as long as I can. Since the places are staffed around the clock, I could keep at it into the evening, if my calls appear to be bearing fruit. Alexander's gone back to London so I can stick something in the microwave for myself and push on through.'

Carol felt the relief wash over her. 'Thanks, Christine – that would be a big help. I'll chase up Louise for that other information, and I'll do my best to clarify this "on holiday" thing. That one seems to be a bit of an outlier to me, so I'm hoping she'll be able to explain it. And I'll be able to give Albert and David a bit of time, too. Thanks. We'll talk in the morning, eh?'

'Absolutely – and I'll upload anything I find to the cloud drive, so you can see it there, and I'll text if there's anything urgent, alright? Oh – hang on, before I go…have we heard anything from Mavis? When I saw her earlier, Althea was moaning about the fact that she hadn't talked to her since yesterday. Any news? I could at least put Althea's mind at rest…without giving away anything about the case, of course.'

Carol chuckled. 'According to Annie, that would be The Case of the Suspicious Sister, Ellie Ramsey being the nursing sister involved. She worked through a huge pile of stuff that Mavis had uploaded to the cloud. Well, she said it was a huge pile, and I'll take her word for it, because all I could tell was that there were large audio and image files, and that was about it. Anyway, Annie trawled through the lot and said it looked as though Mavis was "onto a hot lead", which could mean anything. She said it looked from the photos as if Mavis was following someone through a council estate. An audio file said Mavis was tired, but feeling optimistic that she'd be able to get enough evidence to refer the matter to the appropriate authorities – which is typical for Mavis, but doesn't tell us much. Annie reckoned Mavis had "knocked it on the head and gone to get some kip", which I have to say would make sense. Mavis isn't as young as she once was, and I can only imagine that a twelve-hour shift as a carer – even as a trainee carer – would even be exhausting for someone thirty years her junior.' Carol checked her watch. 'She's probably still asleep – dead to the world, I wouldn't wonder. But she's due back on duty at seven, so we might get an update as she's on her way to the nursing home. Or maybe she's already involved with some sort of police enquiry – but no, she'd have phoned if that was the case.'

'Alright then, I'll let Althea know she shouldn't worry, but I'll send Mavis a text in any case – just so she knows we're thinking of her, even if she's in the Land of Nod. Right-o – we'll talk in the morning. Bye.'

When Chrstine disappeared, Carol heard Albert blow a raspberry. She turned to see that he was fixated on her screen, and guessed he must be wondering where 'Auntie Christine' had gone. She picked up her son and held him close.

'Your Mam's got some brilliant friends, my boy, and she works with some lovely people. I wish my life could have been like this years and years ago…but, there, I wouldn't be who I am today if I hadn't been that workaholic City girl back then, would I? No, I wouldn't…oh no, I wouldn't.'

She squished her son's perfect nose with her fingers, and rubbed his perfect hand on her own, then realized she needed to trim his nails – a job she hated with a passion!

CHAPTER TWENTY-THREE

The majority of the drive from Brecon back to Anwen-by-Wye had passed in silence. Annie was distraught because Gertie had to stay at the vet's clinic overnight; the vet needed to perform what she'd called 'a small surgical procedure' on her darling girl the next morning. Annie hated the idea of Gertie being alone in a strange place all night, and she'd been told that Gertie wouldn't be allowed any food until after the operation, too – which she knew would be awful for her.

'Gert's got to be completely empty by now – she'll think she's starving if they don't feed her, Tude. And them cages didn't look too comfy, did they? All stacked up like that in that big back room. Oh Tude, I hate to think of her there. But what could I do? Why wouldn't they let me stay there with her? Or bring her back tomorrow?'

Tudor kept his eyes on the road as he replied gently, 'The vet said she'd get it done before the clinic opens in the morning; we wouldn't want to be rushing Gertie off that early, would we? And what if she'd managed to get something into her tummy, somehow? You know what she's like. And the vet explained how that can be dangerous when they're under anesthetic, didn't she?'

'I can't bear to think of her out cold on one of those big stainless-steel tables. What if...what if she doesn't...' Annie felt a tear roll down her cheek – she'd known it was bound to come to this, but she'd held it back as long as she could.

'She'll be fine, Annie. The vet's only sedating her because she's such a lively girl, and she needs to be able to examine her properly. The X-rays will show her what's what – if there's some sort of blockage or something that's causing the vomiting. Though I was pleased to hear she didn't think it could be too much bread, which I reckon might have been Gertie's doing at my place the other night. And Gertie's young and healthy – she'll be just fine.'

Annie knew that everything Tudor was saying was true, but she couldn't help herself...she'd never known that such a bond could exist between a human and a dog. She loved Gertie with all her heart. Carol had been right when she'd said that Annie thought of her as her child: a child who'd never grow up to be able to look after herself; a child who would always need Annie to do everything for her; a child who loved Annie unconditionally, and always knew when she needed to be licked, or snuggled, or encouraged to be playful.

Tudor reached for Annie's leg and gave it a squeeze, before needing both his hands on the steering wheel again to negotiate a sharp bend. 'We'll be home before long, and we'll have our dinner, together, in the pub. I can't ask Aled to stay on any longer, he'll need to be getting home soon, having come in early. We'll manage. Then how about you stay at mine, tonight?'

Annie wiped her eyes, and hunted in her handbag for a hankie. Tudor stuck his hand into his inside pocket. 'Have mine. It's clean.'

'Not for long,' replied Annie, wondering why on earth anyone used cloth hankies any longer. She was glad she wouldn't have to wash it; that was Tudor's problem. She blew her nose.

Back at the pub, with Aled released for the evening, and Annie one of only four people in the place, she suggested the salad from the menu for dinner, knowing that Tudor could pull that together in a couple of minutes, while she watched the bar. Which she did – without having to serve anything to anyone.

With her tummy almost full, she contemplated some apple tart for afters, but preferred the ones that Tudor got from a baker in the next village more than the ones he had delivered with the rest of the food supplies – and that wasn't the one he had in the kitchen that night, so she left it, knowing she could pop over to her cottage to raid her supplies of chocolate bars, if needs be, later on.

She moved from the dining table to a bar stool and swirled a gin and tonic with a great deal of ice in it, for her; it really was a warm evening.

'Quiet tonight,' she observed.

Tudor nodded. 'But there are eight sitting outside, so that's something, isn't it. I'll just pop out for the empties; sometimes that encourages them to get another round – though three of them have got cars.'

Annie waited as Tudor did his bit to increase the evening's takings, then waited again while he filled a tray with three shandies, two pints of bitter, and a few soft drinks – plus four packets of crisps and four bags of those prawn-flavored puffs that she thought were delicious…making her mouth water.

Finally back behind the bar, Tudor leaned in and said, 'I know we were supposed to be having private time to talk tonight, but it's not as though it's crowded in here – so, what do you say – shall we discuss our plans for…that place?' He nodded his head toward the snug. 'I'll have it finished before you know it. Then it'll be over to you. Have you worked out how you want it to look yet?'

Annie chattered on about tables, chairs, tablecloths, and how best to display a wide variety of teas. She suspected she was going into such detail as a way to distract herself from dwelling on the picture in her mind's eye of Gertie languishing alone at the vet's, but Tudor seemed to be enjoying what she was saying – until she reached the bit about maybe having a piano in the corner and inviting Wendy Jenkins in to play occasionally, which was when Tudor held up his hand.

'Hang on there, young miss – we're planning a room that's set up for teas, coffees, and pastries, not full-blown soirees.'

Annie grinned. 'But why not, Tude? If people like thc idea they might come in for a coffee and a sandwich in the evening, and you know how good Wendy is. You're always saying how beautifully she plays the organ at St David's – why not the piano at the Lamb and Flag too?'

Tudor said, 'Hold that thought – we'll come back to it. My pocket's vibrating.'

As he listened to the voice on the call he'd answered, Tudor's mouth fell open.

Annie had no idea who he was listening to – and her thoughts immediately leaped to Gertie.

'Is it the vet?' Annie mouthed the words, panic-stricken, and was relieved when Tudor shook his head.

She tutted at herself, *Why would the vet be phoning him not you, you silly so-and-so?* she thought.

But Tudor's expression had her worried, and she was even more concerned when he motioned to her that he was going to step out of the bar to continue talking on the phone.

A few moments later Tudor returned, looking…weird. Annie couldn't read his face at all.

'Who was it? Is something wrong? What's the matter?'

Tudor spoke slowly. 'It was Delyth James. She's agreed to the price that I told her was as high as I could go for the Coach and Horses.'

Annie squealed, 'But that's brilliant, Tude.' She jumped off her stool, raced around the bar, and hugged him tight. 'Congratulations!'

Tudor hugged her back, then nodded at the two remaining customers, who were both staring at the couple, and whispering.

'Hey, put me down,' he said, playfully.

Annie scuttled back to her stool and finished her drink. 'I think that deserves another large one, don't you?'

As Tudor prepared Annie's drink, and gave himself a tot or two from one of the better bottles of whiskey on the top shelf, Annie wriggled with delight.

'If you thought my plans for the snug were good, wait till you hear what I've got up my sleeve for that place, Tudor Evans. The first things we have to get sorted are the main bar, the side bar, and the bit that goes around the side and back toward the old stable block and smithy – the courtyard area. I think that should be a beer garden. I want us to offer a first-class customer experience in the main areas as a priority, then we can focus on the guest rooms…because I know from experience the bathroom set-up up there is going to need a good bit of work, and that won't be cheap, or fast. Do you know exactly what we can and can't do under the terms of the listing of the building? I can't make head nor tail of what they say online. I don't think we'll even be able to find out until we see the paperwork relating to the property.'

Annie was surprised that Tudor looked taken aback. 'All over it, aren't you?' He smiled his biggest smile and leaned across the bar to peck her on the cheek.

'Oi, no hanky-panky in front of paying customers,' mugged Annie.

Tudor rolled his eyes. 'Paying customers? A half of lager and a fizzy orange isn't going to line the coffers very much, is it? See, that's what I have to admit I'm a bit worried about; if they won't come here to spend their money, why would they go to the Coach and Horses? And that's another thing – do I think that the Chellingworth Estate wouldn't just replace me here with another lessee? They'd have someone in here like a shot, and then there'd be two pubs in the village, and no more people to drink and eat in them. I mean, to be honest, both places are much of a muchness – ancient, solid, country pubs. Of course, I'd offer an extended range of beers and so forth there, and I could push the menu a bit…elevate it, if you see what I mean. But, honestly – it's right there, across the green, just a bit bigger. But…but I'll have put all my own money into it, and I'll have much higher outgoings to support. It's…it's a wonderful idea, but a bit of a worry, really.'

Annie looked at Tudor's furrowed brow. She told herself off for having thought about this situation entirely as a way forward for them as a couple, and she'd really not given too much thought to the very point Tudor was now making: would they be able to make enough money at the pub across the green to keep their heads above water, when he was hardly making ends meet at the moment, with much lower outgoings?

She decided to let him speak – she needed to hear his point of view, and not get too caught up in the excitement of planning their lives as a couple, living under the same roof.

She said, 'Well, you're the expert, Tude. What do you think? Have you done any actual sums? Worked out the cost of the overhead, the supplies, the cashflow issues?'

Tudor smiled sadly. 'I have. Several times. I'm hoping they'll add up the way I want them to quite soon…I just have to keep redoing them, that's all.'

Annie felt her tummy tighten. Tudor's face was telling her he was already worried to death about the entire set-up, and they weren't even living through it yet. She set aside ideas of chintz curtains and new shower stalls and said, 'If this is going to be constant stress and worry, then I don't think we should...sorry, *you* should do it, Tude.'

He smiled more brightly. 'It really is *us* doing it, not just me. You know that.'

'But I won't be able to contribute in any way to the takings, and you'll be the one making the investment – so it really is all about you, financially. I'm just the emotional bit, added on.'

'Come on, Annie, don't talk like that. Look, I've got to be honest and say that the one thing I can't really factor into all of this is the impact that Stephanie and Henry's regeneration effort might make to the number of people who visit Anwen-by-Wye. Maybe, with rooms to rent out at the Coach and Horses, we could really capitalize on that; there are no real alternatives in the area, as you know from wanting your mum and dad to stay, but them not really fitting into your cottage. I've heard that one of the houses up on the new executive estate has been put into that scheme whereby you can rent a whole house for short breaks if you want, but, otherwise, the nearest hotels are a good drive away and cost a pretty penny, too. So, yes, if the Twysts can attract more tourists, and we do a better job of lunches and dinners, and can put on some good breakfasts to be able to offer bed-and-breakfast packages, then maybe that would make the difference. But who knows what will happen in reality?'

'Alexander and his partner Bill are reopening the old antiques shop, I know that much,' said Annie, 'but that alone wouldn't pull in the punters. I mean there's the sort who visit Chellingworth Hall and might want to make a weekend of it, or take a midweek break...but maybe we'll have to put our thinking caps on about getting together with local attractions to make Anwen-by-Wye more appealing.'

Tudor shrugged. 'There aren't any, are there? I mean, the duck pond is lovely, but hardly unique. And everything else – except the Hall – is closer to somewhere that already offers what we could. In a way I was glad when Delyth said she wanted more than I could afford, because it sort of got me off the hook of what had been a bit of a pipedream. And – if I'm honest – the main thing I was thinking about was that it would be wonderful for us to have somewhere big enough that we could be together, all the time. But the reality of it is just a bit…daunting.'

Annie didn't know what to say or do for the best, so said nothing, burying her face in her non-celebratory drink, and watching Tudor as he thoughtfully sipped his own.

TUESDAY 6th JUNE

CHAPTER TWENTY-FOUR

Mavis MacDonald opened her eyes, and her first thought was that she'd lost her sight…then she realized there was something covering her face – a smelly, greasy something. She worked out that her hands and feet were bound, and she was lying on her side on a floor that smelled nasty.

Her head hurt, but everything hurt, if she was honest. She did her best to sit up, and rolled about a bit until she found a wall to push herself up against. However, she couldn't get whatever was on her head off it, because her hands were tied, or taped, behind her back.

Taking a moment to catch her breath, Mavis reckoned she could make out daylight coming through a window, but not much else. She did her best to control her breathing, and listened carefully. Cars in the distance, but not many. Voices – where? In the same building as her? Or outside? Definitely inside. Above her. There was shouting, and she could make out the sound of someone clomping around up there. Were they dragging furniture around?

She tried to remember what had happened to her; she'd been following Veronica Daniels, then the bicycle, then – yes, a bang to the head. Now she was here. Could she recall anything else? Vague recollections of being led around by…someone? She could recall stumbling up some stairs and…what? Nothing much else. The pounding in her head and furriness of her tongue suggested to her that she'd been drugged…but for how long? She felt hungry – ravenous even – and thirsty. So thirsty.

A door slammed and she heard feet clattering on what sounded like a bare wooden staircase. They came closer. A door opened noisily, blocking the light she'd been able to see. The deeper darkness of a figure moved toward her.

'You're properly awake then, are you? There's lovely.'

A man. Not old, not young. Strong Welsh accent. Bad breath. A smoker, no doubt about it – and a drinker, too.

Mavis had to make a quick decision.

'Water…water…' she croaked, then slumped onto her side as pathetically as possible.

The man sounded surprised. 'Water? Oh, right…'

Mavis heard him leave the room and was glad she'd decided to adopt the role of a pathetic captive needing help, rather than a strong type who might prove problematic; it had been a fifty-fifty decision. The man was back in a few moments, and she heard him open a can of something fizzy.

'No glasses. You'll have to have this.'

He lifted the bottom of whatever was covering Mavis's face and tipped the can of liquid against her lips. The taste of beer came as a shock to her, but she sucked down as much as she could, because she really was terribly thirsty, and she reckoned anything was better than nothing.

The man was quiet, and seemed patient, helping her drink as best he could quite gently, which Mavis found bizarre.

'Thank you so much,' she whispered when he took the can away. 'I wonder if I might be able to…um…use the facilities. It's quite urgent.'

'You what?'

'I need to pee. Urgently.' She didn't, which suggested to her that she'd been unconscious for only a short time, and therefore couldn't be too far from where someone riding a bicycle had dismounted and cracked her on the head, but Mavis had a plan, and hoped it would work.

'Again? Um…well…um. Hang on.'

She heard the man leave. As he climbed the stairs, she could hear him huffing and puffing. Oddly, Mavis thought he seemed like a fairly decent sort – except for the fact that he had her tied up…somewhere.

She could hear voices above her again, and it was clear that some sort of argument was raging; it was definitely between a man and a woman, and probably connected to her request.

Eventually a door opened and she heard the man shout, 'Well, she might have been stalking our angel, but she's an old woman and she needs to pee. You'd let a dog out to pee, wouldn't you?' A pause. 'No, I'm not doing that. I wouldn't even do that for my mam. You did it for her yesterday, and earlier on today, when she was really out of it and couldn't tell up from down. Go on – you do it again now.'

There was a long pause.

The man continued, 'Well, keep your mouth shut then, and she won't know, will she? Yeah, we can do it with the bag on her head. Oh…alright then.'

Mavis had learned a couple of important, and worrying, things from the exchange. One, she'd been unconscious – or at least 'really out of it' – for a lot longer than she'd imagined; if she'd been helped to the toilet by someone the day before and 'earlier' that meant it must now be, what…Tuesday? Secondly, she reckoned she'd be visited by a female very soon, and maybe someone whose voice she'd recognize.

She knew she didn't have any time to lose, so decided on her exact plan of action. She began by lying down again and forced herself to squeeze out a few tears…which took less effort than she'd imagined it would.

Her rolling about had told her that she didn't have her phone in her pocket, which she knew she had done when she'd last been out on the street, ready to snap Veronica Daniels in action.

She wondered what had happened to her cross-body bag, too. Presumably whoever had snatched her and tied her up had taken it. She quickly pictured its contents; if they had it, they'd know who she was, where she lived, and what she did for a living. And they'd have access to her credit cards and the cash she'd been carrying – which weren't her main concerns at that moment.

Once again, she heard feet on the stairs, then someone entered the room.

'You'll have to hold it for a bit.' The man's voice sounded as though he were apologizing for being the bearer of bad tidings.

'I'll do my best,' she sobbed dramatically, disappointed that her plan hadn't worked…yet.

CHAPTER TWENTY-FIVE

Carol and David had enjoyed their breakfast/dinner together, and she'd decided it was best for her to push on with work on the Uninvited Undertaker case.

With Albert, thankfully, playing contentedly in his playpen, and David relaxing with his gaming stuff in the sitting room, Carol put the washing on the line to dry, then set herself up at the dining-room table.

When her phone rang and she saw it was Ellie's number, she was pleased – she'd been hoping to catch up with her friend who could, hopefully, tell her how things were going with Mavis at the nursing home; Carol reckoned she must have gone back there for another shift the previous night.

'Hiya, how are you?' Carol thought it best to get the niceties out of the way first.

'I'm alright, ta. Bit of a difficult day yesterday, having to talk to poor Mrs Thomas's family. But at least they were expecting it, as I said.'

'She did die, then?' Carol guessed that was what Ellie had meant.

'Yes, sorry, didn't Mavis tell you?'

'I haven't heard from her.' *Odd.* 'In fact, I assumed she'd gone in for another shift last night.'

'No, she didn't turn up, which was the real reason for me phoning; they told me when I got in this morning, and it was a bit awkward for me, see? To be honest, I assumed she'd get in touch when she had some news, so that at least I'd know when she was planning on no longer being here to work.'

Carol sat a little more upright. 'So Mavis wasn't at the nursing home last night?'

'No.'

'And when did Mrs Thomas die?'

'Early hours of Monday morning, during Mavis's shift that night. I sent her a text saying that all the medications Mrs Thomas had been prescribed had gone missing around nine yesterday morning. Should I be worried?'

Carol was, that much was certain. 'I don't know – let me make a few phone calls. Have you tried Mavis's phone yourself?' Carol could feel her heart beating in her chest; she felt instinctively that something was wrong.

'Yes, a few times. Voicemail.'

Carol felt a bit sick. 'Right-o, leave it with me. I'll phone you back. By the way, where are you? At the nursing home or your flat?'

'At work, of course. All Mavis's stuff was still at my flat last night, and I thought she might come back to my place to fill me in…but she didn't, and I fell asleep on the sofa. As I said, yesterday was a difficult day. Sorry.'

'It's alright. I'll phone you back.'

Carol phoned Mavis's mobile number; voicemail. She phoned the Dower House; no, Mavis wasn't there. She phoned both Christine and Annie; no, neither of them had heard from Mavis. Carol assured them that there wasn't a problem, encouraging them to both get on with what they needed to, then spent the next couple of hours trawling through Mavis's cloud files.

When she knocked at the bedroom door, it was ten in the morning. 'I've got to go out, you're in charge of Albert.'

David pushed himself up onto his elbows in the bed.

'What do you mean you've got to out? Where? Why?' His face fell. 'Is everyone alright? Your parents?'

'Yes, they're fine – I suppose. It's Mavis, she's gone missing; no one's heard from her since yesterday morning, and she didn't turn up for work last night. But I've got the address of where her car was yesterday morning, so I'm going to drive there now. Christine and Annie both have their hands full with other things, and I don't want to worry them with this.'

David looked shocked, and finally wide awake. 'What do you mean you're going there now? On your own? I'm sorry, Carol – you know I support your work, but this doesn't sound safe. You said Mavis is missing. Missing from where?'

Carol sighed. 'She's missing from everywhere, because no one knows where she is. However, I know she was in an area west of Cardiff city center yesterday morning because she uploaded photos of a nurse she was following with street names in the pictures, so that's where I'm going to start.'

David scratched his head as though he were trying to burrow down to the bone. 'Carol, love – you're a mother and a wife, not some sort of superwoman. What would you do if you found Mavis's car but no Mavis? Surely this is something for the police – people who can track phones, and things like that.'

'I can track her phone, but it's turned off. And, like I said, she took photos of where she was last…or, at least, of several places where she was yesterday morning. But…yes, you've got a point. If I found her car but not her, I'd need to get the police involved.'

David patted the bed and beckoned to his wife to sit beside him. She did, and he held her gently by the shoulders, gazing at her face, smiling. Carol returned his smile; she loved the way his hair went all squiffy when he was in bed.

He said, 'Why not phone the police now, and let them look into it? They'd do that, wouldn't they? Or do you have to wait a certain number of hours to report a person as missing?'

'No, you can make a report at any time. I could do that, I suppose…' Carol knew that David was being incredibly sensible, so she agreed, and made her way down to the dining room, where she phoned the police station closest to the last location that Mavis had photographed.

Sadly, she wasn't impressed with the response, which was – in a nutshell – 'Come in with all the information we need, and we'll see what we can do'.

It seemed that a woman in her early sixties who'd not been heard of by friends for a whole day, who hadn't arrived for her work as a care assistant – which was her undercover persona as a private investigator – sounded a bit too fishy to the police officer she was speaking to.

Carol took some deep breaths. Annie was off to the vet in Brecon with Tudor, so she was out of the question – which left Christine.

She phoned Christine – who sounded a bit...weird in some way – and told her everything; she was pleased when she knew that Christine would be on the road in half an hour, heading toward Mavis's last known location.

She made one more phone call, to Llinos Trevelyan, apologizing for disturbing her. She filled her in on the situation, too, and Llinos promised to do her best to get hold of a constable she'd trained with who worked in the Cardiff area to try to prime the local police station about the seriousness of the situation. Llinos knew Mavis and her reputation for reliability, so Carol had no doubt the constable understood her anxiety.

She was just about to pick up Albert to give him his lunch when David stuck his head through the door. 'I couldn't get back to sleep. How's it going? Any word?'

'I'm putting the kettle on – but you can only have decaf tea. I'll tell you all about it, then back to bed for you, *cariad*.'

CHAPTER TWENTY-SIX

Annie had hardly slept. She'd crept downstairs and had paced around the pub rather than disturb Tudor, who'd snored for most of the night, which had been more than annoying. Knowing, logically, that constantly staring at her watch wouldn't make time pass any more quickly, Annie did it anyway, hoping the laws of the universe would bend to her will. But they didn't.

When Tudor appeared, she'd already drunk too much tea. Her first words were: 'It's been light for ages, and the vet's clinic opens in an hour. Do you think the operation will be over by now?'

'Good morning to you, too,' replied a sleepy Tudor. He looked at his watch. 'Maybe. Why don't you phone them?'

'They said they'd phone me when there was any news. But they might have forgotten, I suppose. Yes, I'll give them a ring.' She picked up her phone from the bar.

'You didn't need my permission, you know. And have you drunk an entire big pot of tea? I'm making some upstairs, too. But maybe you've had enough already.'

Annie grew impatient as the phone rang out in Brecon, then hit her screen when she heard the recorded message. 'There's no one answering. Do you think we could drive over? So we can get in there as early as possible.'

Tudor sighed. 'I suppose so. I warned Aled he might need to open up here this morning, so why don't we get ourselves fit to mix with the public and get in the car. I know you won't rest until you know how Gertie's doing, so let's get going. Alright?'

Annie felt the relief wash over her. 'Right-o, but I'm going back to mine to get showered and changed, that'll be easier. I can be back in twenty minutes.'

She headed toward the door at the rear of the pub.

'Make sure you eat something,' called Tudor as she left, 'and I'll bring some fruit and so forth, in case we've got to hang around when we get there.'

After Carol had phoned her, Annie wasn't sure whether she should be more worried about Mavis or Gertie, but knew she had to focus on her beloved pup first to be any good to anyone, so she decided to make that her priority.

She did her best to not tell Tudor to drive faster too often as they got caught in the morning traffic snaking through the lanes and roads they needed to use to get into Brecon, and she replied absently when he commented upon the lovely weather, the beauty of the hedgerows, and even the news that there might be thunderstorms coming their way later in the day. All Annie cared about was Gertie; everything else was unimportant.

Their arrival at the vet's clinic was marred by Annie tumbling out of the car and scraping her elbow, which she didn't feel at all as she brushed off gravel and blood. Tudor provided yet another cloth hankie for her to use, saying it didn't matter if she got blood on it, because he had a secret method of getting bloodstains out of cotton, which Annie thought odd, but didn't want to ask about because she was too intent upon getting inside to find out about Gertie.

The receptionist wasn't the one who'd been on duty the previous day, and seemed taken aback by Annie's insistence that she should be allowed to see her pup, then disappeared into the rear of the building for what felt like ages.

Returning, the young man said, 'Dr Brackenfield has asked if you can wait in room four. She'll be with you in a few moments.'

'How's Gert?' Annie hadn't meant to snap, but knew she'd sounded curt.

The receptionist's face creased into a platitudinous smile. 'The doctor will tell you all about the procedure. Let me show you to your room.'

He stepped out from behind the tall desk and walked along a corridor lined with doors. Beyond the farthest, Annie was convinced she could hear Gertie whining and yelping.

Her heart beat faster, and she did her best to smile when the young man left her and Tudor in a small room. It had a banquette seat covered in green plastic along one wall, with a high, wide countertop in front of it. Posters showing happy, healthy cats and dogs enjoying the benefits of having been treated with any number of medications with complicated names adorned the walls, and a calendar – supplied by a leading manufacturer of pet food – announced that it was time to make sure your pet's flea treatment was up to date.

Annie couldn't sit…couldn't stand…couldn't think – except for about how the operation might have gone wrong in innumerable, but vague, ways. When the door opened, she turned and grabbed Tudor's hand, squeezing it until it became completely white, she noticed.

'Hello, again,' said the vet. 'Thanks for coming in – though I have to say we weren't expecting you.'

'How is she?' Annie couldn't wait for niceties.

'Gertie is sleeping. The procedure was a success. We found the cause of her gastric distress and the problem has been resolved. Gertie didn't suffer any complications. She'll just be a bit sore for a while, and she'll need a wet food diet for about a week to ten days. But she's fine. Just fine. A lovely girl – though lively. We'll keep her here until she's fully awake, but she should be able to come home with you by about two this afternoon. We just need to make sure that all her functions are normal – so we need her to have peed properly, and so forth, without any problems before we can release her.'

Annie could feel the tears welling up. 'Oh, thank you. Thank you so much, doctor. I didn't realize I'd be so…I've been worried to death about her. I could picture you slicing her open – all those stiches. Will she have to wear a cone thing, so she doesn't nibble at them? Will we be coming back to have them taken out – or do they dissolve? I know some of them do that.'

The vet smiled. 'There are no stitches, and we didn't slice her open at all. We needed her to be sedated because she wouldn't let us get a proper look down her throat. I could see on the X-rays that there was an obstruction – some sort of foreign object – in her gullet, but I couldn't get to it without the sedation. It's not an uncommon situation, and we were lucky – the obstruction had lodged where we were able to extract it without having to perform surgery.'

Annie was confused. 'What was it? Something dangerous?'

The vet chuckled. 'I have it in the back, if you want to see it.'

Annie glanced at Tudor. 'Is it very…yukky?'

The vet shook her head. 'Not very. It's a hankie…one of those old-fashioned cloth ones. You don't see them used as much these days, though dogs eating paper tissues can be dangerous, too. Do you have any idea where she might have picked it up?'

Annie glared at Tudor. 'Yeah, I've got an inkling. Tude – you've been leaving your hankies around the flat, haven't you? It's all well and good us keeping our socks and things out of their reach, but not if you go leaving hankies lying about the place.'

Tudor was puce. 'I…I don't know how she could have got hold of one, I really am very careful with them. Always right inside my pocket, they are. And I don't leave them hanging around after I've ironed them, either…they go straight back into the drawer. Always. I mean, it's not as though Gertie's the only dog at my place – I'm always careful because of Rosie, too. Yes, if I could take a look at it, doctor, that would be lovely.'

The vet left the two of them to stare at each other. 'I really don't think it could have been one of mine.' Tudor sounded too defensive for Annie to calm down.

Returning with a sealed plastic bag, the vet held it up. Annie gulped at the disgusting item inside – stained with all sorts of things she didn't want to think about. Tudor studied it more closely. 'There. See? Not mine. Mine haven't got anything sewn on them. And certainly not in red. Nor with frilly edges. *Not* my hankie. Not my fault.'

Annie could feel her chin puckering; she'd have forgiven him even if it had been his hankie, but the look of vindication on Tudor's face made her wonder where on earth Gertie could have got hold of a strange handkerchief.

She was grateful when Tudor wrapped her in his arms and kissed her cheek.

He said, 'Well, I'd better get hold of Aled and tell him we won't be back until about three. Shall we take some time in Brecon for a bit of a wander and some lunch? Then we can come back here for the girl herself and take her home. We could always pick up some special dog food while we're in town.'

Dr Brackenfield pounced. 'We have a variety of flavors of a type of nutritionally balanced wet food in tins outside, in reception. Let me ask Michael to talk you through them. I highly recommend the brand we offer – especially given what Gertie's been through. She deserves the best, doesn't she?'

Annie suspected the vet was tugging at her heartstrings, then reminded herself of the quote she'd been given the previous day for Gertie's proposed treatments and answered with a quiet, 'I'll take a look. See if there's anything she might like.'

Having told Tudor that she couldn't do anything as underhand as claim that Gertie was, in fact, the fully-insured Rosie – and, yes, she'd admitted to Tudor that she should, probably, have taken his advice about pet insurance – she was now facing a sizeable outlay. And, while credit cards were invented for such emergencies, their balances still had to be paid off.

Annie glumly surveyed the shelves full of tins bearing photographs of dog food presented in such a way as to suggest that the contents were, actually, fit for human consumption. Chicken? Beef? Lamb? Turkey? With barley, or without? She couldn't decide. She suspected Gertie would gobble them all down, but couldn't bring herself to commit.

'Let's decide when we come back to pick her up, eh?'

Annie knew Tudor was right, so they left without Gertie, but at least with Annie's blood pressure having dropped a bit, for which she was grateful. She'd do her best to not count the minutes until two o'clock.

CHAPTER TWENTY-SEVEN

Althea Twyst had slept exceptionally well. Her morning exercises completed, she planned to make the most of yet another sunny day by…well, she'd start by walking with McFli over to the Hall – he could do with the exercise; then she might drop in on Ivor, just to see how things were going around the gardens – McFli enjoyed scampering along the paths yapping at the visitors, who had no idea he was the dowager's dog, which made her giggle sometimes; then she'd invite herself to lunch with Stephanie and Hugo; she would even stay for tea. Ah yes, tea…with Marjorie Pritchard and Elizabeth Fernley. That was something she was looking forward to a great deal.

A hurried, puzzling phone call from Carol made her believe that Mavis was proving as difficult to get hold of for her colleagues as she had been for Althea herself. Should she be worried about that? She thought not; Mavis hadn't gone into any detail about her latest assignment, though Christine had let it slip that night work was involved. She told herself that Mavis was probably sleeping like a baby wherever she was, having finished an overnight stakeout, or whatever it was she might be doing.

She chose a cashmere emerald cardigan to go over her buttery-yellow blouse and her favorite MacGregor hunting tartan kilt, which she was allowed to wear because of her grandfather, and which always made her smile with its heathery purple and more somber teal colors. She realized on her way out that the kilt would need to be taken up – it was almost at her ankles, she'd shrunk so much of late – but hemming a kilt was beyond her abilities, she knew that, so she made a mental note to have it sent off for professional attention.

The walk was pleasant enough; she and McFli easily matched each others' pace, though he liked to dash off to investigate something or other all the time, returning to her on the path when he'd discounted it as being not interesting enough for his mistress to get too far away from him.

Her arrival at the Hall wasn't as she'd imagined, however. Instead of the usual activity that accompanied the imminent arrival of members of the public, she saw Clementine's car – the red estate one – at the bottom of the steps, and was greeted by Edward who was carrying a great deal of luggage to it.

'Are Clementine and Jools leaving, Edward?' Althea hadn't expected that.

Edward placed the three heavy-looking, and rather aged, suitcases on the pea-gravel of the drive. 'Her Ladyship has asked that all her personal items be brought to her car, Your Grace. I have sent people to try to locate suitable baggage to fulfil her request, though, as you can see, her vehicle is almost full already.'

Althea was nonplussed. 'But why?'

Edward cleared his throat. 'Mr Tavistock left the Hall in the early hours. He…he was most insistent that I allow him and his motorcycle out of the gates at around three this morning, Your Grace. Her Ladyship is returning to the London house. She…' He spoke more softly. 'Her Ladyship has been most upset this morning, Your Grace. She has made it clear that she will never be returning to Chellingworth Hall once she has left it – which she plans to do as soon as all her personal items have been packed into her car.'

Edward's expression trod a fine line between sadness and exasperation.

'Poppycock,' said Althea. 'I shall see myself in, Edward. Do you know where Clementine is at the moment?'

'Overseeing the packing, in her rooms, Your Grace.'

'Very well. I shall go to her, if I must. Come along, McFli…let's not dawdle.'

McFli showed no intention of doing any such thing, and raced up the wide stone steps as though he were a pup, not a senior. Althea enjoyed seeing him being so active, and still so interested in everything; it bode well for him, as did his genetics – she'd bred him herself, and his parents had lived to be seventeen and eighteen, so she hoped McFli had several healthy years ahead of him yet. He was certainly pampered and well-cared for enough that he should do.

Althea chuckled as she made her way up the Hall's grand staircase toward her daughter's apartment; time was she'd have been doing the same thing with more than half a dozen Jack Russells surrounding her. But those days were gone. Now there was only one sweet face, one ringing bark, and one pair of excited eyes welcoming her as she reached the landing.

As luck would have it, she didn't have to plod to the wing where Clementine's rooms were located; her daughter was barreling toward her with a bag in each hand, and an expression that could curdle milk.

'Are you happy now?' Clementine was furious, her mother could tell that quite easily.

'What on earth is going on, Clemmie? Edward tells me you're leaving. For ever. Which, I must say, is more than a little puzzling.'

Clementine dropped her bags, unceremoniously, all the better to be able to wave her arms about, it seemed. She flung them aloft and declaimed, 'I'm leaving all this behind me, Mother. Don't worry, you'll never have to see me again. Just tell me if you're wanting to use the London house and I'll make myself scarce. I understand it must be more than you can bear to be under the same roof as me – as it is for me with you. So, goodbye, and don't give me another thought.'

Althea clutched her chest, and waved a hand in front of her face. McFli was at her heel, yapping, in an instant.

'Don't bother, Mother, it won't wash. You're not about to faint, you're putting it on so that I'll feel sorry for you. Well, I'm not. Yet again you've interfered in my life, and this time? This time is the last time. He's gone. Which is, I dare say, exactly what you wanted.'

Clementine drew breath, sagged, and a tear rolled down her face. 'Oh, Mother…Jools was…is…so important to me. He might be my last chance to find happiness. And you've taken that away from me. Do you hate me, Mother? Are you determined that I shall live my life alone, forever? Why on earth must you always meddle?' She reached for the balustrade to support herself, and Althea watched with deepening sadness as her daughter crumpled into a heap on the landing, sobbing like a small child.

She weighed what she should say. 'I'm sorry, my darling girl. I only ever want you to be happy. This is because of what I said about Mavis investigating someone who had secrets to hide, isn't it? Jools thought I meant him, and he's done a runner.'

Clementine sniffed. 'Done a runner? You could say that, Mother. He left in the early hours after we'd been rowing for hours. And, yes, he did have secrets, but they weren't bad secrets, just things he didn't want me to know about him until he was sure I really was going to marry him. He was planning to tell me once we were in Egypt.'

'That doesn't sound very…um…but he's told you now?' Althea's mind was awash with potential types of secrets the man might have been hiding.

Her daughter gathered her wits, her voluminous skirt, and then her bags. 'Don't think for one minute that I'm going to tell you what he said,' she sniped. 'I'm going to London where I intend to do my best to find him, and to beg him – once again – to forgive me for my family, and to reconsider marrying just me, not you lot. He's the one, Mother. I won't let you stand in my way. And I hope he'll see that we can have a life together without you constantly poking your nose in, and without Henry constantly being snarky and putting me down. I now believe the only way I can achieve that is to never come here again, and to never be in the company of either of you two.'

'But what about baby Hugo? You seem to be very attached to him.' Althea knew she had to try everything.

Clementine sobbed as she flounced past her mother. 'That's going to be the only thing I regret about disassociating myself from this family. I just hope he grows up surrounded by love, not poison. And, whatever you do, Mother, keep your nose out of his business and just let him be him. But, there again, maybe by the time he's old enough for you to really want to mess with his life, you'll be dead. Which will be a blessing in itself. Goodbye, Mother. I won't be telling Henry any of this so you can pass it on.'

Althea felt dizzy. She reached out her hand for support, but found none, then touched the balustrade, and allowed it to take her weight. Looking down, she could see that Clementine was already halfway across the Great Hall, Edward taking the bags from her hands, her kitten heels clattering on the marble floor. Then she was gone.

Althea couldn't quite believe what had just happened: she and Clementine had most certainly had their fair share of disagreements over the years, but her daughter had never wished her dead before – not as far as she could recollect, in any case. That wasn't at all nice. Though, upon reflection, she thought it understandable, given that she had, in fact, been interfering in Clementine's life – though only with her happiness in mind.

McFli demanded, and gained, her attention for a moment, then Althea straightened herself, and made her way down to a private sitting room she knew was not open to the public. She settled herself, pulled out her mobile phone and called Mavis, but there was no answer, only her voicemail message, so she phoned Carol, who sounded a bit puffed.

'Have you spoken with Mavis yet?' Althea thought it best to be direct.

Carol's response didn't come at once. 'No. Not today. Can I help?'

Althea wondered if she could. 'I hope so. I had asked Mavis to look into the background of a Julian, known as Jools, Tavistock. Do you happen to know if she made any headway with that enquiry prior to her departure to…wherever she might be?'

Another pause. 'I could check. Would you like me to phone you back?'

'Yes please, dear, as a matter of some urgency. Thank you. I shall wait for your call.'

'I might not be able to phone back straight away, Althea. I'll…it might take me a little while to get through to Mavis. She's…she's working on a case that means she's not always able to take calls.'

'But this is incredibly urgent. What was not a priority has become an emergency. I need to know all about him. Now.' Althea always believed that sugar was better than bile when wanting someone to do something for one, but, on this occasion, she had allowed her anxiety to show. She added, 'I'm sorry, I didn't mean to sound so…high and mighty. But, you see, the man in question was Clementine's new fiancé, and he's taken himself off during the night, and now Clementine's left too. It's the most dreadful mess, and it's all my fault. Can you help? Please? Maybe you could look into him yourself – while you try to get in touch with Mavis.'

Althea hoped Carol would, because she knew, in her heart, that if anyone could find out about Clementine's missing fiancé, Carol could.

Carol sighed. 'Tell me everything you know about him.'

Althea hurriedly shared all her knowledge and observations about Jools, then asked, 'Will that be enough to find him?'

Carol replied tiredly, 'Not sure. Hold on while I run my custom search program.'

Althea couldn't imagine what Carol was doing; all she could hear was the excited laughter of Albert in the background and a lot of tapping. She perched on the sofa she'd always hated; Chelly had chosen it – a leather Chesterfield, most uncomfortable. She waited, and waited, her phone beginning to feel quite hot in her hand. McFli was curled at her feet with a shaft of sunlight no doubt warming his little body, and he looked quite peaceful – though she felt anything but.

Althea was starting to wonder why on earth she was listening to the oddly calming sounds of Carol working at home, then she heard what she believed to be the phone being picked up again.

'I don't believe he exists,' said Carol finally. 'There's no Julian, Jools, or even Jules Tavistock with an online footprint of any description – not even a website for his business. He's not listed on any database I can access – and I can access a great number – unless he's the four-year-old son of a couple in Derbyshire who's just had a birthday party with a bouncy castle, an eleven-year-old in Walthamstow who's the next great hope of his school's cricket team, or a man of eighty-four who's just managed to run a half-marathon in Leeds. If he's Clementine's fiancé, I dare say he's none of those so – no – your Julian Tavistock doesn't exist. Does that help?'

Althea was speechless.

CHAPTER TWENTY-EIGHT

'Thanks for popping in, Llinos. Is there any news?'

Carol welcomed the off-duty constable to her kitchen table, pushed aside a couple of things, and made space for the teapot.

Llinos nodded. 'I don't know them personally, but I know that two constables from the local station met Christine at the place where she'd found Mavis's car. I believe they're taking the news of her disappearance seriously.'

Carol glanced at her phone; she'd heard nothing from Christine – she imagined she'd be fully involved with briefing the officers in question.

'I really appreciate you getting involved, Llinos. I don't know what difference it will make, except that there are now resources being used that we don't possess, so thanks for that.'

Llinos sipped her tea. 'No worries. That information you gave me about the potential identity of the man we found deceased in the caravan speeded things up for us, so thanks for that. Back-scratching always works, doesn't it?'

Carol nodded her agreement. 'Speaking of which…'

Llinos chuckled. 'Go on then, what now?'

'Any news about how Ed Hughes actually died? Or when, exactly?'

Llinos shook her head. 'Without going into details – except to say that a brand new, just out of the box, constable is currently on sick leave, because he's trying to come to terms with what he found in that caravan – the word is that the deceased could have passed away at any point from Monday to Wednesday, that week. Definitely no later than the Wednesday. There's no indication of foul play at this stage, but the toxicological investigation is ongoing. He was an out-patient at the local hospital, where he'd received a couple of steroid injections for a recurring shoulder problem. The path lab is checking with them about the high amounts of opioids found in his remains. That's yet to be explained.'

'Suicide? Or something else?'

Llinos shrugged. 'You've got something you want to tell me, haven't you?'

Carol finally took the chance to explain the entirety of The Case of the Uninvited Undertaker to Llinos, and the officer agreed that the fact that wreaths were being delivered prior to deaths taking place was 'interesting', especially in the case of the discovery at the caravan park.

'You know I have to report all this, don't you?'

Carol nodded. 'And you know we want to cooperate. The death at the caravan park is the only one that didn't happen at a medical institution – other than this one other case.'

Llinos bit, 'What other case?'

'I was wondering if you could put out some feelers about one Alan Ridley? All I really want to know is where he died, you see, but the client hasn't come back to me on it. And it's annoying me; if he was "on holiday", then how did the Uninvited Undertaker know him, or know enough about him, to be able to deliver a wreath to a local family if the man himself wasn't in the area…or maybe not even in the country? I have no idea where he was, you see.'

Llinos agreed to do what she could, but warned Carol to not expect too much, too soon, because she now needed to pass all the information she'd just received to the team handling the enquiry into Ed Hughes's death. Also, she'd agreed to do an extra shift, because the hot weather seemed to be bringing petty criminals out of the woodwork and everyone was having to lend a hand.

She explained, 'It's all the open windows, see? People don't think about opportunistic thievery, but it happens all the time. If only people would fit those locks that only allow the window to be open a bit, that would save them a lot of distress, and us a lot of work. I've got four break-ins to see to that I know about, and I haven't even clocked in for my next shift yet.'

Carol hugged her chum. 'You go and get those baddies, Llinos.'

'Baddies? Yeah – I dare say that's how they see themselves. But what they usually turn out to be is someone who thinks that the world owes them a living. Anyway – thank goodness they're usually so stupid that they do something, or even leave something behind, that means they're easy for us to find. As for getting them off the streets for any length of time? Now that's a different kettle of fish, and I'm not going to discuss that. Never do – really not a good idea for a copper to talk about things like that in public…nor, necessarily with a friend over a pot of tea. I'll text you if I find anything useful, alright? Thanks for the tea…now, let me just give this little man of yours a big hug before I leave, and all will be right with the world. Come here, Albert.'

Just as she was waving Llinos off at the door, Carol's phone pinged; it was a text from Christine:

With police at Mavis's car. Will do all I can. Wanted you to know – I sent files to cloud about Undertaker stuff. You should look – weird things – more of them. Text me if you have questions. I'll do my best for Mavis. Leave it with me.

Carol settled Albert and accessed the cloud files Christine had loaded. She noted that her colleague had been busy, working long into the previous night; her records showed she'd been speaking to people at various hospices until gone eleven.

The 'weird' thing Christine must have been referring to was that several staff members at various hospices often attended the funerals of those who had been under their care, and quite a few of them had noticed that what they described as a 'rose made out of cast iron' had been present either at the burial site, or among the tributes at the crematorium, when the funeral party had arrived for the observations.

So the Uninvited Undertaker is not only leaving wreaths before deaths, but also iron roses before interments? Yes, weird is one word to describe that.

Carol had an idea, and phoned Louise Attwater. After exchanging brief greetings Carol said, 'I know I'm waiting on other information from you, but can you tell me this: have there been any deliveries of wreaths to families where the deceased has not yet been interred?'

Louise paused. 'Let me check.' Silence. 'Yes, one. Jedediah Williams is due to be buried at a little church about thirty miles or so away from you – I can send you the details if you like. Burial is set for…oh, this afternoon. Half four, which is quite late. Is that of any help?'

'No more bodies "on the books" so to speak? We didn't even have him on the list you sent me.'

Louise paused again. 'Oh, wasn't he? I thought he was. Sorry. No, no others.'

'Leave it with me,' said Carol, and ended the call.

Next, she phoned Annie, who was back at the pub with Gertie and Tudor. Having established Gertie's condition, Carol said, 'Can you get Tudor to watch her, and I'll get David to watch Albert…so that we can go to a church just south-east of Brecon this afternoon? I'd pick you up as soon as possible, and we'd only be gone for a few hours, I hope.'

Annie dithered, which Carol knew wasn't like her. Eventually she said, 'Shall I walk over to you? Tude says he'll be fine with Gert.'

'Please – that'll save a few minutes, and I'm keen to get to the church in question as soon as I can.'

Annie dared, 'Why? What's at this church, then?'

'A funeral, Annie – and I want us to be there for as much time as possible before it starts. See you in a minute, bye…I'm off to wake David.'

CHAPTER TWENTY-NINE

Stephanie Twyst had found herself in many unusual and unforeseeable situations since she'd married Henry and become the Duchess of Chellingworth, but she believed that this was one of the most bizarre; she was having tea with her mother-in-law, Elizabeth Fernley, and Marjorie Pritchard – and she was about to waltz across a minefield.

Bob Fernley was the trusted Estates Manager at the seat, and he'd steered Henry through many a tricky situation over the years. His wife Elizabeth had stepped up as overall housekeeper when Henry's mother had moved from the Hall to take up residence at the Dower House, and both Henry and Stephanie had acknowledged on more than one occasion that without Elizabeth's efforts the role of the Twyst family in the local community, and the role the Hall had always played within it too, could have suffered in the period before the duke's marriage.

However, even Stephanie had to admit that relations between herself and Elizabeth had never been exactly warm, not even when Stephanie had been the PR manager for the Hall. Indeed, she'd got the impression that Elizabeth had felt Stephanie was treading on her toes from the moment she'd arrived, and that impression became more pronounced once Stephanie had become her *de facto* employer.

Marjorie Pritchard was someone Stephanie didn't know as well as she knew Elizabeth, nor, of course, as intimately as she knew the dowager. Marjorie sat on the Anwen-by-Wye social committee and was very much involved in the fabric of the village – which meant she was on every possible committee she could be, and stuck her nose into absolutely everything, even when it was nothing at all to do with her. That said, Stephanie acknowledged that Marjorie was exactly the sort of person who was needed if things were ever to get done; she'd push people to participate, cajole them into volunteering, and get them to donate their time or money to the many good and necessary causes and events in the area. Of course, this meant that the sight of Marjorie often sent people scurrying into their homes to avoid her, but she was the type who never noticed such things, always believing that everyone wanted to hear what she had to say about everything.

As Stephanie poured tea for the quartet, she also allowed herself to give some thought to the reason for her mother-in-law being so keen to be in attendance. Althea hated to miss out on anything that smacked of devilment, and this tea offered just such an opportunity, because its purpose was for Stephanie to try to get Elizabeth and Marjorie to bury the hatchet – and not in each other's skulls.

Stephanie noted the twinkle in Althea's eye as she settled into her seat, urging McFli to lay beside her, which he did after a good sniff of the leg of the chair, and a few turns.

The women were seated in one of the private rooms in the Hall, which were protected from the prying eyes of the public by a series of velvet ropes, and a bevy of well-trained docents. The family always referred to it as the Rose Room, because the predominant color was of muted rose tones, including the hand-woven silk wall coverings which dated back to the seventeenth century. At least, the parts that were original did; the rest of it looked exactly the same, but it had cost a small fortune to have it woven at a convent in the hills of northern Italy. That same wall covering had required the room to be fitted with special window treatments designed to protect it, meaning that it was relatively cool, even on such a warm day, which was why Stephanie had chosen it; she didn't want potentially overheated discussions to be fuelled by overheated participants.

'Thank you all for coming,' she opened, once everyone had their tea.

'It's a great honor,' gushed Marjorie. 'I mean, it's always a treat to come to the Hall for meetings and so forth, but this room? I've never been here before, and it's lovely. Yes, a great honor indeed.' She sipped her tea, realized it was too hot for her, and set it on the small table beside her elbow.

'I oversaw the restoration of the décor,' said Elizabeth airily. 'I believe we did the room justice.'

'Chelly used to sit over in the window looking out at his white rose bushes at night, smoking his cigars,' said Althea mistily.

'Hence the new wall coverings,' said Elizabeth quietly.

Stephanie judged that Althea had pretended to not hear the comment.

The duchess began, 'I haven't told you why I've asked you to join me, but you all know me well enough, I hope, to believe that my intention is never to wound, but that my manner is quite straightforward.' She noticed that Marjorie looked mystified, while Elizabeth's eyes narrowed. Althea smiled so that her dimples showed – always a bad sign.

'Oh, it sounds very exciting,' twittered Marjorie.

Elizabeth sipped her tea – with determination.

Stephanie continued, 'It's been brought to my attention that, some years ago, there was an…unpleasantness…which caused a rift between the two of you,' She nodded at Elizabeth and Marjorie. 'I don't want us to rehash those old injuries, but I do want us to do whatever we can – here, today – to allow bygones to become bygones, so we can all move forward as one team.'

Stephanie could hear echoes of speeches she'd given at meetings in her previous incarnation as a PR guru for corporate types, and inwardly sighed as she did so. Maybe that was what she had to do – imagine that Elizabeth and Marjorie were two companies with a torrid history who now needed to be melded together for their future success.

Yes – she'd steer it all that way. 'In life, it's sometimes best to speak directly to the person who's hurt you, telling them how it's made you feel – then we can move past the destruction and plan a better future together. But let's not forget that we all have feelings, and we don't want to air grievances that will cause fresh hurt. So, on that basis, is there anything anyone would like to say?'

'The Victoria sponge is excellent,' said Althea, dimpling.

'Thank you, Althea. I shall pass your compliments to Cook Davies. Anyone else?'

'It's rich, yet moist,' said Marjorie.

'Her Grace means about something other than what you're eating,' said Elizabeth, managing to make 'Her Grace' sound almost like an insult, Stephanie thought.

'Like what? Like about how you threatened to take me to court for doing absolutely nothing wrong?' Marjorie bit into her sponge after she'd spoken with such vigor that a shower of crumbs fell to the floor. McFli darted toward them, then lay in wait, in case there would be more.

Elizabeth set aside her tea. 'The truth of it is, Your Grace, that Marjorie and her partner in gossip, Mair Jones, put it about that I was…that I was having relations outside my marriage. It wasn't true, and it was extremely hurtful to both myself and my husband – as well as being completely unfair to the other party mentioned in their rumors. I found it difficult to maintain any respect within the area because of what was being said about me, and my husband was being whispered about behind his back. It was a terrible, terrible time. I begged them to stop, but it was like trying to put out a fire with a bucket of petrol. They became more brazen, and Marjorie went as far as telling people she knew there was truth in the rumors because she'd seen me and "the other party" as good has having intercourse in the church. In the church! I had to make them see I was serious, and that was why – when the police told me there was nothing they could do – I went to see a solicitor, and they wrote to both Marjorie and Mair.'

Marjorie wasn't nibbling sponge any longer, noted Stephanie; now she was nibbling her lip, her ears pink – and that wasn't down to the reflected glow of the rose-colored cushions.

Althea said, 'Well summarized, Elizabeth. It must have been terribly difficult for you and Bob. Indeed, I take my hat off to you for having sustained your marriage throughout it, and beyond. Gossip can be caustic for even the most robust of relationships.'

'Caustic?' Elizabeth sneered. 'It was like poison. But, yes, me and Bob agreed we'd do everything we could to stop the rubbish being spread, because we both knew there was no truth in it – none whatsoever. And what I could never work out, was why on earth you and Mair ever even started it off. I mean – other than some horrible sort of sport, what on earth was the point of it all? Were you both bored?'

Stephanie was about to speak when Althea nodded sagely saying, 'Oh dear me, yes – some people are only able to glean joy from the misery of others, you know.'

Hoping that her mother-in-law would spot her glance that was screaming, 'Please stop talking', Stephanie tried to throw a little oil on the rough waters. 'But I'm sure there's another side to all of this, isn't there, Marjorie?'

She couldn't imagine what the woman's justification for causing such unhappiness would be, but she deserved an opportunity to speak her piece, to apologize to her victim.

'I only said what I believed in my heart to be the truth.' Marjorie's statement was made with a straight face, and a gravity that suggested she was – at that moment – being truthful. 'Elizabeth, I realize now that was not the case, but please believe me when I tell you I absolutely believed that you and the Reverend Ebenezer Roberts were embroiled in a passionate affair, that even involved making love on the organ bench.'

Stephanie was speechless; no one had told her what the scandal had been about, and she was only too aware that her shock must be showing on her face, because Althea's nostrils were flaring with delight as she all but hid her face behind a large slice of sponge.

You knew this would come out, and you never warned me, you little minx, thought Stephanie as she tried to control her expression.

Elizabeth reacted in a way that Stephanie had to admit she found very strange. She smiled. Almost kindly. Then she chuckled wryly and said, 'You know – I believe you, Marjorie, I do. Though – come on, be honest – me and old Ebenezer? Get a grip. Do you know that he's still completely oblivious to the fact that this rumor swirled for months? To this very day, he hasn't a clue. He's that innocent. He knew people were whispering about him, but he had no idea why. He even started having more parish council meetings to be able to address what he feared were moves to have him removed from the parish, which there were…but he could never get to the bottom of it. Luckily for him, no one had the guts to tell him to his face. They preferred to snigger behind his back, poor man. And any solidarity I voiced on his behalf was only seen as "proof" that we were at it like rabbits.'

Althea cleared her throat rather loudly, leading Elizabeth to pick up her tea again, stick out her chin, and add, 'Well, that's what folks were saying. Most unseemly. I had to put a stop to it.'

'You were right to do what you did,' said Marjorie sheepishly. 'But I've never been able to build up the courage to apologize to you. But I will now. I'm very sorry. I just…I just…like I said, I thought it was all true.'

Stephanie could almost see a path toward a harmonious future, when Althea piped up, 'But why did you believe it, Marjorie? I never did, I saw it for what it was – utter twaddle. As Elizabeth said – with the Reverend Roberts? Tosh.'

Stephanie wondered what Marjorie was thinking. Her eyes were darting, and she looked…trapped. What was her problem? And Althea was quite right – why on earth *had* she believed such a thing to be true?

Marjorie inhaled for what appeared to be about five seconds, then blurted out, 'It was Mair. All Mair. She told me she'd seen the two of you together…you know, very much together…like two coats of paint together. And she was so convincing that I believed her. She told me so many things that I thought she couldn't have made up: where she'd seen the two of you, and what you'd been doing. She went into lots of details about that. And I was horrified. You see, I'd always thought of the reverend as an innocent, too, so I believed her when she said she'd seen you doing all sorts of things to seduce him. And he's single, so there wouldn't really be anything wrong with it for him – except that you were…are…a married woman, and adultery's a big no-no for him, isn't it? Anyway…there you have it, I believed her. And I felt…well, I felt very let down by him. And you. You were handling all the committees at that time, and you really were lording it over us all a bit – sorry, but I'm being truthful now –

and I didn't like that either. So all I did was mention how I felt about the two of you, and then people asked why, and I told them. I didn't feel as though I was spreading gossip, I felt I was sharing my feelings about something that was real – something that was actually happening. And when I got that letter from your solicitor, well it terrified me. And that was when I went to see Mair. And it all blew up after that.'

Althea was on the edge of her seat, her eyes glittering, which Stephanie thought dreadfully unbecoming.

'What blew up?' Apparently, Althea couldn't help herself.

Marjorie sighed. 'I went to the shop to tell Mair about the letter, but she'd had one, too. And what did she do about it? She laughed. She laughed at you, Elizabeth, and at the letter, and at me. And then she told me she'd made it all up. Well, no – that's not what she said. She called it "embroidering" which was worse, in a way.'

'Mair fed you some old guff and you swallowed it whole?' Elizabeth sounded unconvinced.

Marjorie was beginning to look quite distressed, and Stephanie's heart went out to her; she was watching a woman who was unused to admitting any shortcomings on her own part, and yet here she was, accepting she'd made an enormous error of judgement. Stephanie thought it best to hold her tongue and let the poor woman get through it in her own way.

'Is that why Mair sold the shop and moved away?' Althea sipped her tea innocently.

Marjorie appeared to be close to tears. 'I thought Mair was my best friend. In fact, I sometimes felt as though she was my only friend. People don't seem to ever open up around me, see…so I don't open up around them. But Mair? Oh, she was always so lovely to me. We'd spend hours nattering in the shop, we would, and we knew each other inside out. Or I thought we did. But what I saw in her then was wickedness, just pure wickedness. She'd done it for no reason at all, other than…well, she never said why – because there couldn't be a good reason, could there? But we had a terrible row, and lots of things were said that couldn't be unheard…and, yes, that's when she sold the shop and moved away. Because…' Marjorie sobbed, just once, 'because I said that if she didn't, I'd tell everyone about what she'd done, even if it meant people thought less of me, too. And that's what she did, she left.'

Elizabeth was considering her response – at least, that was Stephanie's guess, and Althea was – thankfully – petting McFli and seeming to be hardly taking notice of anything at all.

Sitting up again, McFli having been settled down, Althea surprised everyone by saying, 'Mair Jones always kept a good shop – always clean, well-stocked and so forth – and she always managed to communicate with her customers in a way that allowed them to think that they, as an individual, were very important to her. Now that's good business, that is, because people like to go somewhere where they feel valued. Her daughter, Sharon, has much the same intuitive gift, but she lacks something her mother had, in spades.'

Stephanie sighed. 'And what's that, Althea?'

'Mair Jones had the ability to drip poison into a person's ear so gently that they didn't even know it was happening to them. She won others to her viewpoint gradually, inch by inch, then, when they agreed with something she'd dropped into the conversation, something about another person, for example, she'd pass that on as something they'd said…something that had originated with them.'

'That's right,' said Marjorie. 'She did that. Exactly that. Sometimes she'd tell me I'd said something that I hadn't – or I didn't think I had, but she was so convincing that I wondered if I had…even though I knew I didn't really feel that way.'

Althea continued, 'She did it to young Ian Cottesloe's father on one occasion, when I still lived here and he was my driver. Mair was quite new to the village back then, and I didn't know her well. Old Ian was an agreeable man – agreeable to the point that he'd avoid conflict of any sort, at any price. And yet word reached me that he'd claimed I was less than supportive of him and his family. So I spoke to him about it, and he explained what had happened: Mair had taken some innocent remarks of his about how he'd much prefer to live at the Hall completely out of context, and the only reason he'd said what he'd said was to agree with an observation she'd made about how much easier that would make life for him, and how much more he'd see of his family. The rumor began that I didn't have the entire Cottesloe family living at the Hall because I wanted him all to myself. Now, both he and I knew that the reason he didn't live in was because his wife quite specifically wanted to stay in the village to be close to her mother, and we discussed it…allowing me to work out quite quickly what had happened. I had words with Mair about it, and no more was said.'

Elizabeth said thoughtfully, 'So the gossip about me was all Mair's doing, eh?'

Marjorie nodded. 'Like I said, all I could think to do was to get her to leave. And I must admit it's been much better since she did. I mean, Sharon's wonderful at keeping the news circulating around the village, but none of it has the…edge that Mair's conversations had, if you know what I mean.'

'And you've never seen fit to tell me all this before now because…?' Elizabeth Fernley leaned toward Marjorie, who receded into her seat.

Stephanie saw Marjorie falter for a moment, then she said quietly, 'Because I felt so terribly guilty about it all, Elizabeth. I've mended my ways, really I have. I mean, I still like to chat to people, and sometimes chat about other people, but I do try to make sure that what I'm saying is positive. And Mair's really turned over a new leaf – she's all about good works nowadays, ask anyone.'

Stephanie knew for a fact that Marjorie was casting as flattering a light as possible upon her continued gossipmongering.

'Yes, Mair's an incredibly active hospital visitor these days,' said Althea nonchalantly, 'as I believe I have already mentioned, Stephanie, dear.'

Stephanie recalled what Althea had said on an earlier occasion, and also remembered Althea's other acid remarks about Mair's so-called 'good works'.

'Yes, Althea, you did mention that.' Stephanie nodded her thanks. 'Well, let's hope the "good" part of Mair's works in the community is effective, because it sounds as though she's got rather a lot of bad to make up for. Now then – do we all feel we've had a fair opportunity to examine the causes of the problems back then? Do we feel able to put them aside, and move on, as one?'

Althea dimpled. 'So why have you been saying that Elizabeth shouldn't be the person to run the antique shop in the village when it opens, Marjorie?'

You just can't let anything go, can you? Stephanie stared daggers at her mother-in-law, but their eyes never met, because Althea was smiling sweetly at Marjorie.

Elizabeth tensed. 'You've what?'

'I haven't,' bleated Marjorie. 'I promise, my hand on my heart, that I have never said anything of the sort.'

'Excuse me,' said Althea, sitting up very straight. 'You were in church on Sunday morning chatting to Iris Lewis, correct?' Marjorie nodded, looking confused. 'And you said to her that you would not be able to support the choice of Elizabeth to run the antique shop – is that also correct?'

Marjorie's brow furrowed. 'I do think I might have said that I couldn't see how that would work out. But what I meant, Elizabeth, was that you still do so much here – how could you fit in running an antiques shop, too?' She spoke directly to Elizabeth. 'Honestly, that's all I said.'

'Then why on earth did Tudor Evans say that you didn't want Elizabeth working in the village every day?' Althea looked truly puzzled.

Stephanie felt she had to step in. 'So, let me get this straight, Althea. Tudor told you, that Iris Lewis had told him, that Marjorie had said she was against Elizabeth running the shop. Is that right?'

Althea shook her head, 'No – I saw Tudor talking to Wendy Jenkins after the service, who'd been chatting with her Aunt Iris after Marjorie had left her…when she'd gone to talk to Carol about something to do with Sarah Hughes – yes, that was it. So I believed that what Tudor said to me about Marjorie's opinion had come through that route. But, you know, thinking about it again, maybe

Tudor said that Marjorie was *bound* to be against it, rather than that she *was*.'

Stephanie sighed with exasperation. 'So when you told Alexander that Marjorie was dead set against this idea, you…*you*…were the one spreading an untruth that had stemmed from an innocent comment. Have I got that right now, Althea?'

'Oh dear, I suppose I was. I say, I'm terribly sorry. Still, if I hadn't made that silly mistake we'd never have got this all sorted out, would we? And we have, and we can all move forward with the air quite beautifully cleared. So let's look on the bright side, eh?'

Stephanie said nothing. In fact, she quite literally bit her tongue, thinking that Althea's dimples should carry warning signs.

CHAPTER THIRTY

As they drove along the A40, having skirted Brecon itself, Annie could feel the tension in the air. Carol wasn't one for using strong language, usually, but Annie had heard her mutter quite a few words under her breath when they'd been stuck behind slow-moving vehicles and, although they were all Welsh words, she was pretty sure they weren't anything Carol would be using if she thought that Annie could understand them.

'For heaven's sake, get a move on,' said Carol irritably.

'Look, I know we want to get there as far ahead of the funeral starting as possible,' observed Annie, 'but you can't drive over that car in front, and if you get past them there's a whole row just a bit ahead anyway. You might want to pull back a bit, eh?'

'Says the non-driver in the passenger seat,' snapped Carol. She quickly added, 'Sorry. You're right,' and slowed the car a little – allowing Annie to stop gripping the seat and crunching her toes in her shoes, for which she was grateful.

'So the plan when we get there—' began Annie.

'*If* we get there, at this speed,' interrupted Carol.

'When we get there we're on the lookout for anyone wandering about the graveyard clutching a cast iron rose, is that right?' Annie sounded skeptical, because she was.

Carol unhunched herself and sat back in her seat. 'Essentially, yes. Christine found out that cast iron roses had been present at several of the interments of those whose families had received wreaths, so at least this opportunity gives us a chance to maybe see someone leaving such an item before the observances begin. This Jedediah bloke is being buried in the family plot, which is why this is all happening in what my research tells me is an otherwise "closed" graveyard. It's essentially full, and people are now interred at the cemetery of their choice rather than in this church's graveyard.'

'Where are you going to end up, Car? Have you and Dave talked about that?'

Annie could tell she'd surprised her friend because she actually took her eyes off the road ahead for a moment to give Annie a quick look. 'Where *what*?'

Annie added, 'Where are you going to be buried, or cremated, or whatever? Have you two talked about it? Eustelle and Rodney were telling me when I was with them last weekend that they're both thinking of being cremated locally, then having their ashes taken back to St. Lucia. They called it "going home". Which I found odd, because I'd have imagined that they'd have thought of Plaistow, or at least London, as "home" by now. They've been away from St. Lucia for twice as long as they were ever there. But, no – apparently that's where they want to end up. In the sea, there. I said I could put them in the sea here – their ashes, I mean – and they could end up going all the way around the world, that way, but they weren't happy about that.'

'That's the sort of thing you talk to your parents about when you visit them?' Carol sounded gobsmacked.

'Yeah – well, we talk about everything. No reason not to. At least I know what they want. Don't you know what your parents want?'

Carol didn't answer, but overtook the car in front with a swerving maneuver that left Annie shaking. 'Gordon Bennett, Car – that was close. Let's get there alive, shall we? It's all well and good me telling Tude I want to be cremated then scattered over the village green, but I don't want him to have to be doing that in the foreseeable future, thank you very much.'

'The village green? Really? I'd have thought you'd have wanted your ashes scattered along a Tube tunnel, somewhere on one of the Underground lines that runs through the East End, if anywhere,' said Carol, smiling. 'But it's nice to know you feel so attached to Anwen-by-Wye that you want to stay there forever.'

Annie sighed. 'All I really want is to be close to Tude, to be honest, and I can't see him ever leaving the place, can you? I know he's from the Swansea area, but our village has been his home for a very long time now, and I think he's taken root, so to speak. And I want to take root with him.'

'Lovely,' replied Carol – distracted by her phone ringing. 'Can you get that?'

'It's Llinos,' said Annie, 'I'll put her on the speaker. Hiya, Llinos – Annie and Carol here. We're on the road.'

'Just a quick one,' said Llinos, sounding a bit out of breath. 'A couple of things: first, there's a detective sergeant who wants to talk to you about this Uninvited Undertaker case, as soon as you can, please – I'll text you his number; secondly, I happen to know why he wants to talk to you. So listen up. Ed Hughes? Now deemed a homicide: yes, he was stuffed full of opioids, but that's not what killed him. It seems he was strangled – which it was hard to tell initially, because of the condition of the remains. Anyway – it's all kicked off at this end – which is why the team wants you in. Any of you, or all of you. Maybe Carol? Anyway, I'll text you his number, and you really need to talk to him, pronto. They've already had a word with Ed's close friend Archie Hammond – the bloke who found, and reported, Ed's body. He's now said that, yes, he had seen an unusual figure hanging around the caravan park in recent times. And I'll just add this – lay off this case until we know more. That whole list of people you gave us? Every death is being looked into as I speak – in case more of them are suspicious. It might be that this so-called "undertaker" is, in fact, doing the deed himself. You won't go doing anything silly, will you?'

Annie and Carol shared a snatched glance.

'No,' they chorused.

'I'll get in touch as soon as I can,' said Carol. 'Thanks for this, Llinos. Talk later. Got to go now.'

'Gordon Bennett,' said Annie. 'That's a turn up. We're still going to this graveyard, right?'

'Here's the turning,' said Carol, 'and here comes the change in the weather they've been promising, too, by the looks of it. You're sure about going through with this?'

'Course I am, doll – we're on a case. Besides, we're just here for a look-see, in't we?'

Annie had noticed that they'd been driving toward the gathering cloud cover for some time, but now she realized that the sky had taken on the bruised look it got just before thunder began to rumble.

'I wish I'd brought a mac, or something,' she noted. 'All I've got is what I'm wearing, and I don't think these thin sleeves are going to be much good if it starts to pour.'

'Let's worry about that later,' said Carol, now hunched over the wheel again. 'Keep a lookout for the church, will you? Check the app – it should be close, now.'

'There's a sign, over there.' Annie slung her arm across Carol's body in the direction of a small signpost.

'Well spotted.'

'They need to cut back the hedges a bit more,' remarked Annie. 'This is more like a lane than a road – just as well we know where we're going. Look, there it is.'

Annie thought that the stone church at the end of the lane looked as though it had emerged from the landscape hundreds of years earlier. Beyond it was a small lake, and the setting was suitably tranquil.

'It looks old enough to have a full graveyard,' said Annie, 'or not. There seem to be lots of areas without gravestones, don't there?'

'Actually, I looked it up, and it's not that old. Built in the late 1800s in the Gothic style, though I agree it's weathered nicely.'

As they pulled into the parking area beside the little lake, Annie swiveled her head to get a better look at their destination. 'It looks like the graveyard goes right around the church. I wonder why there are so many big bits of grass with nothing poking up.'

'Maybe the stones have fallen over, or maybe there are those flat graves, without standing stones, you know?'

'True enough,' agreed Annie.

Carol added, 'Anyway – there aren't any other cars here, and that means we might have beaten the Uninvited Undertaker to the place – or they've already been and gone…'cause I can't imagine anyone walking along that lane we just drove down to get here, can you?'

As the pair exited the car Annie said, 'No, I shouldn't think so. Though they could have parked at that pub we passed and cut across the fields from there. See – there's a footpath just there, giving access to the lake. Anyway, phones out, cameras at the ready, alright? Let's see what we can see.'

The pair entered the graveyard through a lychgate, which reminded Annie of the much more ancient one at St David's, in the village. She spotted something. 'That must be where they're burying him,' she said, pointing. 'Look – they've put artificial grass around the edge of that great big hole.'

Carol and Annie picked their way carefully among the tombstones, then peered into the open grave. It wasn't as deep as Annie had imagined it would be.

She said, 'In't they supposed to be six feet down at least? And then there's the depth of the coffin. Is it six feet to the bottom or the top of the coffin? You know, I've never thought about that before.'

Carol was pacing around the opening, snapping away. 'It's a family grave, so this might be the last coffin to go in, I suppose. Maybe not enough room to go deeper? I don't know – but what I do know is that I want us to have a good look around inside the church, to see if there are any floral tributes or a cast iron rose in there already, because there's nothing at all here. But if the church is open, one of us needs to stay somewhere where we can keep an eye on this spot.'

Thunder rolled in the distance.

Looking up, Annie said, 'Here it comes. Just what we need. As if this place wasn't creepy enough as it is. The sky's going almost black…well, sort of purplish black, anyway. That's not good.'

Another rumble of thunder seemed much closer.

'The weather's coming in fast,' agreed Carol. 'Look, there's a place over there, under the eaves of the church porch – let's at least head there, see if the place is open. If it is, I'll go in and you can keep watch, and stay dry. Oh – here come the first big drops now.'

The women scampered out of the rain, but they were both soaked to the skin before they reached the shelter of the porch.

'I suppose one advantage of having almost no hair is that I don't look like a drowned rat,' said Annie, unable to hide her grin as she looked at her friend, whose naturally curly blonde hair was now hanging down in dripping corkscrews.

Carol pulled a large piece of cloth from her massive handbag. 'Like every good mother, I am always prepared,' she said, rubbing the cloth over her wet head. 'And I have any number of pouches of apple sauce, as well as wet wipes and a spare nappy, if you need them.' She chuckled. 'Right – it's open, I'm going inside – you hang about here and keep your eyes peeled.'

Annie followed the underwhelming instructions as Carol disappeared into what was an echoing gloom, while the rain bounced off the path that led to the porch and thundered on the roof above her head. The rain was so heavy that Annie could hardly see as far as the lychgate they'd come through earlier, and it was so dark that it was as though an immediate twilight had fallen. A clap of thunder made her jump, and was followed by a flash of lightning four seconds later. Annie had learned to time the gap as a child. The smell of the petrichor – Annie loved that word – hung in the air, and she breathed in deeply; after weeks of drought, the ground had to be soaking up the rain, she thought. And she knew the local farmers would all be delighted – because Carol had been banging on about that for a couple of weeks.

Was that someone at the gate? Annie really couldn't be certain. She squinted. Yes, someone was coming toward her, toward the open grave, in any case. She withdrew further under the porch, and was glad she'd happened to be wearing navy when Carol had phoned her, because she reckoned she'd be hard to spot in the gloom and the shadows.

The figure approaching the grave was better prepared for the weather than Annie was; it was wearing one of those long, waxed-cotton coats, and a hat – with a wide brim, a bit like a cowboy hat. *Odd. If we were gong to spot the Uninvited Undertaker I'd have expected a top hat at least,* thought Annie. Could this be the person they'd been hunting for?

Torn between losing sight of the figure and attracting Carol's attention, Annie crouched as low as she could and braved the rain, which was falling so hard that it actually hurt the top of her head. Another clap of thunder followed immediately by a streak across the sky made Annie squeal aloud – alerting the figure to her presence.

Nothing to lose, now. This bloke might have killed someone – I can't let him get away with that. She stood up straight and ran toward the figure. She saw an arm dart out – *throwing something into the grave?* – then the figure turned and came right toward Annie, which surprised her.

As their two bodies met, Annie did her best to wrap her long arms around her target and was surprised to feel the massive coat sag beneath her grasp, until she was hugging a slight figure through the slithery waxed cotton. As Annie's momentum outmatched that of her quarry, the pair staggered, then Annie felt herself losing her footing and she toppled over into thin air – a mass of flailing arms and legs.

Annie screamed. Thunder boomed. The metallic smell of electricity filled her nostrils. She opened her eyes to find herself at the bottom of the open grave with the hat-wearing figure looking down at her, the silhouette against the bruised sky possibly that of a killer. She strained to make out any facial features, but ended up having to shield her face from the pounding rain.

She was also aware that her upper thigh was hurting; she rearranged herself as much as she could to try to work out what was going on and felt about a bit. Her navy trousers had turned black in the rain, but her hand came away with her palm covered with blood, which was immediately washed away. She felt about a bit more and discovered a long-stemmed metal rose – its full-blooming head half broken, a jagged edge protruding.

Above her, the figure had disappeared, but the rain was incessant; she felt as though buckets of water were being thrown onto her. Trembling at the thought of exactly where she was, alarmed by the blood and the broken rose – as well as the splintered wood she'd felt beneath her bum, and the knowledge of what lay beneath it – all Annie could do was scream for help, and hope that Carol would hear her.

CHAPTER THIRTY-ONE

Mavis had reached the point where she really did need the lavatory, and called out as plaintively as possible, 'Help! Somebody help! I really, really need to pee!'

Once again she heard voices above her, then the sound of more than one person coming down the stairs.

The figures Mavis could vaguely make out through whatever cloth was covering her head – *a pillowcase?* – looked to be about the same size as each other, but only the man spoke.

'My mate's going to help you to the toilet. No funny business, right?'

Mavis's pathetic 'I promise' came out as no more than a squeak.

A hand grabbed Mavis by the arm quite roughly, and the man said, 'We're going to cut the tape on your ankles, but don't bother trying to make a run for it, the front door's locked and you need a key.'

Mortice lock, too bad, thought Mavis. *But handy to know.* 'Alright.'

She felt the tightness around her ankles disappear and waggled her legs a bit. The hands holding her pulled her forward, and she felt as though she might topple.

'Hang on, she's been on that floor for ages, she needs a minute to get her act together,' said the man. Mavis heard the other figure, the one holding her – *a woman* – tut and sigh.

'Come on, up you get,' said the man, lending a hand.

Mavis managed to get to her feet, and allowed herself a moment or two to get her balance and make sure she was feeling up to moving, which she was clearly about to do.

'Please…I really need to go,' she whined.

'Yeah, yeah, let's move,' said the man, and he and the woman steered Mavis out of the room and into what she imagined was a darker hallway, then her foot hit something.

'Careful now, you've got to go upstairs.'

The journey was quite exhausting, with Mavis having to work hard to keep her balance without being able to see, or use her hands to steady herself. Finally at the top, she was steered forward. They all stopped, and there was the noise of a door opening.

'In you go. Mind the threshold,' said the man.

Mavis stumbled a little as her foot caught the change of flooring, and four hands grabbed her.

'I'll shut the door, and leave you two to it,' said the man, sounding relieved.

Mavis's mind raced as she stood in the room, a small patch of light ahead of her. 'I don't know who you are, and you might be very happy to help me with the next bit, but I think it's only decent if you let me have my privacy. Please. I beg you. I don't think I could go with you here – no matter how desperate I might be.'

A sigh. The door opened, there was a whispered back and forth, then the man called, 'She's going to cut your hands loose, but you have to count to ten before you take the bag off your head. Promise?'

'I promise.'

'There, she promised,' he said.

Hands fumbled with Mavis's wrists, then she felt them fall free, and she began to count. 'One, two, three…' The door was slammed shut.

Mavis pulled what was, after all, a pillowcase off her head and took in her surroundings. Bath, toilet, sink. She locked the door, shouted, 'I'm running the water so you can't hear me – I don't like that. And I might be a bit more than two minutes.' She added a plaintive 'Sorry,' for good measure.

She stepped to the window which was glazed with modesty glass at the bottom, but had clear glass above that. She balanced on the toilet rim and peered outside. Back gardens – one with a couple of kids in it, kicking a ball around – a row of semi-detached council houses, most of which were in decent shape, another street matching it beyond…and a police car, and Mavis's own little Morris Minor Traveller.

Her sprits lifted; she was just a couple of blocks from where she'd been snatched – and the police were there, which meant that the WISE women must be involved somehow. How wonderful!

She dared to try to open the window, and the bottom half slid up without making a sound. Mavis couldn't believe her luck. But the opening was tiny – she didn't think she'd be able to squeeze through – and there was a sheer drop to the rubble-strewn garden below, which explained why her captors had felt confident that she wouldn't be able to escape.

Mavis considered her options – which were just about nil. Should she shout for help, and hope that someone – other than a couple of small children – might hear her cries? Or would that merely serve to alert her captors, who might then…well, she didn't want to think about that.

There were a few bits of make-up on the counter beside the sink, but not even a medicine cabinet, and nothing useful hiding in drawers, because there weren't any. There was a grubby-looking, massive bar of soap, a towel that could do with a wash – and a boil-wash, at that – and nothing else.

'You alright in there?'

Mavis bleated, 'Please go away – I can't do what I need to do if I think you're listening. You know there's no way out of here, so just let me be.'

'Fair enough.' The man clomped away.

Think, Mavis…think.

Got it!

She grabbed one of the lipsticks from the countertop and began to write a message on the toilet paper; she kept it brief and direct – even so, she needed to use a second lipstick. She wrapped the toilet paper around the soap – which she made sure was dry by rubbing it with the grimy towel first – then wrote: FOR THE POLICE – URGENT!! REWARD IF YOU DO IT on the outside of the bundle.

She stuck as much of the upper part of her body out of the window as she could, and waved a long length of toilet paper about until she caught the attention of the two children playing with the ball. Once they were looking at her, she threw the bundle with all her might, and her best aim, hoping it would reach its target.

It landed in the garden where the children were now standing, which was the best she could have hoped for. Unable to be sure of their ages, she crossed her fingers that at least one of them was able to read what she'd written. She pointed frantically at the bundle as the children eyed it with suspicion from a distance, then one of them turned and ran inside their house.

Mavis pulled herself back inside, took advantage of the facilities – with some relief – and then waited, without flushing, knowing that the longer she could stay in the bathroom, the longer she'd be unbound, and hopefully the closer she'd be to the police knocking on every door in the street she was in. She'd judged she was in the fourth or fifth home along, but might have miscalculated.

Then she had another idea: she wrote HELP in the biggest letters possible on a long run of toilet paper, and stuck herself out of the window again. Below her, a young woman in cut-off jeans and a tank top was staring up at the bathroom window, shielding her eyes from the sun. Mavis waved and held up her 'sign'. The woman looked at the bundle in her hand, dragged her children indoors, then gave Mavis two thumbs up before following them.

CHAPTER THIRTY-TWO

Annie hadn't been happy about being taken to hospital, but the kerfuffle that had followed her falling into the grave at the church had left Carol with no option but to get the fire and ambulance services to come to the site – the first to get Annie out of the grave, the second to tend to her wounds. The chance of a potentially dangerous infection – given where she'd been when she'd sustained a deep laceration – was the only thing that kept Annie inside the ambulance as it drove off. As the doors were shut, Carol could hear her chum speaking to Tudor on the phone.

The mourners for the deceased were already utterly discombobulated when they arrived for the funeral, because they, and the hearse in which their loved one was being transported, had had to back out of the lane to allow the ambulance to get out first – with its sirens blaring.

Carol had to explain why the damage to their ancestor's coffin had happened, which all sounded bizarre, given that she didn't feel it appropriate to tell them about the Uninvited Undertaker. Then there were endless conversations about what should be done. Should the funeral – *could* the funeral – go ahead? Did the shattered coffin need to be removed and repaired before they could bury Jedediah Williams on top of it? Were there laws, or bylaws, or church rules about this sort of thing? Could they all make up their own minds and proceed, or not?

Carol sat in the church, drenched and dripping, worrying about her chum, and only too fully aware that they were no closer to catching the figure Annie had seen in the graveyard. She'd said she wasn't sure if it was a man or a woman, but had emphasized to Carol that – whatever the gender – the person had been small. Given that Annie was six feet tall, that didn't narrow down the range of heights very much, but the size of the body within the large coat had really made an impression on her – which she'd passed on to Carol. A thin 'person' of less than six feet in height? Not much to go on, really.

Eventually, it was agreed that the police were not required, and that the vicar could go ahead with the funeral – a phone call to the diocesan office in Brecon clarified that the family could make their decision as they pleased – so Carol left the party of mourners to get on with the burial, though she did come away with a photograph of the broken iron rose, the piece itself having been taken away by a paramedic out of an abundance of caution.

Placing one of Albert's blankets on the driver's seat, so as not to completely ruin the upholstery, Carol made her way back to Anwen-by-Wye along roads that were still awash after the downpour – the dry ground and overwhelmed drainage systems being unable to cope with so much rain in such a short period. It seemed such a pity that water was running along the road itself, and not able to benefit the grass and crops that so desperately needed it, that Carol did what she rarely did; she phoned the family farm in Carmarthenshire, with the aim of finding out if they'd had rain that far away and, if so, whether it might help their difficult situation.

She left a brief message on the answerphone, unsurprised that no one had been there to pick up, then phoned Christine to tell her about Annie, and hoping for some positive news about Mavis.

'Carol – is that you?'

Carol was puzzled that Christine hadn't recognized her number. 'Yes, of course it's me. Are you alright? Any news about Mavis?'

'Yes, to both questions.'

'And?'

'Well, we know where she is, and we believe she's alright. But we're waiting for some more officers to arrive before we do anything else.'

Carol wondered about the wisdom of having made her call while she was concentrating on driving home. 'You'll need to explain what you mean.' Carol could hear a strange sound at Christine's end. 'What's that noise?'

Christine shouted, 'That's the noise of the rain on the roof of the police car I'm sitting in – it is chucking it down here. Forget cats and dogs, I think we've wandered into cows and horses territory here.'

'Knives and forks,' replied Carol.

'What?'

'Never mind, just a Welsh thing.'

'Oh, right. It's cobblers' knives for the Irish, though I don't usually say that because it sounds so weird. "Knives and forks" is better, as are – in my humble opinion – cows and horses, because cats and dogs don't weigh nearly as much.'

The two women chuckled wryly.

Carol said, 'Come on then – Mavis is alright. Excellent. But *what?*'

'Alrighty – from the top. I came to the place where Mavis's photos showed her last location to be – and there's her car, right enough. It's all locked up. Engine cold to the touch – and this was before the rain began, so I knew it had been standing idle a while. Anyways, I phone up the local Bobbies, as we agreed, and I explain everything to them – including the fact I'm being buzzed by hoodies on bikes the whole time I'm standing here, so I am – which they said I was to ignore…calm as you like.'

Carol usually enjoyed the way Christine was able to spin a tale, but felt herself getting impatient.

'What about Mavis?'

Christine told Carol about a worried mother, a ball of toilet paper, a house-to-house enquiry, and the fact that one of the two constables who'd joined her at Mavis's car had knocked at the door of number thirty-seven, got punched in the face for his trouble, and was now on his way to hospital. She was stuck in the back of a police car – where she'd been told to stay, in no uncertain terms – while the now three officers on the scene awaited the arrival of some sort of negotiating team. Mavis was trapped in a house that was rented from the local authority by a bloke in his twenties, one Frank Spencer.

'Like the character in *Some Mothers Do 'Ave 'Em*?'

'So the council reckons. You've got to wonder about some parents, haven't you? Surely they knew they were naming their son after that idiot of a character?' Christine sounded incredulous.

'Oh, I don't know, Christine, if he's only in his twenties, his parents might be too young to have ever seen that program; it was on in the 1970s, wasn't it?'

'I'm only in my twenties, and I know about it,' was Christine's sharp reply.

Carol sighed – something was making Christine very shirty these days, but now wasn't the time to try to find out what it was. 'Anyway – back to Mavis: is she in any danger? Is this Frank person the one who injured the officer? Is he likely to do her harm? Come on, I need to know.'

'We think it was Frank who punched the officer, sending him reeling. They've taken him off in an ambulance as a matter of course. That's about all we know. The woman who came running out of her house to alert the police who were already in the street said she'd seen someone waving what she thought was a long bit of toilet paper with the word HELP on it out of a bathroom window. That was obviously Mavis, because she'd managed to write a message the same way and get it over to the woman's garden. The message gave her name, rough location, said she'd been kidnapped, and then asked whoever found the note to take it to the police. Which the woman did. They, and I, were almost outside her front door, see, which is where I'd found Mavis's car. By the way, I'm owed fifty quid in expenses, because Mavis's note mentioned a reward. Hang on a tick…yes, this must be them. Right – I'm handling this, and I'll keep you updated. Now, how about you and Annie? Any luck at that graveyard?'

Carol gave her the short version.

Christine replied briefly, 'Give Annie my best. By the way, listen up: the list of florists I sent the photo of that wreath to is in the cloud. I sent it there while I was sitting here twiddling my thumbs and worrying about Mavis. Displacement activity, I suppose. Everyone I got through to said they hadn't made the wreath – so not much help there, but it's a loose end I realized I hadn't tied up. And one more thing: that cast iron rose.'

'Yes.'

'Clementine's fiancé is a blacksmith; might he know about people who make such items? Just a thought. I met him over at the Hall when I was there for a meeting the other day – nice bloke. Big. Bear-like. Massive beard. Jools something-or-other. Althea will know, as will Stephanie. But you could always phone the Hall and ask for him, I suppose.'

Carol's heart sank as she realized she'd let one ball drop. 'Alright, good idea, thanks for that. Talk later.'

She'd almost reached the turning to Anwen-by-Wye when she phoned Althea, which she knew she had to do, not only to pass on the information about Mavis, but to ask if anyone had managed to locate Jools Tavistock yet – who she suddenly thought Annie would no doubt now be referring to as the Fleeing Fiancé, if only she knew of his existence at all, which Carol realized she didn't.

Ah well, I'll tell her when I can talk to her. Now – I'd better get home for a few minutes, feed my child, then phone the police about Ed Hughes…and do a bit more digging into Jools flaming Tavistock.

CHAPTER THIRTY-THREE

When Mavis MacDonald walked into the Dower House there was still light in the sky, despite the fact it was just before ten at night. Indeed, it seemed to Mavis that it was no darker than when she'd finally emerged from Frank Spencer's home that afternoon, into the thunderstorm.

She was feeling tired and dirty, but absolutely delighted to be back in 'her place'. McFli was all over her; Cook had left lots in the fridge before she'd departed for the day, in case Mavis did manage to get back before morning; Althea veered between being helpfully solicitous and uselessly emotional.

Finally bathed and swaddled in a massive fluffy robe, Mavis sat with Althea at the dining table with platters of cold meats, pâtés with crackers, and a massive trifle – an eclectic variety. She enjoyed picking her way through them, and Althea helped out by taking one small portion of the trifle after another.

With the story about where Mavis had been while working on the case, then what had happened afterwards, all told, Althea pressed, 'So how exactly did you manage to get away? Did they send in the SWAT team with flash-bangs and so forth?'

Mavis shook her head. 'You're watching far too much TV, dear. No, they phoned the man who'd been overseeing my captivity on his mobile and they talked. Then he opened the front door and they came in and got me.'

Althea looked disappointed, which made Mavis laugh. 'I'm sorry I wasnae plucked from the hands of a power-crazed captor by a bevvy of gun-wielding men in black – though they were wearing black, but that's by-the-by. There were no firearms involved, and I have made it quite clear to the officers who interviewed me that the man in question – whose name turns out to be Frank – was most kind and thoughtful in his handling of me. It was the other one who was the trouble; she was the one who knocked me out and dragged me to his house, you see. The poor man had to go along with it all after that, I dare say.'

'Who? Who?'

Mavis discounted making any owlish jokes, and replied, 'A woman by the name of Tracy Daniels.'

'Who's she?'

'The older sister of the nurse I'd been following. I told you, dear; I was following Veronica Daniels. Keep up.'

'I'm old, and it's been a long day,' replied Althea, sulking. 'And why did she do it?'

'Trying to protect her sister, no doubt. Frank had mentioned that I'd been following their "angel"; maybe that's Tracy's pet name for her sister, but I didn't think so when he said it.'

'And she was the one dealing drugs? Nurse Daniels?'

'I believe she was in possession of all of the late Mrs Thomas's medications, and she visited the most seedy-looking houses in the area. So, yes, I'd say that was it. Though, to be honest, I'd no' have thought that of her, having met the girl.'

'Are the police going to grill you again?' Althea's eyes sparkled.

Mavis sighed. 'I'm a victim and a witness – so they'll no' be grilling me, dear. But, yes, we all agreed it was best if I came back here to get a good night's rest, and I'll go into the station in Cardiff tomorrow morning. Now – I've spoken to everyone who needs to know I'm safe, and I am rather tired. I've no idea how well I'm going to sleep after that food, but I was ravenous, so had to have something. I suggest we both go to bed now…and I wish you a good night's sleep too – though after all that rich trifle I suggest you keep some sort of digestive aid on your bedside table tonight.'

'I shall sleep very well, thank you. And I was comfort eating. It's been a stressful day all around. First Clemmie, then Jools, then Elizabeth and Marjorie, and then you. I can hardly believe it.'

Mavis was almost at the foot of the staircase when she turned and said, 'I don't understand any of that. Are you going to explain tonight – or can it all wait until the morning?'

She stared at the dowager as Althea took a moment to make her decision. 'It can all wait. Let's make sure you get a good night's sleep. Then we can catch up over breakfast.'

'Agreed.'

As Mavis lay awake in her bed, she allowed her body to fully relax for the first time in what seemed like days on end. She was safe. She was surrounded by all the creature comforts, and she'd broken a case that would, she had no doubt, result in far fewer unlawful drugs being in circulation. Despite the discomfort of her captivity, she felt she'd done a good job, and now that the police were involved, she knew that The Case of the Suspicious Sister was in good hands and she'd play her part as a witness as best she could.

WEDNESDAY 7th JUNE

CHAPTER THIRTY-FOUR

Althea hadn't slept well at all – though she was absolutely certain that had nothing to do with her pre-bedtime over-consumption of trifle. At least the day held some promise: the morning was one of those when it was obvious there'd been recent rain – the sky was a hazy azure, the foliage on the trees looked vividly fresh, and the grass immediately greener. But it was humid and still warm – the thunder hadn't broken the run of unseasonably hot weather the way everyone had hoped it would.

Having agreed with Cook that kippers would not be required that morning, she was nibbling dry toast and scanning the local news on her tablet when Mavis joined her.

'You're in the paper – well, online,' she said gleefully. 'They haven't used your name, but the Cardiff paper says it was "a major incident" involving "several specialized units", so that's quite big, isn't it? You never said there were lots of police involved; you gave me the impression there were just a few. I think you've been keeping things from me.'

'No' as much as you've been keeping from me,' said Mavis. Althea could tell by her friend's expression that she was about to be told off for…something.

'I don't know what you mean, Mavis. I say, could you ring for a fresh pot, please? I seem to have drunk most of this one.'

Mavis picked up the almost empty teapot and said, 'My legs still work, I'll fetch one.'

Althea steeled herself. Why might Mavis be cross with her? She hadn't done anything wrong, as far as she was aware.

They'd thrashed everything through about the disaster that had taken place on May Day; Althea's plan for a proper Maypole on the village green had resulted in chaos when it collapsed before it could even be used, landing on the roof of a car parked far too close to it. So that couldn't be it.

And it couldn't be because of the way things had turned out when Althea had tried to move that beehive in the old Land Rover, on her own. Once the police had found out it was her, they'd been really rather good about it all. *Of course* she'd kept her beekeeper's suit on while she was inside the vehicle – and her decision had been proved correct when the hive toppled over and the bees escaped. When the policeman stopped her for what he – quite unreasonably, she thought, given the circumstances – had called 'erratic driving', she'd tried to communicate to him that she couldn't open the door because he'd get hurt – possibly killed – if the bees all swarmed him. But maybe making actions suggesting shooting, throttling, and – eventually – a massive explosion to him through the closed window, with her face completely covered, hadn't been the wisest decision.

That had been a tricky one, come to think of it. Luckily, she'd been able to poke at her mobile phone with one, ungloved finger and Mavis had come along and had worked it all out. But that had been back in April, so Mavis couldn't want to rake that all over again, could she?

When Mavis returned with a fresh pot, and some extra toast, Althea sat a little more upright in her chair – ready to take whatever her friend might throw at her. But she didn't say anything.

Mavis poured herself a cup of tea and buttered some toast in the way only Mavis could, with a silent subtext of impending doom.

Eventually she said, 'I've been on the phone, and I hear from Carol that Jools Tavistock has made himself scarce, and I gather from Cook that Clementine's taken herself off to London, never to cross the threshold of Chellingworth Hall again.'

Althea poured more tea. 'Indeed.'

'And this would all be because Clementine somehow found out that you'd asked me to look into her fiancé's background? Or was it because you tried to make the fellow uneasy by telling him that was what I'd be doing?'

'Edward's not always as circumspect as one might hope, I fear.' Althea knew exactly how the news-network operated on the Estate, and had no doubt that absolutely everyone knew what had happened – docents included.

'And I further understand from Carol that Julian Tavistock must be an assumed name, or identity.'

'So she said.'

'And does Clementine know this?'

Althea squared her shoulders. 'Clementine told me the man had explained whatever secrets he was hiding, and then asserted her intention to marry him in spite of same. She didn't see fit to elaborate, so I have no idea what he's hiding, beyond whatever his real name might be.'

Mavis nodded slowly, which Althea knew could mean one of two things, neither of which bode well for her.

Mavis's tone was solemn. 'Carol is working hard to establish his identity, given what little we know about him, but it appears that – so far – she's drawing a blank. She's also still heavily involved with another case we're working on. Christine was told she might need to answer some more questions for the Cardiff police, but she's back at the barn, now. Annie has been released from hospital, but Tudor informs me she'll need a short recuperation; he's proposed that both she and Gertie stay at the pub under his oversight so they can both return to full fitness, together. I have agreed. So now Christine, Carol, and I – when I have fulfilled my duty to society by giving the Cardiff police all the information I can pertaining to the theft and distribution of harmful drugs – will have to focus our efforts on our paying clients' needs.'

'I'll pay,' snapped Althea, much more haughtily than she'd meant.

Mavis sighed. 'It's no' about the money, dear. I'm sorry – I put that badly – I meant we have a pressing situation.'

'What pressing situation? You won't tell me what you're up to.' Althea didn't care that she sounded petulant – she didn't like being left out of things. She felt useless enough as it was, and she relied upon Mavis to at least let her think about the cases she was working on, even if she couldn't help.

Mavis tilted her head – which was almost as dangerous as her doing things slowly – then said, 'Aye, well, there can be no harm in it, I dare say.'

As the women continued with their breakfast, Mavis told Althea about The Case of the Uninvited Undertaker. Althea was surprised, chilled, confused but, ultimately satisfied that she understood.

When Mavis had finished, Althea couldn't help but say, 'But I don't see that as an urgent case, Mavis. After all, everyone's dead, aren't they? They aren't going to get any deader. And people saying that a wreath arriving at their front door has upset them? Well, I think that's rather odd. After all, wouldn't one expect them to be much more upset by the death of their loved one? And you've no evidence to suggest that the person delivering the wreaths is killing these people, have you? I mean – how would they do it? They'd have to be knocking people off in places where you can't just waltz in and kill someone. Besides, the authorities would find out, wouldn't they?'

Mavis stared at the tablecloth as she finished her third piece of toast – *oh dear, staring* – then said, 'You're right. Everything you've said, given the facts as I've presented them to you, is quite correct. However, we have a client who is dealing with customers who *are* upset about the wreaths; Sarah Hughes, in the village, is one of those who's been shaken by it, for example, though it turned out to be her husband's uncle who had…died, as I said. And I understand from Cook that everyone who lives close-by is now on edge, the Hugheses' situation being generally known about, of course. I pity anyone trying to make a legitimate floral delivery in the vicinity – they'd be mobbed by terrified villagers.'

Althea gave the matter some thought. She had the distinct impression that there was something Mavis wasn't telling her; sometimes Mavis did that, if she thought there were facts about which Althea didn't need to be informed…which the dowager found irritating. 'Are they nice wreaths? Do you know where they were made?'

Mavis's smile looked…tired. 'An avenue we've explored, with no luck, so Carol tells me. No local florist recognizes them. Here you are – a photo of the one left at Sarah and Steve Hughes's home.'

Althea took the phone Mavis had passed across the tablecloth. 'I say – whoever sent this must really not like the recipient. Look at those flowers. As you know, because of my small contribution to The Case of the Disgraced Duke, I understand a little of the language of flowers, and I know that, for example, this pretty yellow flower is called rue, and in the Victorian era it meant "disdain". These cypress sprigs, of course, mean "death, despair, or mourning", and that foxglove – a very unusual plant for a wreath, I must say, because it flops so quickly without water – means "insincerity". Oh, and the hydrangea? It's a *macrophylla;* they were often called hortensia, and meant "you are cold". I think that your Uninvited Undertaker knows their flowers and flower lore, very well – and this wreath, specifically, has been designed to speak volumes to its recipient…none of which is very pleasant.'

Althea was delighted when Mavis beamed and said, 'You're a wonder, my dear. Let me make a phone call.'

Althea listened while Mavis spoke to Carol, passing on the information she'd just, rather proudly, given her. Mavis then added, 'Yes, I agree, I think these are hand-made by the Uninvited Undertaker. Yes, craft shops and supplies – though, of course, there's always the internet, these days, and we cannae check that. But, yes, whatever you can. And, yes, nurseries too. I don't know, let me ask. Althea – which of these plants do you think would have to come from a nursery, to be grown on in a garden, that would be unusual enough that someone might recall a person having purchased them?'

Althea waggled her hand saying, 'Let me look at the photograph again.'

Mavis pressed her screen a few times then said, 'Carol, you're on the speaker and I'm passing the phone to Althea so she can examine the photo of the wreath.'

Althea gave her attention to the photograph. She bitterly rued the fact she was still a relatively new student of all things botanical, but she was able to identify many of the species, nevertheless. 'None of these are rare, or even difficult to find. Anemones, wild tansy, flowering laurel. Everything here is naturally available, in this condition, at this time of year, too – so they wouldn't have to come from a greenhouse, or anywhere like that. I don't think I can help much, I'm sorry.'

Mavis retrieved her phone and returned to talking to Carol with the speaker turned off, which made Althea feel a bit left out. Again.

'Very well, I'll see you there,' she concluded.

When Mavis disconnected, Althea smiled brightly. 'Anything else I can do to help?'

'I don't think so, thank you. Carol has promised me that she will continue to try to reveal the true identity of Jools Tavistock, and to work out if there's any way we can track him down. But it might not be quick, dear – those who wish to not be found can achieve their goal very easily as long as they stay away from the online world, and she's got a fair few other things to be dealing with at the moment, too.'

Althea knew that her friend was right, but felt she had to do something to help someone, somehow or other. She sighed. 'I have other news.'

'Tell me. I hope it's good.'

'Marjorie Pritchard and Elizabeth Fernley are building bridges.'

'Are they now. And why would they need to do that?'

Althea reported everything that had happened at the Hall the previous day, and was thrilled that Mavis complimented her on her attention to detail in her recounting.

'So the antiques shop will open again? That'll be good for the village, I hope. Now, I'm away to the police station in Cardiff. Carol will work on the Uninvited Undertaker case, Christine will also be continuing her efforts in that direction, and Annie will be…well, resting up at Tudor's. She's no' only got Gertie under the weather, but she's also got a nasty gash to contend with. I understand that Tudor Evans has an opportunity to purchase the Coach and Horses pub from Delyth James, so Annie's very excited about that; I dare say that'll raise her spirits, because it means she and Tudor can finally live together. And another boost for the village – those guest rooms becoming available again. Good for Annie and Tudor, and good for the village too, don't you think?'

Althea didn't know quite what to think. She fussed with the teapot. 'Well yes, of course…but I haven't heard about Tudor leaving the Lamb and Flag. Who would we have running that place? If he left it, I mean. Maybe he's spoken to Henry about it, but no one's mentioned anything to me.' She felt a bit miffed – something else nobody had bothered to inform her about.

It was only when she looked up that Althea realized her companion looked aghast.

'What have I said?' Mavis was spluttering, and it wasn't like Mavis to splutter. 'Ach, I always forget about your lot owning everything about the place. Please forgive me, Althea, I shouldnae have said anything about Delyth James selling the pub to Tudor; I don't know the details – so don't go getting all aerated about it. And please don't talk to Henry either? If it's going to happen, I havenae doubt Tudor will choose the right time and place to talk to the duke and duchess about it. Alright?'

Althea nodded, and Mavis took that as her cue to leave.

Alone, and still seated at the table, Althea felt a bit deserted and wondered what she could do about that.

CHAPTER THIRTY-FIVE

Carol's day had begun when Mavis had phoned her before seven, which she thought was a bit much, but she was at least delighted that Mavis felt well enough after her ordeal to be raring to go. They'd had a wide-ranging conversation, and she knew that Mavis intended to speak to Christine next. The plan was that – as soon as Mavis got back from her time with the police in Cardiff – she'd join Christine at the office, and the three of them would have a video meeting.

Her telephone call with the detective sergeant in Brecon the previous evening had been interesting; of course, he'd told her nothing, but had been at pains to point out how the actions she and Annie had taken that afternoon had been foolhardy, and might even have alerted a potential killer to the fact that they were under suspicion – something about which he was quite clearly unhappy.

Carol had countered with the argument that the police still had no idea about how the death of Ed Hughes and the appearance of a wreath at the Hughes house in Anwen-by-Wye were connected, since they couldn't be certain if the wreath had been delivered before or after the death of the man. To her mind, it sounded as though afterward was more likely, given what she'd heard about the condition of the remains from Llinos. Of course, she couldn't tell the man what she knew about that aspect of the crime, because that would drop Llinos in it – so she'd sounded vague, and realized she'd probably come over as a complete idiot, meddling in things that were none of her business, rather than as a competent professional investigator.

She sighed as she thought of the business, and her colleagues: it had been a week since all four women had met up, because Annie had left for London the previous Thursday; now it looked as though she'd be on the sidelines for a while again, but this time Carol felt she was partially to blame. If only she hadn't left Annie alone, she'd never have ended up tumbling into an open grave, getting such a nasty injury, and now having to take a course of powerful antibiotics because of the potential threat of all sorts of infections.

When Carol had spoken to Tudor late the previous evening, he'd told her that Annie was fast asleep, curled up with Gertie – neither of them stirring – and that he intended to leave them that way, so Carol knew she'd have to wait to talk to Annie personally, and told herself to be patient.

With an early start, and then yet another conversation with Mavis – this time about the flowers in the wreath of condolence that had been left at the Hughes house – Carol contemplated opening a packet of biscuits, but decided she really fancied another bowl of cereal, only to find there was almost no milk left in the fridge. She couldn't understand it, until she realized that David had been using breakfast cereal as a sort of meal replacement at odd times of the day and night; he'd probably helped himself while she'd been on the phone with Mavis, or with Christine, or Mavis again. The nocturnal pattern had suited him at first, but she knew he'd be glad to get back to his normal routine – as would his digestive system.

It was a lovely morning – everything looking fresh after the previous day's rain – so she reckoned a break would be as good as a rest, and she popped Albert into his pushchair; he still wasn't walking well enough to make a trip to the shop by foot a realistic possibility.

Carol picked up a couple of oranges and some apples from the boxes displayed outside the shop, then made her way inside, pushing Albert's chair carefully over the threshold while trying to hang onto her fruit.

'I'll take those for you,' said Marjorie Pritchard.

Carol thanked her for her help, silently wondering if the woman knew she had a home to go to, because she seemed to spend her entire days in the shop, nattering to Sharon.

Marjorie plopped the fruit on the counter, where Sharon began to weigh it. Marjorie said jovially, 'Will you be getting some grapes for Annie? I think she could do with some, don't you? Will you be visiting the sick today?'

Carol did her best to not tell Marjorie anything, ever, so simply replied, 'Maybe not today.'

'I dare say she'll be laid up for a while.' Marjorie was in her element. 'Did you say it was a concussion, Sharon?'

Carol was cross that she'd allowed her surprise to show, having decided that no facial reaction to any of Marjorie's comments was always best. Of course, she rarely managed to live up to her intentions, but they remained in place, nonetheless.

'I didn't say that,' said Sharon, 'I said it was a possible concussion, from falling into that grave.'

Marjorie wrinkled her nose. 'Imagine that. A grave! Were you there, Carol? Or was this another of Annie's solo performances?'

Carol dithered – she hated being put on the spot. 'I was in the vicinity. It was very unfortunate.'

'But it *was* a grave? Oh dear. I must say I found that very hard to believe, but if you were actually there, then it must be true.' Marjorie's eyes sparkled.

Carol was even more annoyed with herself; by answering, she'd confirmed Marjorie's story. Now everyone would know that poor Annie had ended up in an open grave, and Carol wasn't sure that was something Annie would want people thinking about whenever they looked at her – she knew she wouldn't, personally speaking.

'Just the fruit and some milk, please,' said Carol, smiling at Sharon and doing her best to ignore the way Marjorie was cooing over Albert.

She grabbed her supplies and paid, hoping for a quick getaway.

'Was the grave all stinky and full of water? That rain we had yesterday was like nothing I've ever seen. Biblical, it was,' observed Marjorie.

'Yeah, Mum got caught in it,' said Sharon. 'Had to stop on the side of the road because it was so heavy – everyone did…too dangerous to go on.'

'Off visiting one of her hospitals, was she?'

Carol was surprised by the acidity of Marjorie's tone.

'I dare say,' was Sharon's casual reply. 'It was Tuesday, so I suppose that would be…um…'

Carol was amazed as Sharon rattled off a long list of places, then spotted a natural break in the conversation and decided to escape.

'Give my best to Mair, if she ever gets a chance to drop by,' was Carol's parting comment.

Sharon responded in a very flat tone, 'Not seeing much of her these days. Wednesday? That'll be…um…' She listed five more institutions that sounded quite familiar to Carol, but she didn't comment, because she really did want to get back to her desk.

However, by the time she got there, she'd forgotten all about the idea of more cereal, and took an apple to her laptop with her as she checked the list of places where the deceased in the Uninvited Undertaker case had died, then she phoned Christine.

'Look, I know the police are all over the Ed Hughes case, but we're still working on our angle of it, right?' Christine agreed. 'Excellent. So here's a quick one for you: when you were cross-checking staff who might have worked in more than one medical facility, did you also look into people like hospital visitors? I don't mean people who come to visit someone they know, but the people who visit sort of "officially"? And what about other volunteers?'

Christine replied straight away, 'Nope. Got to be honest, that didn't occur to me. But it's a good idea. I can do that. What made you think of it?'

'Sharon at the shop said her mum's been doing a lot of that sort of thing of late; she listed a whole load of places that Mair Jones goes to, and I realized it was almost the same as the list we have. In fact, it sounds as though Mair goes to everywhere on our list…but, as we've established, our list contains almost all the places that exist. And it got me thinking – even if there aren't staff who cross over, what about volunteers? Visitors. Library books. Maybe working in the little fundraising shop. That sort of thing.'

Christine said, 'Do you want to do this, or shall I? Or shall we agree how to split the list?'

'Let's do that, then both hit the phones, alright?'

'Agreed.'

For the next couple of hours, while her son played, napped, and generally got on with the business of being a busy toddler, Carol made phone calls, asked questions, sent emails, and entered data into her beloved spreadsheets. It was only an unexpected visit from Llinos Trevelyan that drew her away from her desk – and she had to admit she was not only grateful for the break, but was gasping for a cuppa, too, so – of course – she saw Llinos's arrival as an excuse to make a pot.

The kettle was almost boiling before Llinos had even taken a seat at the kitchen table.

'None for me, ta,' she said. 'I really can't stop, but I was in the village so thought I'd drop in. Thanks for making that phone call yesterday – I'm not officially working on the Ed Hughes thing, as you know...but I'll keep my ears open, promise. However, I wanted to tell you about that Alan Ridley bloke, face-to-face.'

Carol punched the air. 'Yes! Fantastic. Right, well, you tell me all about him while I make a pot for myself then.'

As Carol prepared the tea, Llinos said, 'He was on holiday – but it wasn't a holiday for him, or maybe it was...anyway, it was certainly a holiday for his son and daughter-in-law. He was at a nursing home so they could have some respite from caring for him, at their own home. He'd suffered a stroke some years ago and needed a lot of help – they did pretty much everything for him. He couldn't even talk much, poor thing. They had a proper hospital bed at their home, with bathroom facilities with those lifts, and everything. Spent a fortune getting it all set up for him, it sounds like. But they just needed a bit of a break, and they'd gone away to a caravan site in Devon for a couple of weeks. They'd arranged for him to be in the nursing home while they were away, then he was due to return to their house when they got back. He suffered another stroke while he was at the home, and they came rushing back from their holiday when they heard about it. So – yes, I suppose he was on holiday, and they were too. Does that help?'

'Where was he staying?'

Llinos gave the name of a nursing home that Carol knew was on the list she already had.

'Thanks for that. It really helps, because if the link is the places where the people died, then that makes more sense, now. He does fall within the pattern. I'd better add him to the list I gave your DS. Oh, and we're also looking into any volunteers who might have offered their services in several of these places, too. Christine and I are putting all our effort into that today.'

Llinos stood, nodding. 'Oh heck – I'd say "good idea", but shouldn't you be stopping work on this now? I mean, we're on it, you know.'

Carol sighed. 'Sorry – you're right…but we can still help, I think, Llinos. We've done so much work already.'

Llinos smiled. 'Can't stop wanting to help, can you? Mind you, I find it hard to think about anything else, too. See, there are possible crossovers with paramedics and medical transport drivers – the ones who might "deliver" people to the hospital, hospice, or nursing home. And the cleaners, of course – though I don't think they're called that any longer, are they?'

'They tend to call it "housekeeping" at the moment, though it all depends on where you are, and what sort of title's in fashion. But we've already discounted that; because of the way shifts and work patterns are set up, no one could have been that wide-ranging in their duties, and the folks who deliver patients – in whichever way – were also knocked off the list, though that was our closest match so far.'

Llinos said, 'Alright then, I'll get on with what I'm doing and say "good luck with it all", Carol. We haven't had this conversation, right? I know what it's like to have your face stuck in front of a computer all day – I did that before I decided this was the career I wanted…and I'm so much happier doing this.'

'Despite having to deal with break-ins all the time, because of the weather?'

'Despite that. Talk soon, Carol.'

'Thanks ever so much for the info about Alan Ridley; I owe you a large…whatever you want, whenever you want it.'

'That would be one of your curries, next Monday night – how about that?'

'You're on. See you then. Come at six, we'll have wine, and plan on getting a taxi home.'

'Great idea. And – please – take care of yourself.'

CHAPTER THIRTY-SIX

When Mavis had entered the police station in Cardiff, she hadn't expected to be greeted like a queen, but she had expected to be taken notice of. But that wasn't what happened at all. The previous day she'd been treated well, with the solicitousness appropriate for someone who'd been through a kidnapping ordeal. Now? She'd been waiting in the reception area for over half an hour. The place wasn't exactly dreadful, but it wasn't where she'd have chosen to spend all that time, drinking coffee that bad.

'I'm sorry for the delay, Mrs MacDonald, but we've been trying to tie up a few loose ends before we got to you. Please follow me to somewhere we can speak privately. DS Brighton…like the place, you know? We met yesterday.'

The young man was, indeed, one of the detectives she'd seen the day before; about the same age as her older boy, and much the same coloring as him, too – pale, freckled, and not too keen on the sun, she reckoned.

'I recall you were there, though we didnae talk too much,' she acknowledged.

'Yes, and that's why it's me and you who'll be doing the talking today; a fresh set of eyes and ears, so to speak.'

Mavis thought it a little odd, then suspected the police might want her to reconsider her statement in the light of a new day, with a good night's sleep behind her, which she reckoned was fair enough.

'Coffee? Tea?'

Mavis checked, 'Is it the same as the stuff in the reception area?' The man nodded. 'Then I'll no' bother, thank you. I tried both, and couldnae tell the difference.'

He chuckled. 'I'm with you, but there comes a point around here when all you're after is caffeine, in any form, so we'll drink anything. But I can also offer you water, if you'd prefer.'

'You may. But no thank you. Let's get on, shall we?'

He looked impressed, thought Mavis.

'Very well. So could I ask you to, once again if you would, talk me through the nature of the investigation you were carrying out that led you to be following Miss Veronica Daniels yesterday morning?'

Mavis obliged, as she had done the previous evening, with a full and detailed background and explanation. She, once again, offered access to all her recordings, and photographs.

As she spoke, the man took no notes, but kept glancing at a tablet he was holding where – she assumed – he was following her original statement. He asked a few questions seeking clarification along the way, and jotted down a few things on a paper notepad when she replied, but – overall – Mavis felt she'd done a good job.

'Sorry to ask you to repeat all this, but could you please tell me again what happened when you regained consciousness in the house where we found you?'

Mavis explained everything and, once more, he nodded as she spoke.

'What made you think of the toilet paper and the soap as a way of getting a message out? It was quite a novel idea – and very effective, too, of course.'

Mavis was about to reply that she'd just come up with it, given what was available to her, when she realized the man's tone had shifted. She couldn't put her finger on it, but it made her feel uneasy.

She, nevertheless, did her best to explain her thought process at the time, and he seemed satisfied enough.

'It was fortunate there was a police presence already in the area,' he remarked. 'But you'd have seen that, through the bathroom window, no doubt.'

'I did. And I have my colleagues to thank for it; as you know they tracked the photographs I had sent them and found my car, alerting your local colleagues to the fact I was missing. Of course, they didnae know at the time that I'd been kidnapped.'

'Yes. About that…the suspects we've been questioning – Mr Spencer and Ms. Daniels – both claim that no kidnapping took place. Indeed, they've suggested that you entered their home of your own free will because you were keen to find out how you could make money from your newfound ability to access essentially untraceable drugs, especially opioids.'

Mavis replayed what DS Brighton had just said in her head. 'They told you that?'

He nodded.

'That's rubbish. Why would they say that?'

'Why indeed?'

Mavis sat up a little straighter. 'If they're trying to get off the kidnapping charges, they'd tell you I went there willingly, I believe. But I have no idea why they would think they could get away with saying I wanted to sell them drugs. And, if I did, why on earth did I make such an effort to get away?'

DS Brighton's smile didn't quite reach his eyes. 'Well, you might have spotted the police when you were using the bathroom – you might have panicked, and decided to paint yourself as a victim rather than as a potential supplier.'

Again, Mavis paused. 'No, that makes no sense,' she said curtly.

'There is something else.' The DS put his tablet on the table and showed Mavis a photograph of several containers almost full of pharmaceuticals. 'Do you recognize any of these?'

'Aye. They're some of the medications prescribed to the late Mrs Thomas, who passed away at the Ty Coch home in the early hours of Monday.'

'And these are the medications you say were taken by Nurse Veronica Daniels soon afterwards?'

'I believe that's the case, aye.'

The DS nodded, and pulled his tablet away. 'I see. You saw them for yourself at the nursing home?'

'I did. I made it my business to, and you'll find the photographs I took of everything that was in Mrs Thomas's room immediately after her death for a comparison.'

He nodded. 'The cupboards where the medications were stored were locked at all times, I thought.'

'A sound system, sometimes sloppily implemented. I found the cupboard open when I was tending to the remains of Mrs Thomas, and took advantage of the fact.'

'That's an interesting turn of phrase. You see, having taken your fingerprints last night, and now having had the chance to do the same for everyone else working at the nursing home, we've discovered something that's quite suggestive: we found several sets of fingerprints on the containers, as you might imagine, but the only ones we found belonging to people who worked at Ty Coch were those of the two night-duty nurses, and of you, Mrs MacDonald. Now, firstly, I find it interesting that it was only the three of you. Secondly, I find it extremely interesting that yours were there at all – given that only nurses are allowed to handle the medications.'

'I handled them when I took the photographs of them: if you examine my pictures, you'll see that all the labels are facing the camera. That's no' the way they'd have been shoved into the cabinet, is it? I handled them when I turned them. I thought it critical to photograph the labels, no' just the containers.'

The DS gave himself away with a little jerk of his head; Mavis knew she'd scored a point. But there was something more pressing on her mind.

'I do have one confession to make, and I think it might change the whole complexion of your investigation,' she said quietly.

DS Brighton didn't exactly pounce, but she could see the gleam in his eye. 'And what would that confession be?'

'When I handled the medications, a little time after Mrs Thomas's passing, I cleaned every container with an antibacterial wipe. This meant that all previous fingerprints would have been removed. I knew that mine would be on there, which was a part of my plan.'

He looked confused. 'And what was that plan, exactly?'

'To have evidence, at some future point, that the only other staff member whose fingerprints were on the containers were those of Nurse Veronica Daniels, proving she was the one who'd removed them from the premises. And it worked.'

More confusion. 'But there *aren't* only her prints on the bottles. As well as your own, we also have Nurse Wanda Gorman's prints on them.'

'Exactly.'

'Exactly what?' The man sounded exasperated.

'Mrs Thomas had died, thereby no' having any need to be administered those pills. So anyone handling them after I'd wiped them clean had another reason for them passing through their hands. To distribute them. And it looks as though Nurse Daniels was no' working alone. If I were you, I'd be reinterviewing Nurse Wanda Gorman, too.'

The DS gave Mavis a sideways glance that she didn't like the look of, so she added, 'And if you want to find out more about me, I suggest you talk to either Chief Inspector Carwen James in Powys, or else Detective Chief Inspector Carys Llewellyn in Swansea; I believe they'll both be able to speak to the likelihood of my suddenly deciding to become a supplier of prescription drugs to the street dealers of Cardiff.'

DS Brighton noted the names, managing to look unsurprised, but then he put down his pen and sat back in his chair.

'I'll put out a few feelers, as you suggest. But there's something else. You see, the suspects are claiming they don't distribute drugs to street peddlers. In fact, they're suggesting an entirely different *modus operandi*, if you will.'

Mavis was all ears, but DS Brighton refused to say more.

CHAPTER THIRTY-SEVEN

Annie had to admit that she'd felt better. Her head was sore, her leg was sore, and the massive antibiotic tablets she was taking to ward off the possible onset of sepsis made her wish she had a bigger mouth. She hadn't laughed when Tudor had suggested hers was big enough already, and she'd made sure he'd quickly understood the foolishness of his so-called joke. Then kissed him.

With Gertie only too happy to keep Annie company on Tudor's slightly worn sofa in the flat above the pub, her only anxieties surrounded the source of the hankie that had caused Gertie's problems; a linen hankie, edged with fine crotched lace, with the initial 'D' embroidered upon it in red cotton, plus, of course, the Uninvited Undertaker case. She didn't know what she could do about discovering the source of the offending hankie, and felt she was letting the team down by lounging about with her feet up. She'd considered phoning Carol to offer her services – even if she just lay on the sofa with her laptop, researching…something.

However, that had been a couple of hours earlier – and now she was peeling open her eyes to realize she'd been fast asleep. Gertie gave her a half-hearted lick and seemed to be doing as well as could be expected, having had a handkerchief yanked up her gullet. Annie felt the same, a bit sore, but willing to consider a tasty meal – if someone would only put it in front of her.

As though he were telepathic, Tudor appeared at the top of the stairs from the pub with a covered plate in his hand. 'I wondered if a nice ploughman's might perk you up a bit,' he said. 'It's early for lunch, I know, but I thought if I brought it now you could pick at it when you fancy. But, first, let's take that temperature of yours, like the doctor said we had to do every few hours…and I'll also get Gertie's lunch ready.'

Having established that she was 'normal' – in terms of her temperature, at least – Annie tucked into the small pork pie that nestled beside slices of gleaming yellow cheddar, a couple of crisp pickled onions, a hunk of fresh, crusty bread, a mound of pickle, and some apple wedges that she fully intended to ignore. *Heaven!*

While she decided on her next mouthful, she said, 'Tude, I've been thinking.'

Tudor chuckled, placed Gertie's small portion of dog food into her bowl, then kept Rosie at bay for the five seconds it took Gertie to demolish it.

He stepped back so both dogs could try to lick the shine off the stainless steel and replied, 'I dare say you have been thinking, and I'm glad to know that all those drugs you're on aren't clouding that wonderful brain of yours.'

Annie tutted, but continued, 'I've been thinking about all our stuff. You know, the stuff we've both got in our current homes. We're going to have to make up our minds about what we chuck and what we keep, because it in't all going to fit into the flat at the Coach and Horses, however big it might be, is it?'

Tudor refilled the dogs' water bowls as he replied, 'You're right. That sofa you're on, for example – that isn't as good as the one you've got. But my table is a better size – bigger than your tiny thing. We're going to have to make lists. But not now. Now's when you rest up and let all those good things get into your blood so they can kill off all the bad things. Yes, I know your temperature's normal, and yes, I know you're feeling good in yourself, other than localized soreness – but you heard what the doctor said, Annie; you cannot risk getting rundown at all, because your body will be using a lot of energy to heal itself. I honestly shudder to think about the sorts of things that open wound was exposed to in that...place. The only reason they let you out of the hospital was because you threatened them with legal action if they didn't – which was a bit strong for my liking. But they briefed me well, and I shall do my duty and make sure you do what you're supposed to do, and don't do what you're not supposed to do. Lists can wait. Your health can't. Now relax. Read a book or watch a bit of TV if you can't nap any more.'

Annie shared her opinions about daytime television with Tudor, who descended the stairs calling, 'I'll be back in two or three hours, after whatever lunchtime rush I get. Mind you stay where you are and rest.'

Gertie had found a patch of sun to lie in, and Annie knew she wouldn't budge until her gleaming black fur was almost too hot to touch, then she'd move to a cooler spot, until she moved back again, always followed by Rosie, her littermate and – at the moment – her shadow.

They'll enjoy sharing the same home, too, thought Annie, before she answered the phone that was vibrating on the little table beside her lunch plate.

'Hiya, Car, how are you?'

Carol replied, 'Forget about me, I'm fine. It's you I'm worried about. It's nice to hear your voice; Tudor's looking after you well, I know, and I get it that he doesn't want you disturbed, but I want you to tell me how you are…yourself. Has he let you have your phone back now?'

'Sort of. He forgot he'd put it on the table, so here I am. And whatever he's told you, I really am not too bad. Sore, of course, and I think the painkillers they gave me are defective, but I can take some more once I've eaten, so that'll probably help.'

'I knew I shouldn't have left you on your own,' said Carol, sounding more guilty than sorry. 'We both watch the films where people split up and then get into terrible trouble alone, and we both tell them how stupid they are – then we go and do that exact same thing ourselves. What are we like?'

Annie laughed. 'Oh don't – that really hurts. Tell you what, if we're ever in a creepy house together, I won't go to the attic if you won't go to the cellar – alright?'

'Agreed. Especially if someone's after us. So you're really going to be alright?'

'I am. Gert's keeping me company, as is Rosie, and Tude's doing a great job as my nurse. He'd put Mave to shame. By the way – I've been worried about her. Tude sort of told me what had happened, but I'll feel better if you tell me. So, go on.'

Carol filled her in.

'Gordon Bennett – what a day we had between us. Was she hurt at all?'

'Tough as old boots, as you know. Gone to see the police in Cardiff this morning, and plans to be back at the office this afternoon.'

'I wish I could be of more help, Car, but Tude won't let me up off this couch.'

'Quite right, too. You need your rest. Mavis has a lump on her head, but no concussion. You? A gash that could go bad – so make sure you do whatever they said you have to do.'

'I can't get the dressing wet, and I've got to take tablets the size of a small car. For a whole flamin' week.'

'As long as it works.'

Annie could hear…something…in Carol's tone.

'Come on, doll, spit it out. What's wrong?'

Carol hesitated. 'It's two things, really. Christine and I had a thought about volunteers who might give their services at all the places where the Uninvited Undertaker deaths have taken place, but it's hard to get information about that sort of thing.'

'Great idea. How d'you come up with that.'

Carol told her about her chat in the shop with Sharon regarding Mair.

Annie said, 'Well, it seems obvious to me then – go and talk to Mair Jones herself. If she's in all the places you need to know about, ask her. Goodness knows she's not backward in coming forward when it comes to "information sharing". Though you'd have to be careful about steering her away from the identity of our clients, because that woman would be all over that like vinegar on chips…and I use the word vinegar advisedly.'

Carol chuckled. 'Ta, Annie – I can't believe neither Christine nor I thought of that. You're right, it's obvious. Yeah, I'll do that – or Christine and I can do it together; we've split the list of places to contact, so between us we really know what's going on. Brilliant.'

'Glad to be of service – even if from my sick bed. And the other thing? Maybe I can help there too.'

'Long story short: Mavis asked me to look into someone's background, because Althea had asked *her* to do it, then Mavis went off to do the Suspicious Sister undercover thing, so I got lumbered with it. Anyway, it turns out the bloke in question was Clementine's new fiancé.'

'Another one? Does that make five now?'

'Only four, apparently. Anyway, I did a bit of digging, and the person he said he was, doesn't exist.'

Annie was delighted. 'Excellent. So have you found out who he really is? I bet you have, haven't you? And Althea's not going to like it, is she?'

Carol chuckled. 'Well, that's the thing – I don't know why on earth he wasn't honest about who he is. He's from a very old family – appeared in the *Domesday Book* and all that. Got loads of land near Gloucester – a place called Middle Monkton. No title, but…well, pots and pots of money, by the looks of it. Althea told me he said he's from Filton, where they build aeroplanes and there's a big Rolls Royce place there, too – but it turns out his family gets its money from designing and making manufacturing equipment. Been in that line since the Industrial Revolution, it appears. Anyway, it was their equipment that was then used to build the stuff other firms made in Filton, so I suppose the bloke only bent the truth in that respect. His family's company is internationally massive, too, hence the pots of money. And there's only him; he's the only child. Initially, Clementine said he was a blacksmith; it seems he lied to her, not just the rest of the family, though Althea says he told Clementine the truth just before he left, then she followed him. I'd named it The Case of the Furry Fiancé to start with…Althea told me he's got one of those big, bushy beards. It was an unofficial name, of course, because you weren't involved. But now I'm thinking that The Case of the Fleeing Fiancé is more appropriate. What do you think? Does that get your stamp of approval?'

Annie managed a chuckle. 'Nice one, doll. I'll second that. But…what else is there? He's killed half his family and he's on the run? Something bad like that? Because from what you've told me about him so far, that all sounds as though you wouldn't need to lie about it.'

Carol sighed. 'Honestly, I don't know. I've found out who he really is, but not why he lied.'

'It's probably the money,' said Annie.

'Althea did say that he'd told Clementine that he'd always planned to tell her the truth once he was certain she was going to marry him.'

'There you go then – he wanted to be sure she wanted him, not just his money. Classic.'

'But, in this instance, disastrous.' Carol sounded really down.

'Have you told Althea yet?'

'I've been plucking up the courage…then decided to phone you instead. You don't mind, do you, talking about work?'

'Anything to take me mind off the pain, and to stop wondering where on earth Gert managed to find herself a frilly-edged, linen hankie, with the initial "D" embroidered on it…or to keep me awake.' Annie couldn't help but yawn.

Carol sounded a bit distant when she said, 'Take those tablets of yours and get some shuteye. I feel better about phoning Althea now, thanks to you. And thanks for stating the obvious about us talking directly with Mair Jones – funny how the simplest path forward isn't always obvious, isn't it? Heal well, Annie – and I'll send lots of emails, so you don't feel too left out; you can read them when you're awake, and I won't disturb you with the phone. Hugs from me, and Albert.'

'Hugs back. Bye for now.'

Annie lay back on her pillows and smiled at Gertie who was doing her eyebrow wiggling thing in the sunshine. 'Oh Gert, I feel about as useful as a lump of lead, me. What about you?'

Gertie stretched to her full length and yawned.

'You and me both, Gert. You and me both.'

Annie had taken her tablets – even the massive one – and was just closing her eyes when Tudor stomped up the stairs. His face was…well, it was usually a face that it was comforting to look at, but Annie could tell he was in turmoil. She sat upright.

'What's wrong? Something's wrong.'

'I didn't want to disturb you, but I…I have to. I just got a phone call from Delyth James's estate agent. Yes, she's serious about selling the pub, but she's just received a better offer than mine, so, unless I can find more money than I know I could – or *should* – raise, then the deal with me is off. I…I know it impacts the both of us, but – in my heart – I knew it was wrong to try to raise the extra money. So I've said I'll step back and let the other buyer move ahead. So that's that. It's off. I'm sorry.'

Annie reached her arms toward Tudor, who came to perch beside her on the sofa where she hugged him tight.

'Don't worry, Tude. You know I had some wonderful plans for this place, and – you know what? – we've got each other, and these two girls, and we're all coping just lovely with the way things are now. Let's put aside the idea of you being stressed all the time, and let's focus on making the Lamb and Flag the very best pub it can be. Of course, when the Coach and Horses reopens, we'll also have to make sure we're the best pub in the village – but you know we both like a challenge, don't we?'

'Annie, I don't know what I'd do without you. You're like a ray of sunshine on a cloudy day.'

'You're welcome.'

CHAPTER THIRTY-EIGHT

When Mavis arrived back at the Dower House she went hunting for Althea; she'd had a bizarre morning and knew that talking things through with the dowager – or even talking about any topic at all – would help her clear her head.

But Althea was nowhere to be found, it seemed. Cook hadn't seen her since breakfast, Ian hadn't been asked to transport her to anywhere, and Mavis had all but given up when Althea finally appeared at the top of the stairs, her hair full of cobwebs. The shapeless garment she was wearing was also grubby – and it looked to Mavis as though it had been made out of an ancient sack.

'Where on earth have you been?'

Althea made her way down to the entryway, accompanied by a happy, but grubby, McFli. 'I went up into the attic-type rooms at the top of the house. I was looking for something and was sure I'd find it there.'

Mavis looked her up and down. 'And did you find it?'

Althea beamed. She pulled up the over-garment and shoved her hand into a saggy pocket in what appeared to Mavis to be a pair of purple cheesecloth breeches she was wearing underneath.

'I did,' said Althea triumphantly, shoving her hand toward Mavis.

In her small palm she held a large lump of green rock carved into some sort of architectural shape. It was quite beautiful.

'What is it? And why did you need to go hunting about for it? In what appears to have been a part of the house full of spiders by the way; you should shake your head, dear, you might have brought some down with you.'

Althea shook, though no spiders fell. 'It's an ornamental carving of a Buddhist dagoba, made of green aventurine. Chelly and I bought it in Nepal. They use a great deal of aventurine there – on the statues of their deities. We loved the look and feel of this piece, and it's supposed to be the luckiest stone of all. I thought it would make a good wedding gift for Clementine and Julian.'

She paused to wipe a few smudges off the object, using her sacking jerkin, then added, 'I think she'll like it. And the pair of them could do with some good luck.'

Mavis wasn't quite sure how to proceed; the last she'd been aware, Julian had been discovered to be an imposter, and there'd been a significant rift between Althea and her daughter.

'I've missed something important, obviously. Why don't we have a pot of tea and you can tell me all about it?'

Althea replied airily. 'Very well, but it will have to wait a little. I want to get myself clean after all that digging about up there. Why don't you ask Cook to get something sorted out for us? I don't think the world will end if we have tea and something sweet earlier than four o'clock, do you?'

Mavis hid her smile. 'I dare say it'll keep spinning on its axis, dear.'

As Althea headed back up the stairs she called over her shoulder, 'And now that the Clementine thing is settled, I want to share my ideas about how we can celebrate the summer solstice here in Anwen-by-Wye, on the very day that my wonderful daughter will be marrying her beau in Egypt.'

Having asked Cook to serve tea, and cake, if there was any – and when wasn't there? – in the sitting room, Mavis sank into an armchair to take stock of her own situation. She'd been allowed to leave the police station after the young but seemingly diligent DS Brighton had spoken personally to both Chief Inspector Carwen James and Detective Chief Inspector Carys Llewellyn, which had relieved her, because she'd not fancied hanging about the place any longer than was absolutely necessary. Not expecting to hear anything more about the investigation – the police service not being renowned for sharing information with members of the public – Mavis had to try to settle her mind to knowing no more, until additional information was made 'public' in the true sense of the word. It was the part of her job that she, and her colleagues, always found the most frustrating.

'Much fresher now, dear. Ah, seed cake, how wonderful.' Althea had replaced the sackcloth with a turquoise shift that allowed for a great deal of air circulation, despite its length, and she'd dramatically wreathed her head with a magenta scarf, hiding whatever mess lay beneath.

As she poured tea, Althea recounted her recent conversation with Carol, who had revealed the true identity of the so-called 'Jools Tavistock' as being Julian Treforest, of the world-renowned Treforest conglomerate of manufacturing companies.

'I telephoned Clemmie when I found out, and am pleased to say that she answered. She confirmed that "Jools" had confessed as much to her just before he left Chellingworth, and he didn't believe her when she said she'd never heard of him, nor his family. That was what they really fell out about, I understand. She's at the London house, where he has now reconciled with her. It appears that he made it his business to speak to several of Clemmie's chums, who all confirmed it most likely that she'd have been totally oblivious of the existence of his family's empire. Once he realized she hadn't been lying, he got in touch with her and…well, the upshot is that the wedding is back on, and they are redoubling their efforts to ensure that the ceremony takes place as they had originally intended.'

'Is he even a blacksmith?' Mavis couldn't believe he was.

'Indeed he is; Clementine has seen him at work and, under his *nom de travail*, he's built quite a good word-of-mouth reputation within the artisanal blacksmithing community. Though I have to admit I find it difficult to comprehend that such a community exists.'

'Aye, well, there's a lot of call for things made by hand, employing ancient techniques, these days. Though if his family's as wealthy as you say they are, he'll no' have to scrimp to make a living I dare say. Nor will Clementine, which must please you.'

'I'm delighted, Mavis. I've always worried about the way she just wanders through life without seeming to have a great deal of purpose. I dare say that my not pressuring her into choosing a path early on has a great deal to do with that, and we all know she doesn't need to work to earn money because, well, because she's Clemmie. But this will be a comfort to me. No grandchildren from her, of course, but at least I believe she'll be happy with this man. He's never married before, either, so they'll be embarking on the journey late in life, but without anything to constrain them.'

Mavis was pleased that Althea was pleased, though she couldn't imagine that marrying a man who had access to an enormous fortune would make Clementine any more focused, or less indolent.

'And she's not the only person whose happiness I've had a hand in helping along, either,' said Althea, innocently sipping her tea.

Mavis felt a tingle at the back of her neck. 'I cannae say that you asking me to investigate a man is a way of "helping happiness along", dear – so what else have you been up to?'

Althea dimpled. 'You'll see. I really don't want to spoil the surprise.'

Mavis sighed. 'Very well, then.'

'Now, about the summer solstice…' began Althea, suddenly fluttering.

'Ach, can you no' leave these things alone, Althea? Was May Day not a cautionary experience for you? That Maypole was far too big for the way it was put into the ground. What do you want to do now? Build a replica of Stonehenge on the village green so we can all gather there at sunrise?'

Althea's little face was deadly serious when she replied, 'Don't be silly. That's not what I mean at all. Wales has its own traditions for the solstice: they'll be gathering at Bryn Celli Ddu in Anglesey at dawn to see the first rays of the day shine through the door and along the corridor into the burial chamber in the mound there, which it has done since it was built in Neolithic times, about five thousand years ago. Chelly and I went there to see it once – a surreal and truly awe-inspiring experience. One almost felt it really was possible for the rays of the sun to bring the dead back to life.' She sighed. 'Anyway, this year, I want to have something special happening in the village; I want it to be something that everyone can enjoy, so I'm getting the village social committee on board to get traditional dancing organized.'

Mavis was surprised; it sounded like a very good idea indeed.

'Will this be at dawn?' She wondered if Althea envisaged everyone getting up in what their bodies would think was still the middle of the night, given the time the sun came up on the longest day of the year.

'No, of course not. Sadly, the solstice falls on a Wednesday this year, so I thought that an early evening event would work best. I've had an initial discussion with Tudor who says he can supply foodstuffs and drinks from the pub; the wonderful Wendy Jenkins has been "volunteered" by her aunt, Iris Lewis, so we have music. And I was delighted – and not a little amazed – to discover that Marjorie Pritchard had something of a reputation as a Welsh folk-dancer in her younger days, so she's going to guide those who don't know the old dances in how to do them…showing everyone the basics, then she'll shout out what they have to do next. Traditionally there should be a bonfire, but we can't do that because it's far too dangerous with the way the weather's been. However, I think I've come up with a way that we can have a representation of fire at the event.'

Mavis was cautiously optimistic about how the solstice celebrations might go, but decided not to breath out until the entire thing was over, and everyone safely in their beds at the end of it. 'It sounds wonderful, dear. And I'm pleased that you've been the catalyst, though it seems you're actually allowing the people of the village to make it their own.'

Althea rolled her small shoulders. 'But, of course, dear. You know how I hate to interfere.'

Mavis was just about to reply, when she was saved by a vibration in her pocket. She pulled out her phone and said, 'Forgive me, Althea – it's Carwen James; I must take this – it could be important.'

She thought she heard Althea mutter, 'Well, he thinks he's important,' as she answered her phone. 'Hello, Chief Inspector, what can I do for you?' Politeness was best – after all, the man had spoken up for her.

'I gather you've been involved with a spot of bother down in Cardiff.'

Mavis wasn't impressed by the man's opening gambit, nor by his supercilious tone. 'If you mean the drug ring I helped them to uncover, then, yes, I have.'

Take that, she thought.

'Ah, I see. Yes. Um…I dare say you know I was approached by a young DS to give you what amounted to a verbal reference earlier today?'

Mavis mellowed. 'Aye, and I thank you for it…though I hope I've earned your trust over the past eighteen months or so.'

Althea was mouthing at Mavis in the most annoying fashion, so Mavis batted the air to try to make her stop.

'Indeed you have, Mrs MacDonald, indeed you have. Hence my telephoning you at this time. I wanted to give you a sort of "insiders' update" so to speak. Should you be interested, of course.'

Mavis spoke through a steely smile. 'Could you hold on for just a moment, please, Chief Inspector? The dowager is trying to get my attention.'

'Ah, she's with you, is she? Well, please, pass on my regards to Her Grace. And, by all means, allow her to listen in to what I'm about to tell you, if she chooses.'

Mavis turned to Althea, having pressed the mute button. 'He says he has news, and you can listen. But you have to be quiet, alright?'

Althea dimpled and nodded, so Mavis hit the right parts of her screen. 'Both Her Grace and I are listening, Chief Inspector,' she said.

'Greetings to you, Your Grace. I hope this call finds you well, and enjoying this spell of weather we've been having.'

Althea rolled her eyes and pulled a face at Mavis, then replied brightly, 'I am quite well, thank you, Chief Inspector, and the weather has, as you say, been remarkable. But, enough of the small talk – we're on tenterhooks to hear what you can tell us about this band of ruffians who kidnapped Mavis as a part of their nefarious goings on. Do tell.'

Mavis sighed – trying to do it quietly. There was no stopping the woman.

Carwen James's reply took a moment. 'Well, I might not characterize the situation in quite that way, Your Grace, but yes, I do have news pertaining to the enquiry, and it's all turned out to be quite interesting.'

'Do you mean there was an interesting reason for Mavis being bashed on the head, kidnapped, drugged – and then having to escape? Or that there was an interesting reason for nurses stealing drugs?'

Mavis shouted at Althea, silently. She judged that it had dawned on Carwen James that he'd clearly bitten off at least more than he'd expected, when he blurted out, 'Both Veronica Daniels and Wanda Gorman have confessed to removing drugs prescribed to recently deceased patients at the Ty Coch Nursing Home, but that they have not been supplying street dealers with the drugs. They claim they have been "dispensing" – their word – the drugs to people who need them, medically speaking. They claim that the only people they have given the medications in question to are those who have been previously prescribed such pharmaceuticals by a doctor, and have – very unfortunately – found themselves unable to cope well when the doctor has stopped prescribing them.'

Mavis sighed. 'The opioids, mainly, I suppose. I have to admit that I've long been worried about the effect they're able to have within society. Daniels and Gorman claim they're supplying those who've become addicted, following a period when they've been properly prescribed them?'

'They do.'

Althea's little face fell. 'Oh dear. Do you think they were telling the truth? Not that people find themselves in such terribly difficult circumstances, I know they do. I had some strong tablets after my hip surgery, and they do save one from a great deal of discomfort, but I recall you being quite strict with me about how long I was allowed to take them, Mavis. The bottle still had lots in it, didn't it, when I gave them up and moved to over-the-counter tablets?'

Mavis nodded gravely. 'Aye, it's all too easy to not realize you're becoming dependent upon that sort of stuff, and to play up your condition to keep getting more prescriptions. It's something that needs attention – but, then, so many things do, and there are never enough resources. Have the people in Cardiff been able to establish if the nurses are telling the truth in this regard?'

'I understand that to be the case. The police in Cardiff have, today, visited a number of homes in the area where they have retrieved a variety of medications. Those in possession of them all made it clear that they were unable – they felt – to get through the day without the drugs they craved, and that the illicit supply they had in their possession had been provided to them, free of charge, by Veronica and Tracy Daniels, and Wanda Gorman. The man who was one of your captors, Frank Spencer, is the boyfriend of Veronica Daniels. The house where you were held is rented from the local authority by him. He himself is one of the addicts in question; after injuring his back at work he was given opioids for his pain, and was utterly addicted to them by the time his doctors stopped prescribing them for him. It was to support his addiction that Veronica Daniels began stealing – and it grew from there.'

Mavis realized that the seemingly substantiated claims by Daniels and Gorman put a totally different spin on things.

'So, if they weren't stealing for profit…what would the charges be?' Mavis dared to ask.

Carwen James sucked in air for a good few seconds – a very unattractive sound. 'Theft is unlawful, whatever the thief chooses to do with what they have stolen, and they did supply the drugs, even if they didn't make any money from doing so. Then there's your injury and confinement to consider, Mrs MacDonald, as well as the assault of a police officer. It mounts up. However, not only is it not for me to say what will happen to whom because I'm Powys and they are Cardiff, but I'm also not the Crown Prosecution Service. At the end of the day, they will decide. I suspect that the nurses will not be allowed to continue in their profession, however.'

'Thank you for telling me. Us. It means a great deal. I dare say this will all take a long time to come to court – whatever the charges.' Mavis was a realist.

The senior officer chuckled, wryly. 'If I had a crystal ball, Mrs MacDonald, I'd tell you. But I thought you deserved a little closure – given your ordeal. This seems to be a case of good people breaking the law for what they believed were good reasons, but I and my colleagues are here to uphold the law, as you know. And, once again, I am happy to acknowledge that you have been a worthy ally in this case. Thank you. Now, if you'll forgive me, I have a pressing appointment. Your Grace. Mrs MacDonald. Until we speak, or meet, again. Goodbye.'

Mavis felt terribly flat when she'd disconnected. Althea was almost in tears.

She blubbed, 'We have so much, when so many have so little – and people can so very easily find themselves in a dark place, without anyone to help them find the light.'

'Aye,' replied Mavis. 'And when it comes to people who will help us when we need it, we have to be very careful about how we let them do that. Maybe, instead of supplying them, those nurses should have concentrated on finding support for those people to help them overcome their addictions; treatment, not enablement.'

'If it's available, Mavis…if it's available.'

CHAPTER THIRTY-NINE

Christine drove to Carol's house so they could share her vehicle for the journey to Mair Jones's home. The music was blaring, and she was thinking about Alexander, and the shop. As she passed it, she could see activity inside – bodies moving around in the shadowy interior. Soon, the place would be overseen by her fiancé, which he'd already made clear meant he'd be able to spend more in Anwen-by-Wye, but working, rather than just relaxing, or tagging along with her.

Christine thought of all the times when Alexander's 'tagging along' meant they'd enjoyed an adventure together, and wondered just how settled he wanted their future life to become. Maybe too settled? She did her best to set aside her concerns; she had work to do, with Carol, and needed to focus on that.

With Carol finally installed beside her, they set off toward Mair's home.

'She's only a few miles away, but – in village life terms – that means she might as well live on the moon,' observed Carol as she turned off the music and relaxed into her seat. 'The thing about being in a village is that its life is all around you, all the time. You get used to its rhythms…its heartbeat. Even out at the barn you're removed from that, aren't you?'

Christine agreed. 'You're right. Whenever I'm in the village I still feel like a visitor – I always feel as though I've missed…something. It's weird, because you and Annie keep me fully informed about what happens, so I suppose what I'm really missing are the nuances of exactly how it all happened.'

'Mair must notice a big difference, having been at that shop for so long,' said Carol. 'Anyway, let's hope she's not lost any of her legendary observational skills, eh? Maybe she's spotted the person we're after without realizing the significance of their presence.'

They chatted through the information about the scandal that had forced Mair to leave, which had reached them from Althea via Mavis – agreeing that it really did sound as though the ex-shopkeeper had found a new direction in her life, then Christine told Carol about her additional findings regarding the list of the deceased.

'I don't know if it'll make any difference to know this, but what I've heard several times is that the patients whose families got the wreaths weren't noted for having had a lot of visitors. Some did, but they weren't visited by the people who received the wreaths, which I thought odd. Did you hear that at all, with the enquiries you made?'

Carol acknowledged, 'You were the one having all the early conversations, I've only started to talk to people recently. No one mentioned it – though Llinos telling me that Alan Ridley was at the nursing home where he died to give some respite to his family would indicate they didn't visit during the couple of weeks he was there; the whole point was for them to be able to take a holiday for themselves. Imagine that, Christine, caring for someone who can't look after themselves at all, can't speak, and has to be fed, washed, and cleaned…and yet you love them so much that you upend your entire life to give them the support they need.'

Christine grinned. 'Like you and David do for Albert, you mean?'

'Aw, come on now, that's different. He's our son.'

'Not so different; Alan Ridley was the father. The cycle of life.' Even as she spoke Christine pictured her own father – still in his prime, and still knocking them dead in the City. She couldn't imagine him ever needing her to tend to his every need – her mother would do that happily. But…what about Alexander? He was fifteen years her senior – how would that work? When she was seventy, he'd be eighty-five and might need more care than she could give. *Give your head a shake*, she told herself.

'Nearly there,' she said, as they turned into a narrow road that was no more than a one-track lane. It was tarmacked, but needed attention, and seemed to lead nowhere.

'Is that it?' Carol sounded unsure. 'The GPS says it is.'

Christine rolled her eyes. 'Not that any GPS has been wrong, ever – eh?'

'Let's stop and take a look. Over there, there's a sort of widening – we could park without causing too much of a problem for anyone else. That big old navy Volvo Estate is taking up the whole of that tiny driveway.'

Christine pulled over. 'Where would they be going to, or coming from, Carol? There's nothing beyond this cottage except that field. Mind you, it's a nice quiet spot. Really tucked away. Picturesque cottage, too – just look at that garden, it's amazing.'

The two women walked toward the cottage. Christine was delighted by the variety of flowers and plants. 'Now this is perfect,' she said. 'Not fussy, not primped, just all running wild…no, not wild, you can tell it's tended, but it looks so natural. It's grand. I'd like a garden like this – and even a cottage like this. It's a good size, don't you think?'

Carol's response told Christine she wasn't really listening. As they walked along the path to the front door, Carol was even muttering under her breath.

'What's up with you?' Christine hissed as they approached the door. 'I'm knocking now – are you alright?'

As Christine knocked, Carol sighed heavily, then said, 'Follow my lead, Christine. Please?'

Unable to do anything else, Christine slapped a smile on her face when Mair Jones opened the door. 'Mair,' she said, 'did Sharon phone you about us maybe popping over?'

Mair was looking as smart as she ever did; she often visited her daughter at the shop, popped into the Lamb and Flag alone, or with Sharon, and while she and Christine had never had a good old natter, they'd passed the time of day often enough for the visit to feel comfortable.

Christine had no doubt that Mair would try to get the pair to divulge information they weren't supposed to, and she and Carol had discussed how they'd both need to be on their guard against that. Christine just hoped they were up to the task; they were both relatively new to the private enquiries thing, whereas Mair had decades of experience under her belt.

As they entered directly into a delightful sitting room that overlooked the front garden, Christine commented upon the fact that the windows were large enough that you really did feel as though there was little difference between the outside and the inside.

Accepting the compliment with a smile, and suggesting the seating arrangements, Mair was clearly in her element. Christine noted her trim figure, well-coiffed hair, and smart clothes. She admired women who made the best of themselves – as she hoped she always did herself. On this occasion both Christine and Mair giggled as they noted they were each wearing the same shade of cobalt blue with their white trousers, and agreed it was a crisp combination for the warm weather.

'You settle down, and I'll bring the tea,' said Mair, dismissing Christine's offer of help. 'I don't get a lot of visitors, so it's nice to give the good china a bit of an airing,' she joked as she bustled off to what Christine assumed was the kitchen.

Christine looked around; every ornament was perfectly positioned, there wasn't a speck of dust in the place, and the décor was subtle – giving a feeling of elegant countryside living, as opposed to traditional rural life. She noticed how Carol was still giving her attention to the garden.

'Lovely, isn't it?' she said, 'even from in here. Very well designed.'

Carol was transfixed. 'Mmm…' she muttered in reply to Christine, but Mair's arrival meant Christine couldn't prod her friend to say more.

The tea was, indeed, served on good china, and Christine was delighted to find it was almost as strong as she liked to make it for herself.

'Is this Irish tea?' She sipped and thought she recognized it.

Mair almost blushed and stage-whispered, 'I like everything to be Welsh, usually, but the Irish blend is what I prefer. I made the Welshcakes myself, mind you.'

Christine didn't know how long the small-talk would go on for, so eventually said, 'Thanks for letting us come to chat to you, Mair. I dare say you understand we can't really tell you why we're doing it, because it's on behalf of a client who wants us to keep their identity confidential.'

Mair leaned in. 'It's all very exciting – being able to help proper private investigators with a case – but, yes, Sharon told me as much. So – what is it, then? Someone been up to a bit of shoplifting in Builth? I could tell you a thing or two on that front, I dare say. Or what about a certain someone whose teenaged son likes to do a bit of joyriding now and again? Or the people who don't mind getting behind the wheel when they're over the limit? You ask – and I will tell. Then…' She mimed locking her lips shut and throwing away the key.

Christine tried to get Carol's attention, but she was still staring at the blessed garden, so continued, 'Thanks. Yes, confidentiality is very much the name of our game…not that it's a game to us, of course. No. Right – so we've heard that you're doing a fair old bit of hospital visiting, and we wondered if there was anyone you could think of who you see everywhere you visit?'

Mair looked puzzled. 'You mean specific people – not just ambulance drivers or nurses?'

Christine nodded. 'Yes, specific people. We're trying to find people who, like you, visit pretty much every hospital, hospice, and nursing home for about thirty miles or so around. Does anyone come to mind? Anyone at all? It doesn't matter what they do.'

Mair nibbled a Welshcake, her brow furrowed. 'The only one who comes to mind would be the bloke who rides the motorbike; he picks up the blood tests and stuff like that and takes them to a laboratory where they're all "done". Whatever they do to the samples, you know? There's him. I see him everywhere.'

Christine felt the first real hope of a good lead. 'You don't happen to know his name, do you?'

Mair sipped her tea. 'I think it's Dylan, or maybe Wayne. I know they're nothing alike, but I always get those two muddled up in my head. He's young, not bad looking, I suppose – if you're young, too. But I dare say any of the places he goes to would know more about him. I don't even know who he works for, exactly. I suppose I've always thought it's the health authority, but he hasn't got any logos on him, or anything like that. Just ordinary motorcycle stuff. Does that help?'

Christine was elated. 'It does, doesn't it, Carol?' She went so far as to kick Carol's ankle, finally managing to drag her colleague's attention from the garden.

However, instead of sharing Christine's excitement, Carol said, 'I'm sorry – could I use your loo, please?'

Mair smiled, and put down her tea. She rose, waving toward the stairs. 'Up there, on the right.'

'Thanks.' Without another word, Carol left.

Mair looked concerned. 'She's alright, is she? She seems a bit…off. Hasn't even touched her tea.'

Christine was thinking much the same thing, but replied brightly, 'I'm sure she's fine. She's a working mum with a baby who's just started toddling, so I think that might be it.'

Mair sat and picked up her cup and saucer. 'She's so lucky to have such a good husband. Talk of the village, he is, with his high-flying work – clients all around the world, I hear. She's lucky to have him.'

Christine felt annoyed on Carol's behalf. 'She used to be his boss, you know?'

'Really?'

'Yes, Carol headed up the systems management for one of the world's largest reinsurance agencies. She's head and shoulders above David when it comes to computing – but she so very much wanted to be a mother…and now he's able to consult while she works with us.'

'Now, isn't that interesting,' said Mair over her cup. 'His boss, you say?'

For some reason, Christine felt she'd been duped into giving Mair a piece of information that wasn't generally known in the village, and was immediately concerned by the fact that Mair found it so fascinating. Her mind grappled with any ways that the knowledge could be used as a weapon by the woman whose eyes glinted in the sun reflecting off the bone china.

'Speaking of interesting,' said Carol, who'd appeared at the door without a sound, 'this is what I call interesting, Mair.'

Christine struggled to work out what her colleague was holding in each of her hands: a roundel of black wire-mesh tubing…what on earth was it?

Carol sounded grave. '*You're* the one who's been leaving wreaths of condolence at people's homes, aren't you, Mair? These forms, and all the other supplies you'd need to make the wreaths, were in the spare bedroom. And your garden? Laurel, foxgloves, anemones, hortensia and cypress – all there, ready for you to use…to fashion a wreath with a message of hatred. There's even a tailcoat upstairs.'

Christine was listening, and hearing, but still not quite understanding.

Carol continued, 'I wondered how Sharon had known about Annie ending up in an open grave. You told her, didn't you? And who would know about that except for someone who was on the spot? And that navy Volvo you've got parked out there? Yes, someone could mistake the back end of that for a hearse.'

Christine dared, 'Are you saying that Mair is the Uninvited Undertaker?'

Carol nodded.

'The who?' Mair sounded more than surprised.

Carol replied, 'That's our name for the person who's been leaving all these wreaths, and the iron roses at the cemeteries and graveyards. It was you who shoved Annie into that grave, wasn't it? She's going to be laid up for at least a week because of that – and there's every chance she might develop a really nasty infection, too.'

Christine was quite taken aback by the anger in Carol's voice – though she understood it well enough, and felt the same emotion bubble up inside her, too, as the cogs all fell into place.

Once it all made sense, she said, 'Of course! We came to ask you if you knew of anyone else who visited all the places you did – when it was you all along. Bloke on a motorbike, my eye. That was just to put us off the scent. What have you been playing at, woman? Do you know how many people you've upset? And what about poor Ed Hughes – did you…did you kill him?'

Mair Jones chuckled, then put her cup down and laughed heartily. Christine and Carol stared at her, both fuming.

When she gathered herself, Mair said, 'Look at the two of you. Overheating because I've put a few floral tributes in front of a few people's homes. Good grief, what a fuss. And all over nothing. The fuss should be about those poor people who lie in their sick beds with their family ignoring them. Yes, some of them pop by for the odd guilt-visit, but if it wasn't for people like me – those who really care – they'd have no one to talk to at all.'

Christine said, 'Hang on a minute, Mair. Whatever you might think was going on, the fact of the matter was that you delivered the wreaths before the person in question died. So how did you manage that, eh? Is there something you want to tell us? Specifically about Ed Hughes, to start with. Or we could stay with you until the police arrive, if you like.'

Mair snapped, 'The police? Don't be so ridiculous. It was only my bit of fun. Well, not fun, really – I wanted all those families to know how they'd let their loved ones down. And I delivered all those wreaths when there was still time for them to go to see them, before they died. But it didn't even occur to any of them to do that much. They thoroughly deserve any upset I caused them. And as for Steve Hughes's uncle? He was already dead when I visited his caravan. I'd met him when he was in the outpatient's department getting some treatments for his shoulder. There more often than made good sense, he was. And always needing a chat. No one in his family cared about him at all. That Sarah and Steve Hughes needed to be taught a lesson. Abandoning him when he needed his family like that. Had to catch two buses to get to his appointments, he did.'

'How did you know?' Christine still couldn't work it out. 'How did you know they would die? I don't believe you about Ed Hughes. Did you kill him? Did you kill them all?' There, she'd said it.

'Just like all the Irish, aren't you? Thick as a brick. No, I didn't kill him, and I didn't kill any of the others, either. I didn't need to – they were all dying, as their families would have known, if they'd bothered to turn up. It's rarely a surprise to those who work with people who are terribly ill that they die when they do; they've seen it before, so many, many times. I'd talk to the nurses and doctors when I went visiting, and they'd tell me who was likely to go next, and I'd deliver a wreath to the family members who could never be bothered to visit. The poor patients lying about in their sick beds were always only too happy to give me chapter and verse about the "loved ones" who never came to see them, right down to their names and addresses. Most of the time the people who got wreaths from me didn't even phone up to find out how the sick, old person they "loved" was faring. I haven't done anything wrong. They did.'

Christine got the impression that Mair Jones truly believed what she was saying. And she didn't know quite how to handle that information.

It seemed Carol did, though, when she shouted, 'You're a bitter, selfish woman, Mair. You have no idea why the people who didn't make visits acted that way. There are sometimes very good reasons why people can't visit. Steve Hughes didn't even know where his uncle was, for example – in fact, he'd never met him in his life. You can't blame him for that. Besides, Ed Hughes wasn't ill, and he certainly didn't die a natural death. So what do you have to say about that?'

Mair had a tinkling, musical laugh, and she trilled down several annoying scales. Christine could feel herself getting hotter as the woman continued to find what was happening funny. She also wondered just how angry Carol might get; she was definitely getting there – pink as the sunrise that morning she was now.

'Shut up!' snapped Carol.

Christine was pleased that Mair did, then said, 'If you found Ed Hughes dead at his home, why didn't you phone the authorities – or at least speak to someone at the caravan park about what you'd seen? Oh no, you let the poor man lie there for days, while you took the opportunity to send a wreath to the Hughes family that meant nothing to them – except to scare them about the health and wellbeing of Steve's parents.'

'Well, that's something, I suppose. But you're wrong, I did tell someone; I told his friend Archie about what I'd seen. He was hanging about the place, and even challenged me when I knocked at the door of the caravan. He saw what I saw; I can't imagine why he didn't report that his best friend was as dead as a doornail straight away, on the Wednesday. Nothing to do with me. Maybe you'd better ask him about that.'

Christine said, 'Even if you think you haven't done anything wrong, Mair, maybe you could apologize to all the families? It would be helpful if they all knew it was you who'd been doing it.'

Mair shook her head and spoke smugly, 'I delivered the wreath, but they did nothing. So I apologized to the person who died for not having been able to get their family to take notice of them by leaving an everlasting rose at their funeral. I won't be doing anything else.'

'What about stopping?' Carol's voice sounded weird to Christine.

'I don't see why I should. I'm thriving now: visiting people who are so ill that they're happy to chat to me, or even just lie there while I chat to them, is wonderful. And the people who work at hospitals? So glad to have someone to have a natter with when they get a break, you know? And the things they tell me about would make your hair curl. Mind you, with that hair you've got, I doubt it, Carol…no room for more curls, is there? So it would make your hair curl, Christine.'

'But why all so elaborate, Mair?' It sounded as though Carol were pleading. 'If you're intent upon gathering gossip from hospitals, that makes sense; the threat of legal action by Elizabeth Fernley and your subsequent rift with Marjorie Pritchard, which eventually led to you selling your shop, meant you weren't at the heart of the village any longer. Living out here you must have almost expired without the oxygen of the "little chats" you were used to having in your shop. We've all seen how you like to keep on top of what's what by visiting Sharon, but it wasn't the same, was it? Not only couldn't you gather as much ammunition as you were used to having, but you couldn't see the effect of any of the little attacks you made. So…you found a new hunting ground.'

Christine couldn't stop herself from saying, 'You're a horrible woman, underneath all this stylish veneer, aren't you, Mair? Thinking about it, I've only ever heard you say nice things about people with a sneer in your voice. A snake in the grass, that's what you are. And when you were all but tossed out of your home field, you went looking for pastures new, didn't you? You wicked woman.'

Mair smiled coldly. 'I've. Done. Nothing. Wrong.' She stood. 'Now, please leave.'

Christine could see that Carol was breathing heavily – in fact, she looked fit to burst – so she also stood, then made her way to her friend, shoving her out of the cottage and along the path.

Carol didn't resist being steered by Christine, but – at the gate – she turned and took dozens of rapidly-shot photographs of the garden.

Christine hissed, 'Come away with you now, Carol. Let's be leaving her in her own bile. She's not a person anyone should ever spend time with – she exudes poison, so she does.'

The drive back to Anwen-by-Wye was largely silent. As they entered the village, Carol said, 'I need milk. Could you drop me at the shop, please? David will be wanting some for his breakfast.'

Christine thought Carol sounded…*disconnected?*...but agreed. They pulled up a little way along from the shop, and Carol had her seatbelt off and the door open before they'd stopped properly, making alarms ping loudly.

'Hang on, Carol,' called Christine as her colleague jumped out and stomped toward the shop. She didn't even check for other traffic.

It suddenly dawned on Christine that Carol was on the warpath, quite literally, and was probably going to tell Sharon exactly what was going on. She grappled with her own seat belt, then managed to escape and cantered to catch up.

When she finally entered the shop, it was clear she was too late; Carol was waggling the photographs she'd taken in front of Sharon's face and she was saying, 'When that wreath arrived at Sarah Hughes's door, the whole family was impacted, Sharon. You saw Sarah –

worried to death, she was. As was Steve, about his parents. And the reason they never visited his "uncle" in hospital? He'd never met him – didn't have a clue where he was. The man had been estranged from his family since before Steve was even born. But that didn't stop your mother, did it? Oh no. Nor did it stop her having a go at a lovely couple who'd done everything they could to look after his father…all they needed was a bit of a break.'

It was clear to Christine that most of Carol's points were going over Sharon's head – the girl didn't look as though she'd grasped the basics of the situation, let alone any of the details that Carol was shouting about.

Why is Carol acting like this? She's usually the one who keeps her cool? was what Christine thought; 'Let's all take a breath, shall we?' was what she said aloud.

She did the first thing she could think of to try to change the mood; she gave Carol a big hug, then did the same to Sharon. Sharon looked grateful, while Carol looked surprised, but it had the desired effect in both cases.

Sharon walked to the door, clicked the lock and turned the sign to CLOSED. 'Right then, how about you start again, and this time maybe you could start at the beginning and go a bit slower because, to be honest, Carol, I have no idea what you were talking about then.'

Carol sighed deeply and Christine began to explain while her chum gathered herself. It took a while to give the sort of detail that was really needed.

WEDNESDAY 21st JUNE

CHAPTER FORTY

Carol, David, and Albert were already nicely settled on the large blankets Carol had hauled out of the house and onto the village green. The sun was still quite warm, but she'd brought a cardi, in case she needed it later on. David was playing with Albert, who seemed keen to run off as fast as he could; it amazed Carol that what had been rubbery legs a few weeks earlier were now capable of such speed. He fell down quite a bit, but she'd decided she wouldn't make a fuss when he did, so his routine was now to get back up and carry on as though nothing had happened.

They'd had a lovely weekend down at her parents' farm, and they'd talked about all sorts of things when Albert had gone to bed – including her mum and dad's plans to make their best efforts to sell the farm, so they could be released from their daily grind.

Carol had suggested to her mum that they could continue to live there, but just not have the sheep, then they'd ended up having a conversation long into the night about the impact of taking land out of the farming and food production picture. But they'd all parted happily, and Carol had even planted a seed that her parents might consider moving from Carmarthenshire to Powys, to be closer to their grandson – which had received a warm reaction.

She waved to Sharon, who was setting out a stall in front of the shop with all sorts of snacks. Sharon and her mother had had a major falling out about the business with the wreaths, which Carol was – in one way – quite pleased about; Mair deserved some sort of comeuppance because of her poisonous actions. However, she also felt sorry for Sharon, who'd really been 'friends' with her mother as well as being her daughter. That said, Carol reckoned that Sharon would come to terms with it all – and had noticed that her gossiping had died down a bit of late, which wasn't really a bad thing, either.

Carol resealed the insulated bag which held the sandwiches and the bottle of squash she'd made up for her and David to enjoy as they watched whatever was going to happen; no one was really clear about the evening's schedule because the posters dotted around and beyond Anwen-by-Wye had been enticing, but a bit vague.

She saw Llinos Trevelyan, in capris and a midriff-revealing top – so, not on duty. Llinos appeared to have someone with her, though Carol couldn't be sure if it was a male or a female. In any case, Llinos crossed the green toward Carol, her arms open and a broad grin on her face.

'Lovely to see you, Carol. Come and give me a hug.'

Carol was a bit surprised by the greater-than-usual warmth of her friend's greeting, but hugged back for all she was worth.

When they were still close, Llinos whispered excitedly, 'We got him, Carol. Well, actually, I got him. The bloke who killed Ed Hughes. Can you believe it? I was having a drink with Sandy over there –' she waved at her abandoned friend – 'in Brecon a couple of nights ago, and there was this bloke as drunk as a skunk, singing his lungs out as he sat on the pavement against a wall.'

Carol was puzzled, but Llinos hung onto her, only letting her pull back a bit. 'And?'

'Well, he was singing "You are my Cardiff, my only Cardiff" to the tune of "You are My Sunshine".'

Carol was still in the dark. 'So?'

Llinos finally released her grasp. 'It's a Cardiff City football chant, you know?'

Carol didn't, but tired not to show it. 'Go on.'

'Well, he looked up at me – completely glazed expression – and he said, "Old bugger had it coming – shouldn't have said he'd tell them about me and the club's money, should he?" And it just clicked.'

Carol finally gave in. 'I'm sorry, Llinos – I haven't got a clue what you're talking about.'

It was Llinos's turn to look puzzled, then she chuckled. 'Of course, you wouldn't know, would you? The Ed Hughes murder case? The investigation uncovered the fact that there'd been a great deal of money going missing from the social club at the caravan park where Ed lived. I wasn't on the murder team, of course, but I got roped in to do some initial examination of the club's books, because I used to work in an accountancy firm before I joined the service – a cubicle-dweller, that was me. I'd seen the photos of all the people they'd interviewed, so I recognized Archie Hammond, Ed's best friend – the bloke who discovered the body on the Friday morning and called it in – even though we'd never met. When I saw him on that street, saying what he was saying, I picked him up and took him to the station – citing the condition he was in. I made my views known that he might be the one who'd stolen the money we knew had gone missing, and then killed his friend who'd threatened to tell about it…based on what I'd heard him say. It took a day for him to be sober enough to be questioned.'

'Did he confess?' Carol was all ears.

Llinos shook her head. 'No. He claimed that he'd found out that *Ed* had taken the money, and said *he* was going to tell. He did, however, confess that he'd confronted Ed about the thefts, at Ed's caravan on the Tuesday night; the two of them had rowed, Ed had attacked him, and he'd fought back. He claimed that it looked as though Ed Hughes had passed out when he left him. Felt awful about it, he said, but still planned to force Ed to own up to having stolen club funds when they met at the social club on the Thursday, as usual. When he found his friend's body on the Friday morning, he was in a right state – said he didn't know what to do, so "omitted to mention" the fight. He broke down in the interview, crying like a baby, and said it was "an accident". So, the upshot is that we have the killer, and I got the praise for bringing him in…even though it looks like the charge won't be murder.'

Carol finally understood. 'Well done, Llinos…though, listen – you might want to talk to whomever is in charge, because I happen to know that Mair Jones – you know, Sharon's mum – told Archie Hammond that she'd found Ed Hughes dead on the Wednesday that week. Might that mean his story isn't true? Maybe what you heard him say when he was drunk was the truth, and what he claimed when he was sober, without Ed Hughes around to protect his name regarding the theft of club funds, was Archie trying to save himself from a more serious charge?'

Llinos's mouth fell open. 'Mair Jones told Archie Hammond that she'd seen Ed Hughes dead on the Wednesday? But Archie told us, categorically, that he was surprised when Ed didn't turn up on the Thursday night. Most emphatic he was that *that* was why he went to Ed's caravan on the Friday morning, which is when he claimed he'd found the body, and immediately – he puffed himself up about that bit – reported the death. I should talk to her. Will she be here this evening, do you think?'

Carol shook her head. 'I wouldn't have thought so. But I have her address; I'll text it to you. I bet she'd be only too happy to confirm what I've told you…though she might have a bit of a shock when you turn up at her house in your police car.'

Llinos's brow furrowed. 'What's going on? There's something you're not telling me, isn't there?'

Carol shrugged. 'You should ask Mair why she was at Ed Hughes's caravan…about how her newfound role as a volunteer visitor to those in hospitals and hospices in the area has helped her form certain views about family relationships.'

'No! Mair Jones…the Uninvited Undertaker? You're kidding?'

Carol nodded. 'Yes, she confessed when Christine and I confronted her. Laughed about it, she did. Poisonous so-and-so that she is. But – well, there was no point telling you about it because she really hadn't done anything wrong, had she? Just left flowers at people's homes – that was it, really. But – yes – if you could roll up, maybe with the lights flashing…that would be…something. And, as I said, you might find she's able to clarify that Archie Hammond has been telling a few porky pies. And who knows how many, exactly?'

Llinos hugged Carol again.

'Text me that address, will you? I'll grab Sandy and we'll go to the station to let them know. We're just constables, see, so we don't really get to do the glory stuff, but being helpful in this case might get them to notice me – in a good way. Mair's evidence would give them a chance to break Archie Hammond's story. Thanks, Carol. Enjoy the evening – got to go.'

Carol texted, then waved.

'Lovely evening, isn't it?' David had finally retrieved Albert from his wanderings, and popped him into the portable playpen they'd brought with them so they wouldn't have to be chasing after him all the time. 'How's Llinos?'

Carol answered simply, 'Doing well, I believe.'

David waggled his fingers toward Albert. 'I know we were all complaining about how dry it had been, but the last ten days or so I feel like I haven't seen proper daylight at all. Still, all that rain will have helped those who needed it, I dare say.'

He reached into the cooler bag and pulled out a packet of sandwiches.

'Oi, they're for later,' said Carol, playfully slapping at his hand.

'But I'm hungry now,' whined David, grinning and sliding the sandwiches out of Carol's reach. 'Besides, what are we waiting for? Who knows what's going to kick off, or even when…not me for one.'

Carol chuckled. 'And not me for two. Mavis seemed to know what the plans were, but she wouldn't say, and she's been tied up with that case over in Lampeter for the past week.'

'What's Annie called that one? I love what she does with all those titles.'

'The Case of the Lost Luggage – an easy one, really, when a client wants you to trace a couple of bags they left behind when they were taken ill at a holiday home they were renting.'

'Did she find them? The bags.' David sounded more than mildly interested.

'Oh yes. It turned out that the brother-in-law of the bloke who owned the place had been in there before anyone else, and had swiped them for himself. Took them back to his place in Birmingham "for safe keeping" he claimed – where Mavis saw one of the bags in a spare bedroom when she had to "pop to the loo" during an interview the man agreed to give…to help his family's reputation.'

David shook his head. 'The things people do, eh?'

'Yeah – but if they didn't, we wouldn't have this chance to be living here, would we? And it is lovely, isn't it? Despite the fact there are a few idiots, like Mair Jones, who live here too. Though, I suppose she's not really a villager any longer, is she?'

David gave Carol a hug. 'The Case of the Village Idiots?'

Carol punched him, playfully. 'Hardy-har-har, husband. Aw, come on, the people here are all wonderful, really, aren't they? And we all have our moments – though I hope I never lose my temper again the way I lost it with Mair Jones.'

David chomped into a sandwich and chewed thoughtfully. 'Christine said you were like an avenging angel; I wouldn't have minded seeing that, because it's so not like you. However, on balance, this is the Carol I prefer – the normal one. Love you so much, Carol…and this one too, of course.'

'That's the David I prefer, too – back to a normal daytime pattern and not stressed out because of an annoying client.'

'Yeah – we're never going to work for him again, all three of us agreed. Nasty piece of work. We all got a bit immune to his way of talking after a while, then you find yourself thinking that way…then you revolt, so to speak. There won't be any Christmas cards exchanged, I don't think.'

'His loss,' said Carol. 'Come on, now, let's clear those crumbs away, and I'll inflate the cushions so we can be a bit more comfy. Oh good – there's Joan bringing Doris over in her wheelchair. I did wonder if they'd be coming. It's nice to see them out and about again.'

Joan Pike was, indeed, pushing her mother toward the Hill family, and she was smiling broadly, as Carol knew she always did, despite all the challenges presented by being her mother's carer.

She greeted the women with a broad smile. 'You're both looking as smart as ever. Did you make those matching dresses, yourself, Joan?'

Joan nodded, her natural copper curls making her flushed cheeks look even more ruddy. 'I did. Do you like them? Mum picked the design and the fabric; it was a dress her own mother made for her when she was a child, so I had to scale up the pattern, of course, but it turned out alright, and the blue suits us both, don't you think?'

Carol and David agreed that both women looked a picture in their lovely cotton frocks.

'I bet you're glad we had all that rain,' observed David. 'Carol's been telling me that you suffer with terrible hay fever, Mrs Pike, and that you can't take anything for it. Is it better now?'

Just as Doris Pike was about to reply she was taken by an attack of sneezing.

'Oh heck, Mam – here you are, have a couple of these.' Joan handed two linen hankies, edged with crocheted lace, embroidered with the letter 'D' in red, to her mother, who promptly dropped one as she sneezed into the other.

Joan tried to catch the hankie before it was picked up by the breeze and fluttered away. 'Hang on to Mam's chair, will you,' she called as she chased after it. Carol did, knowing that she'd finally solved The Case of Harmful Hankie on Annie's behalf, and couldn't wait to tell her about it.

Christine had been truly proud, and surprisingly overwhelmed by emotion, when 'Anwen Antiquities & Curiosities, curated by Coggins and Chellingworth' had been opened with an elaborate ribbon-cutting ceremony – performed by Stephanie – at ten that morning; indeed, at one point she'd thought she might faint. Or maybe it had been the humidity, or the fact that she'd drunk a bit more than usual the previous night – for which Alexander had chastised her, even if only playfully.

It had been interesting to have him staying with her for the past week; he'd been the one up and out early every day, first to run – despite the rain – then to be at the shop to oversee all the final setting-up and stock-taking.

As a general rule, she was able to pop down to the office to start work each day with a minute to spare before Mavis arrived, but even she'd been gone for the past several days. That had meant that Annie and Carol had worked from home, while she'd rattled around inside the big old barn on her own. All day. Every day. It had been…odd. And not especially pleasant.

That was why she was planning a visit to her parents in London, and would be leaving early the next day. Which meant sticking to soft drinks for once, because she didn't want to end up with her head stuck in the loo like she had for the past couple of mornings. It wasn't normal for her to react to having over-indulged that way, but she realized it was all self-inflicted, and she'd hidden it from Alexander knowing he'd give her no sympathy at all. Why should he? It wasn't his fault.

She was fully aware of the fact she could choose to not drink alcohol whenever she wanted, so opened a bottle of fake champagne – fizzy grape juice, really – popping the cork with a joyous 'WOW!' and causing Alexander to finally join her at the chairs and table he'd set up outside the shop on the road; the traffic around the green had been blocked for the evening.

'You look happy,' he said as he kissed her. 'In fact, you're glowing; the sun looks fabulous shining on your hair.' He looked at the bottle, then looked at her. 'Oh, right, you're driving to London first thing – good idea. And you don't mind me staying on in the flat while you're away? I'd say I'd get a room somewhere, but you know there aren't any, which you know also means that Henry would feel compelled – no, duty-bound – to invite me to stay at Chellingworth, and I don't want to do that, really. I can cope with working with him – mainly through Bob Fernley – but to have to see him at breakfast every day? Not my cup of tea, as they say around here.'

The pair shared a hug, and Christine felt the sun in her heart as she saw the smile on Alexander's face.

'We're really very fortunate, aren't we?' She touched his hand, gently.

Alexander returned her caress. 'We are indeed, Christine. But…well, you don't seem as happy as I always hope you're going to be. Maybe now that I have a purpose here in the village we can sort out a bit more of a settled situation. I know I have to be on hand to oversee my construction projects in London, as well as making sure all my tenants are well looked after, but I'm well on my way to doing what the best managers do – finding good people I can direct, rather than having to do it all myself. Of course, finding people I can trust and who I believe will do a better job than me is a bit of a challenge, but I'm getting there…and then we can really decide what shape we want for our future; where we'll live, how we'll introduce balance.'

Christine was certain that she loved Alexander and knew she wanted some sort of balance, but couldn't quite work out how it was all going to fit nicely together for them – *and* allow her to have a bit of fun when she felt like it. Maybe time would tell?

'We'll work it out – together,' she said, pouring a glass of fizz for her fiancé. 'If I'm having this stuff, so are you,' she said cheekily.

'I'll toast to that,' said Alexander.

Their raised glasses caught the mellow sunlight as it played across the village green.

Annie and Tudor had brought the pups with them, and were both struggling to keep them entertained until the festivities really began. Having agreed that a walk around the green, then over to the duck pond and back, would help, they finally had to pass the still boarded-up Coach and Horses. Annie couldn't resist looking up and sighing.

'I know it would have been hard work, but maybe we could have made a go of it, Tude,' she said sadly. Really, she was picturing the two of them in the flat that occupied the spacious upper floor.

Tudor glanced at the building, then gave his attention to Rosie. 'I've been thinking about it, too, and I'm not sad about it really, because we've managed to get that snug at my place looking so inviting. I know we've already made more money than I spent doing it up; we've managed to get quite a few in for teas and coffees who never came into the bar – locals, as well as tourists – which is fantastic. And I know you're back to being one hundred percent now, but you've got your work, and that's important to you, so you don't have to worry that you can't help out at a place that would probably need both of us putting in a full-time effort to cover the costs. Don't fret – we're managing alright, really, aren't we?'

Annie chuckled. 'Well, I've been managing a bit better since you gave me a whole two drawers at your place, plus three hangers in the wardrobe, to keep my bits and pieces, that's for certain.'

'And I've got used to my bathroom smelling like a field of lily of the valley after you've been in it. It's nice, to be honest – it smells like you.' He stuck his nose beside Annie's ear and mugged deep sniffing noises.

'Oi, down boy,' Annie said. 'Oh, hang on – look, Althea and Mavis are making a beeline for us. I bet she'll want you to magic up something she hasn't thought of for this evening; I know Althea has some good ideas that build community, but she's even better at making sure that everyone else does the work.'

'Aw, come on now, this is going to be lovely; dancing, music, food and drink – and the summer solstice is being very kind to us after all that rain we've had.'

'It didn't know when to stop once it started, though, did it? Hello Althea, Mave. How are you? Lovely night for it, in't it?'

Annie wondered why Althea looked so excited, and Mavis so apprehensive. Mavis stood behind Althea and shrugged, so Annie let it pass. 'Something you need me or Tude to do, is there?' She thought she might as well ask.

Althea twittered, 'More something I can do for you, I think.'

Always on her guard when Althea seemed this excited about anything, Annie exchanged a glance with Tudor and said, 'And what would that be?'

Althea grabbed Tudor's free hand – his other was hanging onto Rosie's lead trying to control her as she gave McFli, Althea, and Mavis a good sniffing. The dowager shoved something into Tudor's palm, closing his fingers around the object.

'There,' she said, almost hopping with excitement.

Tudor opened his hand and both he and Annie examined its contents.

They were both puzzled. 'Keys?' they chorused.

'What are these for?' Tudor's brow was deeply furrowed.

Althea beamed. 'They're for the Coach and Horses. I bought it. For the Estate. And I've talked to Henry and Stephanie about it and we've all agreed that we'd like you to take it on. The rent will be at the same rate we charge for the Lamb and Flag…and we have plans for that, too. We're going to make the whole place into a tea shop – a proper one. You've done so well with that snug, and so many people have said how lovely it is to have a tea shop in the village again, that we think that's what it should be, going forward. But the Coach and Horses will give back the village something it's been missing for too long – a place for people to stay. Henry and Bob Fernley have talked about renovations within the rules allowed by the building's listing, so nothing will be instant and, of course, we all want your design input. Both of you. So…what do you think? Will you do it?'

Tudor and Annie stared at each other open-mouthed.

Annie managed, 'Gordon Bennett, Althea – you and your lot don't muck about, do you?'

Tudor replied more soberly, 'I'm so touched and delighted that you think I'm up to it. Yes, I'll do it – but not just because it will be good for me and this wonderful woman to be able to better share our lives, but because…yes, your ideas really will be good for Anwen-by-Wye, and I want to do whatever I can to make this the best village it can be.'

As Althea and Tudor hugged – which looked a bit scary because Tudor almost completely enveloped her – Annie felt her tummy tighten with excitement. Even Gertie seemed to know that something momentous had just happened because she turned her attention from McFli's rear end and jumped up at Annie, yapping.

'Yes, Gert – we're going to be a family: me, Tude, you and Rosie – in't it fabulous?'

As Althea and Mavis made their way around the green, heading toward the area where Marjorie Pritchard was head-to-head with Wendy Jenkins beside her keyboard, Mavis said, 'You kept that quiet, dear. What a surprise.'

Althea dimpled. 'That's not all I've been keeping quiet about.'

Mavis sighed. 'Alright then, out with it – what else have you been up to with all that to-ing and fro-ing up to the Hall you've been doing, that you think I've no' noticed?'

Finally reaching the seating that had been arranged along one of the four sides of the green, Althea settled herself and said, 'You being away for a few days helped, because I didn't want it all to be going on under your nose, but it's sorted out now.'

Mavis sat beside Althea and kept a weather eye on Marjorie and Wendy – who seemed to be waving their arms about rather a lot for two people who were theoretically merely discussing the running order of the music to be played in a few moments' time.

'And are you going to tell me about whatever it is?'

'No,' said Althea intriguingly. 'But he is.'

She nodded across the green toward a man in shorts and a linen shirt who Mavis had never seen before – at least, she thought not, until he was close enough for her to make out that it was Carwen James. Mavis was taken aback to discover that he even had legs, let alone that they should be such a relatively fine pair.

'And what's he doing here? No' going to dance, is he?'

'He's more than welcome to stay for that,' replied Althea, 'but that's not why he's agreed to be here. I didn't expect mufti, though, I have to be honest. I'd rather hoped he'd do it in his full-dress uniform – but I won't pull him up about that.'

Mavis was still very much in the dark, and realized there was no point pressing the dowager, because she'd clearly planned this whole thing – whatever it was.

With the arrival of Carwen James, Tudor made his way across the green, and a general hubbub between Tudor, Marjorie, Carwen, and Wendy resulted in a few loud chords from Wendy on her keyboard causing a hush to fall among the not inconsiderable crowd that was surrounding, and spilling onto, the green.

Tudor welcomed everyone very nicely, thought Mavis, then introduced the chief inspector, to whom he handed the microphone.

A fairly dramatic throat-clearing on the part of the officer was followed by his opening words: 'My thanks to Tudor, and to those who've invited me here this evening. I know you're all keen to get started with what might well – by the looks of it – become an annual summer solstice celebration, so I shall be brief. I, more than most, understand the challenges of policing in today's society, and I certainly don't intend to talk about that, as such. But I want to mention that we at the front line are often able to see where there's a problem, but are unable to do anything about it. We just have to deal with the fallout as best we can, so to speak, rather than having a meaningful opportunity to get to the root cause of a problem. Yes, there are other agencies who can get involved, and they do – to the fullest extent of their capabilities and resources, in most cases. But sometimes immeasurable good can be done by those who offer support of a type that's not readily available from institutions. I'm talking about community support groups, small charitable efforts, that sort of thing – things that happen *within* communities, not *to* them. And this evening I am delighted to announce the formation of just such an organization. The MacDonald Trust has been established to offer advice, counselling, and – where necessary and possible – treatment programs for those suffering from addiction to prescription medications. The plan is to start small, creating launch pads for centers within communities where there's a need, across Powys, but who knows where it might lead.'

As applause rippled around the village green, Mavis stared at Althea, who was beaming, tears in her eyes.

Carwen James continued, 'Now, you might not think that such a set-up would be needed in our wonderful county, but I can tell you that it is – very much so, I'm sorry to say. The founders of this trust have worked with, and will continue to work with, an excellent mixture of existing community groups, as well as my specialized officers and the health system, to ensure that the right gaps will be filled, in the right way. I am happy to announce that Her Grace, the Dowager Chellingworth, will be the trust's patron. However, the financial backers of the trust wish to remain anonymous. Be that as it may, and speaking as someone devoted to upholding the law, I can tell you I have every belief that, by working with those with addictions, this trust will not only help people at the mercy of this blight on our society, but will also help alleviate the crime that is associated with it. There, I've said my piece, and I'm sure you're all keen to get on with the festivities, so I'll hand you back to Tudor Evans now, who I know is your compere for the evening. I wish you all well – and here's to the MacDonald Trust.'

This time the applause was more enthusiastic, and Tudor milked it a bit, as Carwen James made his way across the green to be close to his car.

Mavis hissed, 'You've done this, haven't you?'

Althea nodded. 'You're not cross with me, are you? I thought it would be nice for you to have your name on it – because I think it's something you'd like to be involved with, in some way. Those long chats we had after The Case of the Suspicious Sister left me in no doubt that this was something about which you cared passionately.'

Mavis felt herself choking up. Before she couldn't control herself, she hugged the small figure beside her and said quietly, 'Althea Twyst, you are quite an amazing woman. You never cease to both infuriate and delight me. Thank you – not from me, but from all those who will, I hope, benefit from what you've done. By using your title and resources to get this going, you're going to change people's lives, Althea. And I promise I will do my best to ensure that there's no money wasted as good is done.'

Althea whispered back, 'I never had any doubt about that last point, dear, which is why I'm so keen for you to head up the board of trustees. But let's enjoy this for now, we can talk about all that later on. Have you noticed that Marjorie is wearing her full Welsh costume, including the hat, for the dancing?'

Mavis replied, 'I have – though I have to say it all looks a bit hot for this weather. Mind you – you're not being outshone by her, are you? That yellow kaftan is quite sharp on the eye, dear.'

'It's as close as I could get to what Clemmie wore this morning at her wedding. Didn't she look lovely? It was so clever of her to get someone to record it so we could watch it here in Wales. I must say, the temple at Karnak was looking a lot better tended than when Chelly and I visited it, many moons ago. She looked a picture, didn't she? And what about Julian? Who knew he was such a handsome chap under all that fur on his face? I'm so pleased he chose to shave it all off for the wedding.'

'Aye,' agreed Mavis, thinking to herself that he'd looked better with the beard, if she was honest, because he lacked enough chin to balance the rest of his head. 'Though he'll have to be careful in the Egyptian sun, his skin having been protected for so long.'

'Well, I dare say he can grow it back. I've never been a fan of beards myself – far too tickly in the clinches, if you know what I mean. Chelly decided to grow one of those droopy mustache things at one point, and I had to put my foot down about it…I got a rash whenever we…you know.'

'Ach, Althea, you scamp – please don't make me imagine things I cannae unsee in my head, dear, please? Now, come along, they're about to begin.'

Between them, Tudor, Wendy, and Marjorie hosted the most unexpectedly wonderful evening: dancing was rehearsed – sometimes with great hilarity – then proceeded with many entanglements and fun, despite Marjorie barking what were, to be fair, useful and clear instructions. During breaks, the offerings of Tudor's pub and Sharon's shop were enjoyed by the families present, while Wendy played enough modern and traditional tunes to entertain people of all ages.

Ian Cottesloe's storytelling about the meaning of the summer solstice for the children present went down very well – with adults stepping in to hold up the models of the sun and the planets that he'd been busy making in the shed at the Dower House for the past week. And Althea's idea that he should dress in red and orange then leap about the place like flames was also heralded as both engaging, and much safer than having an open flame about the place, despite the recent rain.

The conclusion of the event was a toast to Clementine and Julian – which was recorded, and the video emailed to them by Christine, which everyone agreed was a delightful way to end the evening.

Carol and David toasted each other, then Albert; Annie and Tudor toasted each other, the pups, then the Coach and Horses; Christine and Alexander toasted each other, then the antiques shop; Mavis and Althea toasted each other, then Henry and Stephanie, who'd brought Hugo with them to enjoy his first real experience of Anwen-by-Wye.

Henry turned his head on his pillow from the sight of his son, asleep in his crib, to face his wife – who he was quite certain couldn't possibly be asleep yet – and whispered, 'I still can't believe that Clemmie is a married woman. The marriage in Egypt will count back here, won't it? She's not going to suddenly discover she's not really married and throw a fit, is she?'

Stephanie turned to face her husband and whispered back, 'No, she's not. She and Julian have been most diligent in their preparations, and their marriage will be as valid here as ours is, dear. Never fear – Clementine really is now Julian's wife.'

'So will she become plain old Mrs Treforest now, do you think?'

'Her form of address will be her choice, Henry. Maybe Clementine, being Clementine, will choose to never be referred to as Mrs anything…but we'll find out, when she's decided.'

Henry settled back. 'The opening of the antiques shop went rather well, don't you think? I believe Alexander said we might need somewhat more stock to supply the place than we'd originally thought – but quite a few people came to the village for the evening's celebrations, and we can't expect there to always be so much outside interest in Anwen-by-Wye, can we?'

'I don't see why we can't give more thought to that, dear. With the plans we've agreed with your mother for the tearoom, and the renovations of the guest rooms at the Coach and Horses, plus the reopening of the Market Hall as an interactive center for the historic record of the area, we now have an opportunity to make the village itself more attractive to visitors – encouraging them to add a side trip to Anwen-by-Wye, proper, when their primary destination is here, Chellingworth Hall. But, please, let's get some sleep, dear? Tomorrow is another day, and you know I have that meeting planned with the social committee about repainting the duck house at the duck pond.'

'Ah yes, the poor old duck house. Tudor was telling me this evening that it might need more than a lick of paint. Something about some of the structure needing repair?'

'Goodnight, Henry. Ducks tomorrow.'

'Indeed.'

ACKNOWLEDGEMENTS

My thanks to my mum, sister, and husband, for their unwavering support, which allows me to continue with my writing.

My thanks to Anna Harrisson, my editor, and Sue Vincent, my proofer; we've all tried to make this the best possible version of this story.

To Joan Pike: my thanks for allowing me to use your name in this book. I hope you don't mind that I've knocked a few years off your age, and I trust you feel I've given you an interesting character profile (thank you!). Now you'll have to keep reading…because, who knows, "you" might return!

My thanks, as always, to every blogger, reviewer, librarian, bookseller, and social media user who might have helped – in any way – to allow this book to find its way into your hands.

Finally, thank *you* for choosing to spend time with the women of the WISE Enquiries Agency.

ABOUT THE AUTHOR

CATHY ACE was born and raised in Swansea, Wales, and migrated to British Columbia, Canada aged forty. She is the author of The WISE Enquiries Agency Mysteries, The Cait Morgan Mysteries, the standalone novel of psychological suspense, The Wrong Boy, and collections of short stories and novellas. As well as being passionate about writing crime fiction, she's also a keen gardener.

You can find out more about Cathy and all her works at her website: www.cathyace.com

Made in the USA
Columbia, SC
24 July 2023

20847267R00148